Unbecoming

Advance Praise for Unbecoming

"Lesley Wheeler's *Unbecoming* is a delightful, beautifully written 21st century gothic novel set at a Virginia university and also in the borderlands between the literal and the metaphorical, between the realistic and the fantastic. Like all universities, this one is a school for wizards and conjurers. Professors offer portals to undiscovered countries and enchanted lands. Portals lead to demons and horror and death too. Cynthia has recently become English Department Chair. She's perimenopausal and coming into her blood-magic, witch woman power. The English Department is a tiny realm, fighting other more powerful realms at the University that would swallow any beleaguered humanities discipline. How do we survive each other, resist the demons or easy escape to a deadly realm that could destroy us? How do we conjure a path to the world we want? Lesley Wheeler says, ask the poets and the painters!"

Andrea Hairston, author of *Will Do Magic for Small Change* and *The Master of Poisons*

"The story of a woman leading an ordinary life who discovers within herself extraordinary powers, *Unbecoming* is sage, funny, and warm, like a long conversation with your best friend about all the strange and wonderful things that have been happening to her lately. Lesley Wheeler's writing is so deft and magical that I'm convinced that she must have learned it from the fairies. This smart, beguiling debut fantasy casts a spell that readers won't want to break."

Emily Croy Barker, author or *The Thinking Woman's Guide to Real Magic*

Unbecoming

by

Lesley Wheeler

Aqueduct Press
PO Box 95787
Seattle, Washington 98145-2787
www.aqueductpress.com

Library of Congress Control Number: 9781619761674

ISBN: 978-1-61976-167-4

First Edition, First Printing, May 2020

Cover Illustration courtesy the University of Michigan Special Collections Research Center. Canis (Vulpes) Fulvus. Desmaret. Var. Decussatus. American Cross-Fox. (v. 1, no. 2, plate 6), From *The Viviparous Quadrupeds of North America* by John James Audubon, F.R.S. and the Revd. John Bachman, 1851, New York, V.G. Audubon

Book and cover design by Kathryn Wilham

Acknowledgments

Wild gratitude to the editors and readers at Aqueduct Press, without whose help this novel would never have become itself, especially Kath Wilham, Lauren Banka, and L. Timmel Duchamp. Several friends also read early versions of the book and gave transformative advice, including Emily Croy Barker, Laura Brodie, Sally Rosen Kindred, Ellen Mayock, and Stephanie Wilkinson. Chris Gavaler helped me think through the plot long before I ever typed a scene, encouraged me to write, and gave insightful feedback at several crisis points in the book's development. I owe him the most.

Lenfest Grants from Washington and Lee University supported this project. Thanks, finally, to the friends, family, and colleagues who believed I could accomplish impossible things.

for Chris

One

Alisa's name lit up my phone while I sat in my car, waiting for a hot flash to subside.

"I need you to make a stop," she said in her new voice, high and dreamy. My best friend was about to head to Wales for the year on an obscure faculty exchange program, and she was changing. "There should be a fax waiting at the office."

"Since when is there a fax machine at the office?"

Since always, she insisted, so I promised to look. Every element of this process had been peculiar. Prickling with misgivings, I hung up, reversed out of my driveway, and detoured to campus.

There were no spots, so I made a risky place for my Hyundai at a yellow curb and scurried to our building. A print-out waited in a corner of the mailroom, on top of a hunk of beige plastic I would have sworn I'd never seen before. I squinted at the sheets, so often copied that the print was fuzzy, each page crested with a dragon.

When I grabbed them, the last page leapt up and opened a red slit in my thumb. Cursing, I jammed the cut into my mouth and sucked. Later I would have a vision of an empty socket next to the dusty machine, plug lying idle, but I must have misremembered.

I shoved the papers into my messenger bag and jogged back to the car, climbing into the driver's side as a vengeful parking enforcement officer raced up in his golf cart. "Not this time,"

I whispered, inserting the key with uncharacteristic dexterity and revving out. My rearview mirror reflected his scowl.

Speeding for a couple of blocks, I turned down Lord Fairfax Street and slowed. The poshest avenue in our Virginia town began not far from its small college, past a run of boutiques and farm-to-table bistros. The first houses were red-brick aristocrats, built just after the Civil War and set standoffishly beyond cool front lawns. Then came wooden Victorians with turrets and tin roofs and smaller but exquisitely maintained gardens. Alisa's Arts and Crafts bungalow sat further along, after a gentle incline began to falter downhill toward the river. Parking by her elderberry hedge, I took a deep breath of air-conditioned chill before killing the engine.

I would get through this day by force of will, putting one foot ahead of another, delivering my dearest ally to the airport, picking up her inadequate replacement.

The door stood ajar. I hesitated in the August heat. Then I rapped the brass knocker before ducking in.

Alisa lived by herself now. Her once-overstuffed rooms, painted in blossomy colors, seemed sparsely furnished. Tumbleweeds of dog fur were long swept away. She kept a tidy house, mostly because domestic efficiency gave her more time to write. Still, the space seemed preternaturally neat, almost expectant. Chenille throws were folded over the backs of chairs. Photos of nieces and nephews had disappeared from end tables, although pretty watercolor miniatures still hung around, islanded on the walls. Marked-up article drafts had been packed out of sight.

Alisa was standing in the middle of the living room. A petite woman in her early fifties, she usually vibrated with impatience, the kind of person who rested from research by running half-marathons, who talked more brilliantly than anyone in the meeting and laughed louder than anyone in the bar. She had been all self-assurance and appetite, with claws. Now

Alisa had one toe in another world. She seemed unaware of me, clutching a clump of long reddish-brown hair in each fist, so I shifted my weight from foot to foot. "Forget something?"

Alisa widened her eyes in my direction. "Almost certainly."

As I watched her, guilt blew through me. Alisa's partner of thirteen years dumped her last winter, and a blunt-shaped misery had squatted on my friend since. By June, I'd been sick of her grimness, just as I felt exhausted by my husband Silvio's depression. I fantasized about a break from both of them—but not so far, for so long. I wouldn't have wished for this.

Now Alisa trembled, despite the heat. "Was the fax there?"

Kicking off my sandals, I pulled the folded pages out of my satchel and handed them over. "Last-minute paperwork?"

Grasping sheets in each hand and peering at them, she said, "They booked me on some airline I've never heard of. I couldn't *find* online check-in. But these are supposed to get me to Wales somehow." Then Alisa came back into focus and smiled.

Oh. She wasn't withdrawn, at least not the way she had been since Sunshine moved in with that plain-as-kale farmer. She wasn't even fretting about the trip. Instead, Alisa looked lighter. Surprise, and chagrin at my own surprise, made me glow back at her. Alisa's dreamy voice, so different from her recent sadness—there was weird confidence in it.

The pre-breakup Alisa would have noticed bloodstains on her documents and interrogated me. Now she just slipped them into a tote on the side chair and waved me deeper into the house, touching the frame of an English-looking landscape as she passed. She spoke over her shoulder as she crossed the dining room.

"You know," she said, "I was about to apply for medical leave when this exchange came through." The coffee machine was a new single-serve device, not the stovetop espresso maker Alisa had always used. Nor did she prepare to beat sugar into crema, a practice learned from her grandmother, one of Alisa's countless varieties of arcane expertise. She used to enjoy an audience for performances like brewing Cuban coffee. Now, she lifted a full cup from its plastic platform and shoved it at me. "I just didn't think I could get my act together for another September."

"I was worried." I watched as she dumped the cartridge and set up another. The businesslike machine gurgled and spat.

Alisa carried a sugar bowl and carton of half-and-half to the counter, where I pulled out two stools. "My therapist would have testified to mental derangement, for sure," she said. "I've been in a stupor most of the time, but every once in a while I imagined myself as Bertha."

"*Jane Eyre*'s Bertha?"

"The mad wife Rochester stashes in the attic," Alisa explained with irritating condescension. I had been her colleague in the English department for nearly twenty years. "First Sunshine, who is basically a witch, persuades me to stay here in the *boondocks*"—I winced—"then I get dumped. When I think about Sunshine shacking up with the cute young governess instead of me, I want to set fire to something."

That sounded like the old Alisa.

When she fell silent, I tracked her gaze around the kitchen, which was as immaculate as the rest of the house, and as foreign. Someone had wiped the small window over the sink clean of soap spatters and erased fingerprints from cupboard doors; a fug of spices had dissipated. Already signs of Alisa had evaporated like mist. I turned my eyes from the room back to her face, half-expecting the freckles to start winking out.

Suddenly I felt bereft. "I can't believe you're leaving."

Alisa wasn't looking at me. She lifted hair off her neck, auburn threaded with gray, then stared at a small, dark painting of trees. I didn't remember it, and the placing was odd, right next to the window, but her next comment distracted me. "I needed to make this happen."

Alisa clasped her mug with both hands as if to warm them. I sweated.

Instead of asking what "need" meant, I pulled over the sugar bowl. She had started taking coffee bitter, but I still believed in consolation. "I can't believe you did everything in a week—not only paperwork and packing but setting up your house for a tenant. I get a migraine just thinking about it."

Alisa shrugged, pleased, maybe, to hear her competence praised, as if an ego still kicked inside this oddly relaxed person. "The house was half-empty anyway. Besides, it's easier to leave knowing they're sending over another professor to babysit the place. A Victorianist, even."

She leaned back. I followed her eyes down to my wrinkly gray clothes as she asked, "Did you find out anything else about her? Beyond her resume?"

I copied Alisa's shrug. Two things I knew about this doppelgänger, Sophia Ellis: one, the Welsh dean had testified in print that the woman was qualified to teach all three of Alisa's previously scheduled fall offerings. Two, she couldn't replace Alisa in any other way. "She comes up online as the author of a few articles and poems. But no, nothing else. Their university website keeps crashing." I paused. "I'm still picking her up today, right, when I drop you off?"

"Yep." She pointed at a folder lying next to the sad new American coffeemaker. "I collected all the appliance instruction booklets. You just have to show her around and give her my keys. I even stocked the fruit bowl. Want something?"

A couple of bumpy-skinned lemons gleamed among shiny pears and nectarines. I thought of apples of knowledge and goblin fruit. "No, thanks."

I downed some tepid coffee, chucked the rest, and rinsed the cup at the sink, where dappled light heaved and subsided. Alisa followed and patted my damp back. She was already a ghost of linen and warm air.

We rolled Alisa's baggage into the airport, chewing over details of the unusual fellowship. "Did I tell you?—I did find one thing online," Alisa said, heaving the larger case onto the scale. "The cottage I'll be living in, Sophia Ellis's house. They finally sent me the address and I looked it up." As she accepted her boarding passes, proffered by the agent with a puzzled expression, and we moved toward security, Alisa pulled up a satellite picture. "Here."

I stared at her phone. "It's thatched! And look at that red door, and the apple tree, and all those flowers." My pitch rose with the escalator. "It's so *cute*."

"Cute like the roof leaks, probably, and the heat doesn't work." But Alisa beamed.

Near the start of the cordoned security line, she dumped her purse and carry-on to embrace me. "Listen. I know I'm leaving at a terrible time, with the dean plotting a coup and all. And Silvio gone."

"Silvio," I repeated, as if the name were a spell.

"And everyone left in the department is either untenured or useless or an agent of destruction."

"Heads up their asses."

"You can kick them into shape." Alisa straightened. She was never more herself than when diagnosing my problems and telling me how to fix them. "But it's hard in ways you don't expect, becoming the chair."

"Surely I know the worst," I protested. Alisa had done a yearlong stint once and depicted it in epic Technicolor.

She shook her head. "No, it's not just extra work. Everyone changes. People seem different, especially the people you thought you knew best."

"Not me, though?"

Alisa snorted. "No, you were always the same. But you have to change now." She stared right into my eyes. "It's really, really important to pay attention."

I blinked and pulled my head back. "What are you talking about?"

"You refuse to see things that don't fit whatever story you're spinning about the world. Keep playing that game, and problems will creep up on you."

"There's no *game*," I said. Before I could assemble a more coherent response, her attention swiveled elsewhere. Alisa balanced mismatched bags and removed her passport from a pocket. Fluorescent lights hummed. She kissed my cheek and headed into the security line, bumping and dragging the weight of too many books and shoes. Soon she was feeding those bags into a scanner's black mouth and stepping into a portal, arms raised.

She was gone. No one was left to tell me how to live.

I stood alone for a minute. The so-called Arrivals Lounge, one of those nowhere places, contained a single row of mean-spirited chairs, but it would be an hour until Alisa's surrogate arrived. I finally sat down and stared through a giant pane of glass for a while. Beyond it, worn mountains, hazed by heat, turned their backs to me.

Soon I was twitching through work tasks on my phone and messages related to my promotion. The scrolling emails must have sent me to sleep, because I started dreaming of a dark-haired woman carrying a knife, running uphill, pursued by blurry figures—until I caught an unlikely scent. It reminded me of crushed grass. I woke and saw a stream of exiting passengers.

A few swift loners darted though the gate. A cluster of travelers with clumsy carry-ons followed. After a blank moment and another waft of coolness, there she was.

At the security threshold, gazing right into me, stood the most stunning creature I'd ever had the ill fortune to behold. Tall and glamorous in a tailored dress, she held an aqua suitcase, the retro kind without wheels. She seemed unburdened.

I knew, sure as summer always ends, this was Sophia Ellis.

"Call me Fee," the visitor said. Her accent was crisp but not quite placeable.

How old was she? As we bypassed the checked-luggage conveyer belt and strolled to the parking lot, I stole glances at her. Not young. Twenty-somethings had a touch of softness still; Fee looked definite. When we arrived at the car, she planted herself on the asphalt, staring skyward, as if she had grown there for centuries.

Yet her skin was unlined, black hair unsilvered, figure lean. She lifted a single case to the trunk in an easy motion.

I babbled the whole time about how magical the logistics of this exchange had seemed. Somehow I was confiding, too, my bewilderment at becoming chair. "The part of the budget under my control is pretty small," I found myself explaining, "but let me know if you need anything, and I'll do my best."

Fee responded with a calm expression just this side of a smile and answered mundane questions as if surprised. Yes, the flights did go smoothly. She slept the whole way across the gray Atlantic. (Her words, "the gray Atlantic.") No, she had never traveled to the States before. About chairing, she observed there were always ways to work a system, no matter how Byzantine the rules.

"Orientation?" Fee asked during the drive to town. I had been describing activities scheduled for new faculty members, beginning, alas, Monday morning—tomorrow. She stared directly east and nodded. She was already oriented.

The afternoon blinked past. I brought her to Alisa's house, where she would be living, as well as sitting in Alisa's office. I showed her the fruit bowl, two upstairs bedrooms tucked beneath the roof, and the landline, because she hadn't brought a mobile phone. She liked the screened-in porch best, reaching out to the steel mesh without quite touching it, skimming her fingers over the hammock.

Here is the thermostat and here is the router, I said, as if chanting a nursery rhyme. Fee was fascinated by the controls for the shower. She peered down the drain. No, thank you, she did not need me to drive her to the supermarket today. She would take a stroll this evening. The downtown was so close.

Time in Fee's company passed jerkily, in ellipses and vivid dilations. Alisa would be high above foreign waters now, but I had crossed some kind of border, too.

My airport dream revisited me that night. When I caught a glint of the knife in the woman's hand, I told myself, *Blood. There's no crossing between worlds without blood.*

In the morning, still half-asleep, I faltered on my front stoop, grasping a watering can. I only meant to duck outside for a second, for a chore I had forgotten, before the construction guys started up across the street.

A garbage truck was clanking in the distance. I had no desire to confront sanitation workers in misbuttoned pajamas. Yet some kind of darkness hunched at the end of my walkway, near the recycling bin. Had the cat escaped? I stepped forward, squinting, unable to make sense of what I saw.

It seemed to be the vintage telephone from our spare bedroom, the room I was supposed to use as an office. The telephone was never hooked up, and I hadn't touched it for years, except with a dust cloth. I certainly hadn't lugged it to the curb on trash day. Yet there it sat, Bakelite handle knocked from the cradle, brushed-metal rotary dial gleaming in the half-light, a crescent moon of numbers. Who had moved it?

The cast-iron telephone was one of many quirky presents Alisa had given me, often apropos of nothing, as if filling some kind of hole in our friendship or my personality. Most were useful as well as beautiful. As well as outclassing me in professional accomplishments, Alisa had taste. This gift, however, had languished upstairs. I would have said its pointlessness annoyed me.

Brakes groaning, the garbage truck finally rolled into sight. A man riding the rear leapt off, seized a bin, emptied it. As he turned to claim the telephone, I dropped the watering can and ran flat-out across the lawn, arm flung across my chest for decency. "No, no, don't take that!"

He stared at the crazed woman rushing him, down at the antique, up at me again. He backed off.

"It's a mistake," I said, as embarrassment or fear welled up hot, dampening my cotton nightclothes. After a beat he nodded, climbed onto his vehicle, and signaled the driver. Wheels turned.

I stood there, panting, while the truck shrank into the distance. Then I gazed down at my wandering appliance.

I willed my heartbeat to steady as I examined, one by one, the possibilities. Had my son dragged it here? I couldn't think why. My daughter had liked playing with it as a child, nattering away to imaginary people, but she was too grown-up for that now. Silvio was out of town. I had been exhausted after helping the kids get organized for their second week of high school—so many forms to sign—but I couldn't have moved the phone myself without noticing. "I don't sleepwalk," I said to it, "or practice telekinesis."

From the lilac, a mockingbird rang and rang.

I crouched next to the stranded hunk of iron. Picking up the handset, I flashed a glance around to make sure no neighbors were watching, then placed it next to my ear.

The receiver was cold and dead. Why so much upheaval? Why now? What did I want to happen next?

Maybe silence was preferable to answers. I dropped the receiver onto the base and hoisted the whole contraption with a grunt.

The day was brightening, but as I limped back along the walk, having skinned an ankle against the curb, shivers forked through me. I sidled indoors and dumped the telephone on a table in the front hall, not where it used to live, but never mind.

I showered, harried the kids through breakfast, urged them upstairs to dress, then called them down again. They had missed the bus twice last week; it was Teddy's fault, but Rose covered for him. "Get a move on! You still have lunches to make!"

Teddy stumbled into the kitchen behind his sister. I thumped into a nearby chair and was smoothing a plastic bandage onto my ankle when a rumble shook the house. Startled, I lurched to my feet. The clocks had blinked out, and the dishwasher was no longer grumbling.

Contractors were demolishing a damaged garage across the street—had they knocked a line down? Heat kindled in my gut and licked up my chest.

In the sudden silence, Teddy looked up from looting the pantry. "A cosmic sign."

Rose rolled her eyes. "Just another blown circuit." Unfazed by shadow, she resumed layering slices of rare beef onto grainy bread.

Teddy checked his phone, probably for notice of a last-minute school cancelation due to apocalyptic collapse of the electrical grid. Disappointed, he resumed raiding the cupboards. Rose must be right: a circuit breaker had flipped. The power in our old house was becoming excitable, prone to surge and collapse. But the box was in the creepy, cricket-infested basement, and I didn't want to go down there.

I paused in front of the cellar door, the cat rubbing against my legs, then shook my head. It would be perfectly reasonable to use the toilet first.

In the bathroom, I glimpsed a perspiring woman in the mirror. She was repeating a pointless ritual, calling on indifferent forces, and hoping for a different outcome. Powerless and bleeding out.

My period had hit the night before, and I was coping with slasher-film quantities of gore. Actually, slashers were predictable. This was blood I'd never seen before, not on screens or in books. Perimenopause: more taboo than serial killings, less plausible than vampire tales. And with Silvio and now Alisa gone, I had no one to gripe to. Middle age, so far, was all about involuntary secrets. I flushed then compressed what remained of my dignity to get my pants fastened.

Cleaning up, listening to the clatter of teens in the hall, I felt lightheaded again. There was also a sensation I didn't have a label for. The word *eagerness* came into my mind, but I batted it away.

On the rug sat my only witness. The cat was waiting for me to conjure water from the tap. No creature looks at a woman my age with personal interest; I was merely the vehicle of his will. I reached for the faucet, but for all Pluto cared, the handle might as well have rotated supernaturally.

When I finished in the bathroom, the kids were already by the front door, shrugging on their knapsacks. Teddy's drooped on his slim back, empty except for overpriced snack bars and the paperwork I'd shoved in. Rose's pack strained at the seams.

I considered asking the twins about the iron telephone, but though they were standing right next to it, I couldn't figure out a way to phrase the question. Instead I followed them, picking up an empty potato chip bag, a dirt-stiffened hoodie, a doodle of a winged woman.

"See you later, Mom," Teddy said.

"Have a tolerable day."

"You, too." Rose, a pace behind, turned to frown at me from behind a blonde tangle. She glanced up and down, presumably surveying my gray tee-shirt and baggy charcoal trousers, so similar to yesterday's. She called this a "groutfit." Rose clamped her lips, but her eyes said, *Change.*

Lamps came on and appliances ground into action. Rose's pupils shrank to points, then she turned to follow Teddy. The screen door banged behind them.

Two

After work, I parked in my driveway and listened to the engine tick as it cooled. My feet throbbed, my ears rang, and my belly kept cramping. I shot a message to Alisa, whom I hadn't heard from yet, wondering how a year's freedom might alter her. It might undo me completely.

Although I never noticed my cell chirping, I found two texts from Silvio. *Sorry we got our signals crossed last night. Alisa get off okay?* Then, *Should be home by 8. Call if you can.* My husband's part-time North Carolina apartment was already "home," apparently. It was unnerving how quickly he had settled in.

Silvio had decamped for his new faculty orientation only ten days ago, but our grass looked unkempt, as if the whole property were pining away. The possum who lived under the front steps was chomping my basil, unless it was the groundhog, or the rabbits. It was hardly worth growing even the sturdiest herbs. I should get out there and pinch off flowers, I told myself, but I was afraid of bleeding through my clothes if I moved.

Alisa was always the person who got me off my butt—insisting I put my file in for full professor two years ago, for instance, when I was unsure my credentials were good enough. "Look how many men have sailed through with shorter resumes," she said. "Unlike the service jobs everyone wants you to waste your life on, promotions in academic rank come with actual raises. Step up and demand the money!" Alisa had been right, as usual.

I wanted to dislike Fee for supplanting my friend, but as Fee's new supervisor I was bound to help her. Today I brought her to the office then handed her off to Harriet, our administrative assistant. I wondered if Fee turned heads at the orientation meetings. She wouldn't charm Alisa's students, though. A challenging professor, Alisa magnetized talent.

The kids would already be home. This was the first year Silvio and I weren't juggling schedules so one of us would be home to meet them at three. I mentally rummaged the vegetable drawer for things to sauté. I shouldn't be eating so much pasta, not if I wanted to stop accumulating pudge, but it was the only common ground between the nearly vegan pacifist and the carnivorous fighter. I would rather fatten than choose between them.

The front door opened and Teddy leaned out, longish hair with its one blue streak damp in the humidity, to call, "Mom!" Twisting like smoke, Pluto bolted between his feet. Teddy sprang after the cat, who was bounding across the lawn in discrete hops, aimed, as always, toward the road. Maybe Pluto had been watching rabbits through the window and, being an animal with limited outdoor experience, imagined lawns must be traversed that way. I dumped my phone and bag and joined the chase.

"Fee?" Rose repeated the name as we cleared plates and loaded the dishwasher. It was her turn to scrub pots. "I forgot to ask last night. What's she like?"

"Taller than me," I answered, bending over the wine rack to choose a cheap Malbec. I left the wine store's price tags on the caps so I could know how much money I was drinking. "Although most people are taller than me. Elegant. She reminds me of someone, I can't think who."

"But what's she *like*?" Rose, haloed by sunset light, was eyeing a frying pan. Finally, she exhaled and picked up the sponge.

"I hardly know yet. British people don't exactly tell you their life stories when you chauffeur them home from the airport. And I only saw her for a few minutes this morning. She somehow gets me to do all the talking." I peeled off the foil and jabbed a corkscrew into the stopper. "She is the opposite of needy, which is good, I guess. Finally a person I don't have to take care of."

Teddy remarked from behind a bank of pillows, "You're *supposed* to take care of her."

I extracted the plastic cork and poured a glass. "I don't know how universities work over there, but when I started describing HR forms, she just blinked. Like bureaucracy was below her pay grade."

"Must be nice."

"I couldn't nail her down about the teaching, either, whether she needed to order different books. She just quoted Christina Rossetti at me. She's more of a poetry person than Alisa, but maybe that's good, shake up the usual offerings. I don't know. She's so gorgeous no one will be able to hear a word she says."

"*Mom,*" Teddy protested.

"At least Alisa's house is walking distance to everything. Europeans never understand how bad our public transportation is." Our house stood further out, at the edge of town.

Casting an eye around my kitchen, which unlike Alisa's looked better when the light failed, I sat in a scuffed but comfortable chair. "Oh, and the dog!" I cried. "When I picked Fee up this morning, the neighbor's big fat Labrador bounded up to the fence, stopped dead, and then started barking himself hoarse until Mr. Mukherjee came out to calm him down.

Right out of a Lovecraft story. Mysterious stranger comes to town. Horror ensues."

Rose's pointy chin lifted. She brought her own edge to the evening, upset about some high school trouble I would never hear the details of. "Sounds as if you resent her."

As my blood pressure spiked, I gulped down the wine I'd been warming in my mouth. "What?"

"For messing up your life. You're making her sound terrible." Rose, who usually did the dishes more scrupulously than Teddy, was already wiping her hands on a cloth. "She was probably just jet-lagged."

I flushed, but before I could retort, Teddy intervened from his nest of striped sofa cushions. "Listen to this. These psychologists did an experiment to tell whether children could judge the difference between fantasy and reality." Blue light shone on his face as he leaned over the laptop screen.

I turned toward him, away from the omniscient goddess at the sink. "What are you reading?"

"Dad sent me an article," he said with an impatient wave, and I felt the usual pang at family members having interesting conversations without me. "So, even three-year-olds know the difference between reality and imagination," he went on.

"Duh." Rose depressed the switch on the electric kettle and browsed tea flavors with an appearance of concentration.

"Yet they can totally get scared of monsters they know are imaginary. So researchers put two large black boxes in a room."

Rose made an impatient noise, but she was paying attention.

"They get a bunch of kids, bring them into the room one by one, and have them look in each box, make sure they're empty. Then they say to some of the kids, now visualize a nice, fluffy, white rabbit in one of the boxes."

He lifted his legs onto the sofa and crossed them, tucking a streaky lock behind one pierced ear, scrolling through results, eyes flicking back and forth. "The others are told to imagine a horrible, mean, black monster."

Rose's eyes widened. "*Racist.*"

"Yeah, right?" he agreed. "Then the adults *leave the room* for two minutes and videotape what the kids do. A few kids beg the researchers not to go, they're scared, although they insist they know it's just pretend. Half of them go up and touch the box they were pretending about, even though they were told to stay in their chairs.

"And then," he finished in triumph, "in the final interview, they admit, yeah, they did wonder if there was a rabbit or a monster in the box. Most of the kids know they can't pretend it into existence. They don't have the magical skills, they say... but they think it's possible *other* people do."

Rose's tea released a scent of peppermint. "So, knowing what's real," she said, "they still recognize holes in what they know."

"Doesn't that seem like the definition of intelligence?" Teddy asked.

I had been swirling my wine around, but now I leaned my achy body against the chair and let one hand fall to the seat. Touch wood. "Why did Dad send you that article?"

"We were talking about how petrified Rose and I used to be of her bedroom closet."

"Ah." I hauled my body up again, feeling bloated and way too factual, but the chores never ended. On my way to the sink, I was startled to glimpse the iron telephone—I had already forgotten its early-morning expedition, as well where I'd parked it.

"Thinking about things does seem, sometimes, to make them come true," Rose said, bobbing the sachet up and down by its string. "No one knows for sure a monster hasn't materialized in the closet since the last time they checked. Saara says that's how her parents think about ghosts. You shouldn't talk about them, because that will draw them to you—or maybe it occurs to you to mention ghosts because they're already there."

She hesitated, cocking her head. "Like I just did."

Returning the corkscrew to its drawer, I found a spoon bent almost into a loop. What the hell? Glancing at Rose and thinking of poltergeists, I shoved the spoon to the back and slammed the drawer shut.

Teddy leaped up and drew the curtains. "We always have these conversations at nighttime when Dad's not home."

"What, you don't think I could protect you?" I waved a mostly clean pan in the air before swiping it with a rag and returning it to the cupboard.

"You're scared of *mirrors*," Rose answered, raising pretty eyebrows and scooping up her bookbag to retreat to her lair.

"Mirrors are terrifying."

Standing in the back yard, barefoot again, I ignored a voicemail from my mother—she probably wanted to gloat over my abandonment, or maybe tell nightmare tales about latchkey kids. Instead I tried to call Silvio. He picked up after a few rings, but we could hardly hear each other. He was at a bar with his colleagues, he said through background laughter that fizzed like static. Was everything all right? he asked. Fine, I lied. Talk tomorrow.

I didn't want him to have fun, although that was unfair. I had badgered him to apply for the job, exasperated by his gloominess. The local Psychology Department would only hire him as a part-time replacement. The more perfect a colleague he became, teaching their ill-designed intro courses to rave reviews while serving up uncompensated committee work and home-baked banana bread at meetings, the more they took him for granted. He talked about the professors in Psych so obsessively, with such mounting distress: couldn't he see this was a dead end?

Silvio scoured the ads. He applied around the region and scored a one-year, full-time, renewable position a few hours' drive away. I had felt such relief.

Hadn't I? My stupid heart stumbled.

Rust-brown flashed through the woods across the stream, with a rustle of leaves. I wanted it to be a fox, a small, lurking creature that seemed powerless but was clever enough to outwit every dog in the neighborhood. It was probably some gray scavenger, instead. I wiggled my toes in the grass while electricity thrummed through my limbs, seeking an outlet.

Three

Entering the English building after an hour in the library, I checked my phone in the hall and found the message from Alisa I had been wishing for. *Fine but having Wi-Fi problems. Don't worry if I'm out of touch.*

"Hey, Harriet!" I stuck my head in the main office. "Just heard from Alisa. She got there safely."

Our administrative assistant was straddling a whirlwind of paperwork, but she paused to clap and call out, "Hallelujah!"

Juggling an armful of books, I pushed my office door open with my back. When I saw Fee standing inside, cool in a pressed cotton skirt patterned with ivy leaves, I jumped.

Fee smiled and gestured with the framed photograph she had picked up. "Are they twins?"

The children were about nine there. Silvio stood with an arm around each, and grassy dunes rose in the background. All three were sun-bronzed, an invisible breeze lifting the kids' hair, still tow-blonde. Teddy's had turned a streaky sand color since, enlivened by Kool-Aid dye-jobs. Rose bleached hers, clinging to a vanished era.

I nodded and took a slow breath to calm my banging pulse. "They looked very alike then, but they're fourteen now. Teddy is almost as tall as Silvio."

"And Rose will be blooming. What a golden family." Fee surveyed me for a long beat. I was brown-haired, wide-hipped, and five-two when I straightened my scholarly stoop. Mismatched to my husband and kids, though she didn't say so. "Will I meet them on Friday?"

"The twins will be there," I replied, reclaiming the photograph and returning it to the bookcase crammed with sideways volumes I had been meaning to organize. The shelves resembled gappy rows of crooked teeth. "Silvio may or may not get back from North Carolina in time for the pot-luck."

"Ah, yes, I heard he was away for a year, working at another university. What a preposterous thing."

That stiffened me, and my irritation resurged. My voice rose. "It was a lucky opportunity, actually." I lifted the watering jug and eyed the straggly plant on my windowsill, its leaves edged with tan. "Did you leave family behind?"

She stayed my hand before I poured. "No, no, it is not thirsty, see?" She poked a finger into the soil and raised it covered with damp black crumbs, which she rubbed off, back into the pot. I smelled something like juniper, earthy but bright. She stepped to the door, then before sashaying out, said, "I will bring mushrooms."

Mushrooms. All right. Is that what she came to tell me? Part of me hoped Silvio *would* be late, although I hadn't seen him for two weeks. From what I was already observing in meetings, men liked Fee way too much.

I sagged into my chair and felt a sharp pain on my calf. Bending over, I found a thin red line, beginning to ooze blood. How had I cut myself now?

"Tap tap," said the next voice at the door. It was our Shakespeare specialist, wiry and bald as a potato. He made a show of looking furtive, blue eyes darting in the direction Fee had strolled off in, and echoed in a loud, delighted whisper, "Mushrooms!"

I dabbed at my leg with a tissue. "How was your summer, Ralph?" I wanted to change the subject, even if it meant hearing about his precocious grandchildren and all the marvelous shows he had seen at fringe festivals.

"I would cast her as Titania, queen of the fairies! She is absolutely otherworldly."

"From the otherworld of *Wales*." I tossed the tissue and neatened my desk, jamming stray pencils and a pair of scissors into a metal cup.

"Oh, my," Ralph said. "I see someone is not completely enchanted." His amusement became sly. "Have you seen Alisa's office?"

"No."

"Transformed into a woodland bower. Our Titania has a green thumb. The house is looking sprightlier, too—she weeded the beds and planted new flowers. Helen walked by early this morning, with the dog, you know, and she swears," here Ralph assumed a stage whisper, "Fee was sleeping on the porch, in the hammock!"

"It's hot," I snapped. "That house has window units, and only upstairs. Maybe Fee isn't used to air conditioning."

"Maybe she prefers to be at one with nature, like her magical people."

"The magical people of *Wales*."

Ralph chuckled, fluttered his fingers in a wave, and vanished.

That night, when Silvio called, I carried my cellphone out to my favorite spot, the folding chair that faced the creek at the end of our sloping backyard. Sometimes I envied my colleagues who lived in the village and could walk to local restaurants, although I liked some distance from the students. I coveted Alisa's house especially, the one she had abandoned without looking back.

Evening's colors were fading, and when the back door slammed, a murmuration of starlings rose from a distant tree. The birds flashed and swarmed into a shape that almost resembled a curvy woman.

"It's good you finally heard from Alisa," Silvio was saying.

"Just two sentences." I stood on the bank, eyes following a thread of water. The creek was only a trickle this time of year, heading toward the James River and the ocean. "I've emailed and texted a few times, and so has Camille." Camille was our specialist in African American and Caribbean literature, one of only three black professors at the entire college and the youngest member of the English department. I adored Camille, finding a weird relief in her hyper-alertness. I loved Alisa, too, but she could be self-absorbed. *Pay attention,* indeed.

"Alisa is probably having connection problems," Silvio continued. "Remember, when I went to that conference in England, my cell worked erratically. And you said she's living in some little cottage?" With a cast-iron telephone, probably.

"Yeah, I know. And the school year starts later, so maybe there's no one at the office yet who can help her get set up." I kicked a tuft of grass. "How's your first week going?"

"Good!" he exclaimed and launched into praise for his students, Broome State classroom technology, the inclusive vibe of the first faculty meeting, blah, blah. I sank into a chair. I couldn't get over the oddness of Silvio's disembodied voice. I wanted this opportunity for him, I reminded myself. Finally he got to be the sparkly new person everyone took out for coffee. Happiness resurrected the old Silvio, the version of my husband I had lost and missed.

And after all, life could be easier without a fourth personality in the house.

A pause fell, and Silvio shifted topic. "Do you feel like a real department head now your term is in gear?"

The sky had turned deep blue, alive with bats; tree frogs chanted. "Well, sort of. I didn't get to tell you yesterday—we had our first blow-up. Between Camille and Sandra." Since last year's retirements, Sandra was the oldest of our old-timers, a mousy medievalist but high-maintenance, I was learning. "Camille wanted to challenge the custom that desks must be returned to rows at the end of every period, so she wrote a group email."

"Oh, no." I could almost hear Silvio blanching. English professors' emails are long and inflammatory. The smaller the problem, the more heated the rhetoric.

"The message called them 'fascist rows,' actually." He started laughing. "It was a joke, I guess. Next thing I know, Sandra is in my office sobbing about how Camille is so mean and Sandra needs the desks in rows because she's hard of hearing and she's not a fascist, she's *not*. But of course, before she came to cry on me, she hit reply-all with a scathing response, which resulted in Camille rushing to my office an hour later, also weeping, sure Sandra would torpedo her tenure case now and she'll get fired and have to move back in with her parents or starve to death."

"Oh my god. What did you do?"

"I reassured Sandra that no one thinks she's a fascist and reminded her how everyone gets wound up during the tenure year. I reassured Camille that Sandra would never be so petty. Then I told everyone they could arrange the chairs however they wanted and leave them that way, for the next professor to move, or not. Facilities Management will probably get mad now, but the department seems calm."

"Brilliantly handled, Professor Rennard."

"I thought so, Professor Pagano. But I also thought about how Walt"—meaning our former chair, now golfing in Georgia—"never had to deal with tears. He seemed busy and important, you know? No one expected *him* to take care of anybody's *feelings.*"

Silvio grunted. "Strategic social incompetence."

"There's power in it."

"Well, you're good at, I don't know, repositioning things. Nudging people along. That will make you way better at chairing than Walt ever was." Here was the kind of story I liked, I realized, and Silvio was particularly good at telling it: describing me as the dogged heroine, triumphing over adversaries. Was this how I smoothed over anxiety, by living in fairy tales? Alisa's warning to pay attention nagged at me.

Aloud, I said, "We'll see." I slid my feet out of my sandals and planted them in the grass. The cut on my leg stung. "So, Friday."

"Yeah. Normally I'll come home Thursday night, but there's a department colloquium this Friday at one, and I feel like I should show my face."

"Of course you should." This meant cleaning, shopping, and cooking for the party solo, as well as whatever parental stuff was on the docket—I had a vague memory of some event after school Friday and Teddy not being able catch the bus. "Absolutely, you should."

"I'll get right on the road from there, though, and even if there's traffic I should be home when everyone arrives, in time to form a human barricade between Sandra and Camille."

In time to meet Titania and eat her magic mushrooms, I did not reply.

Come Friday, an itchy rash had sprouted all over my arms and legs, even though I hadn't been weeding; who had time? I managed to see the doctor before his office closed for the weekend to score steroids. The physician wore an impossibly pink polo shirt and wanted to chat about Dante and midlife crisis. Afterwards I picked up Teddy plus two trays of the best local fried chicken, with biscuits. Beer and lemonade nestled on ice in the cooler; wine stood next to paper cups and plates and a bottle of bourbon. Bowls of chips and nuts decorated every table, and I put out a quinoa salad. What had I forgotten?

"Rose! Teddy!" I shouted up the stairs. "Could one of you shut Pluto in an upstairs bedroom?" Our last cat had been run over by a student in a black SUV who hadn't even stopped. We'd all run out and witnessed unforgettable gore, the cat mangled but not yet dead, the road reddened. The poor animal died wrapped in a towel in Silvio's arms.

While I marshalled salt, pepper, butter, corkscrew, ice bucket, the twins played chase with Pluto. I glanced out the window often. Still no Silvio.

Ralph and his long-suffering wife Helen arrived first, with an elaborate cheese plate, followed by the dean, a.k.a. the Ice Maiden, whom we suspected of unmaidenliness lately, given her melting around our recently tenured fiction writer. All went straight for the bourbon. Sandra the not-fascist-medievalist, a superb gardener, entered with a gorgeous green salad full of nasturtium blossoms and tiger-striped tomatoes. Our raucous pair of composition specialists swarmed in with partners and brownies and pasta and more beer, as well as five children who ran around the backyard, screaming. I missed that, getting together with friends and watching our kids flock and wheel. Beth-Ann, the senior of the compositionists, was married to a red-bearded, friendly IT guy, and Robin, the younger, to a woman who taught poetry workshops for us most years. She was part-time, as Silvio had been, but she seemed resigned to perkless impermanence. All of them grabbed beverages and turned their backs to the windows, exhaling with relief.

It was nearly seven and the party in full swing by the time Camille, who in her pre-tenure panic volunteered for every task, delivered Fee, this year's guest of honor. Fee's fricassee of herbs and wild mushrooms, I had to admit, looked delicious. Camille glanced down at her small, wilted salad of supermarket greens, then over at Sandra's gleaming masterpiece of small-plot agriculture, and sighed.

"Want a drink?" I asked.

"Oh god yes," Camille answered.

Fee looked fresh in a sleeveless blouse of immaculate white linen with cropped green trousers. I was wearing long sleeves to cover my weepy pustules. I watched her attract a crowd of friendly colleagues, including Dan Kuo, the fiction writer, easily the best-looking eligible straight guy in town. She told a story—from her childhood, maybe?—about staying at a commune. A negligent uncle left her for a while among the cultists or hippies or whatever they were, and strange rituals ensued. Everyone around her laughed and sputtered questions.

The Ice Maiden, also observing Fee, rested her hands on a chair-back. I pictured frost branching down cherry wood in lacy patterns as the air crackled.

My teenagers heaped food on their plates. They were no longer savages, evidently, who fled at the sight of adult strangers. I half-attended to Beth-Ann's latest humble-brag while I watched my kids circulate. Rose was chatting with Sandra as she captured a couple of pieces of fried chicken. Teddy said hello to Fee and her entourage. Both twins soon made their way to me.

"That must be her." Rose popped a grape into her mouth and nodded toward Fee.

"She smells good," Teddy said, and then blushed, making Rose's eyes light up. I tried to rescue him before his sister started teasing.

"I noticed that too," I said. "I should ask what perfume she uses."

"Perhaps European women have a natural floral bouquet," Rose began. Then Fee suddenly looked right at Rose, across the crowd, as if she knew she was under discussion. My daughter mystified me by depositing her plate on the counter, peeling off her summer cardigan, turning it inside out, and putting it on again. Fee watched with narrowed eyes, then tilted her head toward Dan again with dazzling intensity.

Before I could ask Rose what that little performance was about, she remarked, "Dad hates perfume." This sent my eyes to the oven clock. "So where is he?"

"I don't know. Should have been here by now." I watched Fee as I answered, unsure what felt so menacing about a beautiful poet flirting over drinks.

By eight the Ice Maiden was carving up her fragrant Earl Grey cake, after which the exodus began. Kids swarmed in, swept the brownie platter clean like locusts, and streamed out into the dark. Their parents lingered longer than most, savoring the company of adults, but eventually shepherded little people into minivans and were off by nine. The twins astonished me again by helping clean up. Rose grabbed empty glasses and Teddy lugged trash to the curb. Camille and Fee, meanwhile, were closing down the party, relaxing with libations. They looked so different—dark-skinned Camille in a colorful off-the-shoulder blouse, white-on-white Fee—but they were harmonizing fine.

I sat down near them with a huff of relief and an amber ale. "I keep losing time. I don't know where the evening went."

Teddy said, "Down the hatch." He was scarfing down mixed nuts and the last smears of chèvre, scraped onto a paper plate by Helen before she left with her cheeseboard. It was good to see him eat something with nutritional value. When he'd declared himself vegetarian, he had replaced the meat in his diet with sugar.

Fee, sitting next to me on the couch and delicately, avidly forking up a second slice of cake, said, "Cynthia. I haven't yet puzzled out everyone's research areas. What's your specialty?" She had the gift of making small talk sound serious: I could have sworn her interest was genuine.

"American lit. The long nineteenth century."

Fee cocked her head. "Aren't all centuries long?"

As Camille snickered, I finally heard Silvio's tread. I stood up as the kids flung themselves at their father.

Silvio looked older, somehow, but more handsome. He might have even dropped a few pounds around his equator—was that likely in just a couple of weeks? He apologized, saying something about a delay leaving North Carolina, a pile-up on the highway he barely swerved around, and forgetting to charge his phone.

"It's okay." I kissed him on the cheek.

Then I stepped back, gesturing to Fee, who had also stood. "Silvio, this is Fee."

"Hello," she said, giving him a graceful hand. "I'm glad you arrived safely. Clearly you have been missed," she added, with a smile at the golden children.

Silvio did not swoon like Ralph or blush like Teddy. He just thanked her with the expression of a practiced host, polite, concealing tiredness. Teddy fetched him a chair and I cracked him a beer.

We chatted about his new job while Silvio ate the last of the salad (Camille's) and a drumstick. Rose kept a pipeline of cold biscuits flowing in his direction. At some point Fee excused herself. I hardly noticed her absence until Teddy, whose chair was angled for a view of the front door, leaped up with a cry.

"What?" I followed his lunge.

He was down the hall and the outdoor steps in a couple of bounds while Fee stood next to the vintage phone that never rang, holding the screen door ajar, lips quirked up in a bow. "Your cat wanted to explore the night," she said. "The black cat."

How had Pluto escaped the bedroom? I walked out onto the stoop and saw a shadow dash, as he always did, across the lawn and toward the street, not hopping now but steaming ahead fast. Behind that small shape, my son was running, shouting, "Pluto, no!" Focused on the cat, he didn't scan for traffic.

There was a car coming, engine rattling.

I shouted too, and heat surged through my body in an unbearable, nauseating wave, the hottest hot flash since Krakatoa. I imagined the shape of the dark vehicle, extrapolating its size and speed from the arc of its high-beams, and pushed it away from Teddy with my mind. The car veered, more sharply than seemed plausible, with a squeal of tires, and stopped.

I stood in the middle of the road next to Teddy, who was shaking but safe and holding the cat, who was also safe, but indignant. A blue-haired lady rolled down the window of her sedan. She asked in an affronted tone if the boy and his cat were all right.

All right, all right, everyone said, Silvio behind us now, pulling Teddy and me back onto the grass where Rose stood, staring first at me, then back at Fee, then at me and Teddy again. I stumbled at the road's verge, feeling rubbery. I was dripping.

Four

The next day I woke with a headache and sore muscles. Had I really pushed the car *with my mind?* I replayed it: first sensing a crackly connection pulsing from my gut through my fingertips to the iron in the Buick, then, without self-doubt, reaching out with my body's power.

I heard Silvio puttering in the hall, collecting laundry. I imagined how he would respond to a story of magical abilities, and I deflated.

When he and I headed out for an early morning walk, we chatted about nothing more consequential than the fancy new garage, with a second-story guest room, being framed across the street. The twins rolled out of bed and onto the living room couches for a *Buffy the Vampire Slayer* binge. Silvio went back and forth to the washer-dryer between episodes. We scrounged for leftovers. Yet I could tell I wasn't the only one feeling jolted. No one mentioned homework or going out with friends. No one holed up alone for hours or moped around, islanded by headphones.

Teddy and Rose made a fuss of Pluto, who was not a lapcat but would consent to being picked up and scratched for brief durations. He ran hot and spent summer days stretched like a shadow across an air-conditioning vent, close but out of grabbing range. They also performed Voice of Pluto, a trick I hadn't heard since our last cat died. Teddy used to talk to our old ginger tabby, and Rose would answer from the cat's perspective in a crabby old lady's voice. Now Pluto manifested a radically different personality. Rose gently chastised the cat for running into the road, stroking his fur, glancing up at her brother with wild mischief. Teddy delivered by assuming a deep male voice and a New Jersey accent to reply, "Yeah, I don't know what the fuck I was thinking."

"Teddy!" I protested, elongating the syllables.

"Yeah, I'm sorry, Mom," Teddy said in his normal voice, sharing my disapproval, while Rose snorted. "Pluto has a really foul mouth."

Pluto also kept announcing, extended full length over the vent, front legs sticking out like a stone lion's: "I am massive and magnificent. It is right that you worship me." At least someone felt formidable.

Sunday, Silvio and I walked again in the coolness, pacing up a long country road and down again, mistaking real cicadas in the grass for my cricket ringtone, while the twins slept. We avoided the hard subjects, instead analyzing schedules and to-do lists. We both had courses to prep, Silvio for his second week of classes, me for my first. He insisted he would take care of the grocery shopping after breakfast, since I had been doing so much, and I smiled at him, meeting his eyes for once.

I went into the house ahead of him. Rose stood with her arms crossed, tapping her foot, waiting for Teddy's bagel to finish toasting. They were friendly, discussing Buffy's little sister, the one who materialized out of nowhere in the fifth season.

"I had an imaginary sister," I said, prying off my damp sneakers with my toes so I didn't have to bend over.

Their heads swiveled toward me. Silvio was outside watering plants, but he already knew this tale.

"Sister Fox."

"Sister *what?* When was this?" Teddy plucked the hot bagel from the toaster slot, and Rose shouldered him out of the way.

"I don't remember when it started, but she was around for years, through grade school, anyway. Someone must have told me Rennard means 'fox.'"

"You've always had a thing for them," Rose said.

"Trippy," Teddy murmured, slathering obscene quantities of butter on his bagel. "Was Sister Fox an animal?"

I sat down to wait my turn. All week I had been breakfasting on an egg and a handful of berries like a forest creature, but this morning I was determined to consume carbohydrates. "Mostly she looked like a girl, normal size or very small, sort of buzzing around my head like Tinkerbell. But she told me she had a tail under her skirt."

"Wait," Rose interrupted. "Are you saying you actually saw her?"

"I don't remember clearly, but yes. Sometimes I just felt she was around."

My daughter frowned; my son's head was practically immersed in a giant mug of orange juice. "She was real?" Rose corrected herself. "I mean, did you think she was real?"

"I knew other people couldn't see her, and it didn't worry me that my brothers called her imaginary. She wasn't real like a toaster or a school bus. But she had a kind of reality. Maybe like the monsters in the box."

Silvio banged in and wiped his hands, grinning. "Teddy told you about that?"

"Being a dork, he read us half the study," Rose said, deploying a decorous quantity of cream cheese. "But I still want to know about Sister Fox."

I refilled the kettle and cut bread while Silvio explained. "It probably had to do with your mom being so much younger than her brothers. They were a team, and she didn't have an ally. Usually it's the eldest child, or an only child, who has an imaginary friend. And girls have them more often than boys."

"The weirdest thing was, she would surprise me." I paused while the coffee grinder pulverized beans, then picked up the thought as I assembled the French press. "She made me jump, materializing out of nowhere. I'd give a little scream and say, 'Oh, it's just Sister Fox, she startled me,' and my parents would look at each other, like, who is this spooky demon child."

"Your mother still thinks you're a demon child," Rose said.

Teddy was more interested in the imaginary friend. Nobody liked my mother. "So where did she go? Do you still feel her?"

"On the first day of middle school, I was in a stall in the girl's bathroom. Sister Fox was trying to give me sensible advice, and I decided I wasn't having any of it." I paused, staring into space. "I didn't want the responsibility. I wouldn't even look at her. She was in tiny mode, and when I turned around, I accidentally knocked her into the toilet."

"No way!"

"Then I flushed." I began laughing so hard tears sprang into my eyes. "Flushed her right down the john. Never saw her again."

Silvio banged in with an armload of groceries and said, "Cyn, there are flowers on the stoop."

Beneath a blue ceramic vase, plain but graceful, filled with foxgloves, daisies, and other colorful blooms, lay a card. I set the bouquet next to the iron phone, opened the envelope, and read the note. "It's from Fee." Rose made a rude noise and went to fetch more bags from Silvio's trunk.

"She says thank you for a lovely evening, and she's sorry it ended in a scare."

"That's nice," he commented, his tone neutral, and followed Rose while I turned the card over in my hand. The paper was thick and soft, the handmade kind with frayed edges.

Fee's handwriting was old-fashioned and elegant. Even the ink looked antique, a walnut-brown of uneven darkness.

As we finished unloading food into the refrigerator and cabinets, Rose declared, "What Fee did was malicious."

I halted, suspending a box of cereal over a pull-out shelf in the pantry. "What Fee did?"

"I was watching her. I think she let him out of Teddy's room herself, to stir up trouble." There was a bite in Rose's voice.

"She should have asked. But she couldn't have known what would happen." Making space for the muesli, I slid the drawer back and shut the cabinet.

Then, remembering, I asked, "Why did you do that thing with the sweater?"

"That thing?" she repeated, pouring herself a glass of water. Tree-dappled light was playing over the walls, over Rose.

"You know. Friday night. When you turned your cardigan inside out."

Rose put on her stubborn face. "I wasn't wearing a cardigan."

"Yes you were, the yellow one. You looked right at Fee while you took it off, pulled the sleeves wrong-way out, and put it on again."

"No, I didn't." Rose sounded pissed-off. "I didn't do that." She left the room while I held empty grocery bags to my chest for a moment.

From the hall came the sound of pottery smashing. Pluto could never resist frondy plant-stuff and must have knocked Fee's vase over while dragging a few stems free. I grabbed dishtowels and headed to the front of the house, yelling. The cat met me with round eyes and tried to squeeze his bulk under an easy chair, as if he were still a kitten. It was gratifying to see someone flee my wrath.

I was meeting only one class that Monday, the ever-popular American Gothic. The third-floor room, just a few doors down from Alisa's office, was packed and boisterous by the time I arrived. I knew only a few faces. In the back sat Royall, hapless kayak-mad son of a big donor. Royall was also enrolled in my yearlong honors thesis discussion group, even though he remained way behind on his major requirements and might have to stay for an extra semester. Anna and Persis, who had sat together all through my first-year seminar last year, were still traveling as a pair, although Anna had a punky new haircut, bleached silver. Tim, a tall biology major from Jamaica who kept choosing my courses to round out his schedule of labs, sat right up front.

I looked at them, then out the window at a line of purple mountains. When I opened my mouth, the old magic happened, and we were off. For the first time in ages, I forgot my secretive children, my troublesome body, premonitions. I even forgot Alisa.

To break the ice, the students had to introduce themselves by telling an uncanny tale. As in previous versions of the class, most students told ghost stories, often revolving around a dead grandparent acting as guardian. Royall's was set on an ancestral plantation in Mississippi and populated by a large household staff. He recounted it unselfconsciously.

A young woman I hadn't met before, Julene, offered a new spin on the eerie-twin-tale. Twin stories were common, since college meant the first extended separation for many. Julene, it turned out, had been relieved to leave her multiples back home, attending community college together in New Jersey. She was one of triplets, originally two sets of identical twins. Julene's twin having died in utero, she was always on the margins of the threesome, excluded from her siblings' confidences and their special language of looks and signs. Meanwhile, she suffered a recurring dream that her own double lived inside her, hiding in her belly like a malformed baby, waiting to hatch out and wreak retribution.

"Good god," I said, and the class laughed.

I considered what tale I could tell about myself. I thought of Sister Fox, but we'd heard about a couple of imaginary friends already, including a whole invisible family that once lived under Tim's kitchen table. Friday evening flickered into my mind, when I imagined saving Teddy. I found myself recounting something half-repressed.

"When I was a little kid, I believed I could make things happen if I just willed them strongly enough."

"What kind of things?" Persis asked. She was the talkative member of the duo; spikey-haired Anna hardly ever spoke in class, though she wrote beautiful papers.

"What I remember best is wanting a pet and trying to wish it into existence. I visualized a gray kitten walking right up to the house. My mother didn't like animals, but I thought she wouldn't be able to resist its cuteness and would let me keep it. The next day, I opened the front door, and a kitten was sitting on the porch, mewing for food, its big eyes shining. It was ginger, though, kind of a rusty color."

Someone said "aww" and I paused, uncomfortable. "Well, my mother wasn't impressed. She trapped the kitten in a box, took it away, and I never saw it again." Had she taken it to the SPCA, where it had charmed some pet-friendly family into adopting it? It wasn't impossible.

"Professor Rennard, that's a terrible story," Tim said.

"Yeah," I said. "I suppose it's like those tales of three wishes—if you don't frame your wish carefully, it does more harm than good. I really did think I had magical powers, though. I just assumed I needed to get smarter about using them."

At the end of the period, I signed forms for students who had sat in, hoping to add the course. One of them had told a story about a haunted girl's bathroom and wanted to confess its origin in Japanese urban legend. "Hanako-san," she said. "You can look it up."

When the room cleared, I remembered that I should check on Fee. I needed to thank her for the flowers, make sure she knew that no one blamed her for Friday's strange non-accident, and see how she was adjusting. It was late afternoon, the hallway desolate. Alisa, and now Fee, had the third-floor office furthest from the stairs. A line of golden light showed that the door was ajar. Hearing soft fiddle-music, I tapped the door and stepped in.

Dan the buff fiction-writer was lounging in a side chair looking addled, his shock of wavy hair raked into disarray, his dress shirt rumpled. Dilated pupils turned his light-brown eyes black. Fee was sitting on the edge of her desk with an amused expression, one bare calf angled so it nearly touched his knee. She was offering him cherries dark as rubies from a pretty bowl.

I wondered if I should back out with apologies, but Dan spared me by struggling free of the chair with what looked like superhuman effort. He mumbled something about an appointment and fled.

Still amused, Fee looked at me, and I was relieved she did not offer me the cherries. "How is the fair family, Cynthia?"

"Fine. Thank you for the lovely bouquet. How are you, Fee? Are you settling in?"

"Oh, yes." She placed the bowl on the desk. "Everyone has been so *friendly.* Well, except that dean of yours. I don't think she likes me."

I laughed before I could stop myself. Snarking at the Ice Maiden was a handy way to unify fractious college faculty members: nearly everyone, excepting flirtatious Dan and ambitious

Beth-Ann, seemed to loathe her. Yet it was a dangerous subject, and I was surprised Fee broached it. "Well, she is reserved," I said. Then I looked around. "Did Alisa clear out enough space for you? It was such a quick transition."

"Yes, the whole desk except for office supplies. And a few shelves. I travel light." The desktop was pristine except for the cherries and a few old books; the computer was dark, and no cellphone was in sight. So where was the music coming from?

"It looks different. I suppose because Alisa's desk was always buried in paper." The light in the room was greener, too, and the air fresher. "You managed to get that window open!" I said. "I thought it was painted shut."

Fee picked up a flat-edged screwdriver, waggled it, and dropped it into her bag with a laugh. No Celtic incantations, then? Ralph would be disappointed. His Titania was played by MacGyver.

"I worked it free this morning. I can't bear to be cooped up, can you?"

Reminding Fee to call on me if she needed anything, I excused myself. In the hall, I felt a sharp pain at my right ankle and bent over to find another bleeding scratch, this time on the opposite leg. What the hell? I limped downstairs.

Five

As September sped along, Alisa's silence got louder. She had lost track of the world before, during writing binges. Her talent for single-mindedness had once awed me. Now I kept trying to reach her through every means I could think of: email, text, Facebook message, Skype. I called her cellphone and sent a handwritten letter into the void. As I left home each morning, I glanced at the iron telephone, but it remained inert, gathering dust. At work one day, I located a number for Alisa's host university in Wales, spoke to a man there, and was transferred to dead air.

When I went searching for someone to grouse to, I found Harriet in the main office, erect at her highly polished desk and rapping it with a pen. An African American woman, local, amid a sea of mostly white and self-important academic nomads, she made sure even the furniture respected her. When my rant ended, she delivered instructions. "You go try again and tell that man at the switchboard what's what. Don't let him be so lazy."

I stomped back to my lair. Before I punched in the digits, I chanted, "You *will* put me through. You *will* put me through."

A delay ensued, full of rustling, but eventually the same man picked up. Hearing my voice again seemed to make him nervous. "Let me give you the direct line to her, um, division," he said, and spat out a long number. I commanded him to repeat it slowly.

Jab, jab, jab. The static before the ring was louder this time and dragged on longer. The noise verged on a recognizable pattern. Was the hissing in my earpiece more like wind in the trees, or rippling water, or traffic on a busy road?

After a click came a small voice, distant but recognizable. "Hello?"

"Alisa! Is that you?"

"Cyn? How did you get this number?"

We were both laughing and speaking simultaneously, but I overrode her. "Wait, wait, you have to tell me you're okay."

She assured me she was fine, aside from the most persistent jet lag ever. As Silvio had speculated, phone and wireless were posing difficulties. Her school year was about to start, and I'd caught her during her first day in the academic building. "I haven't met any students at all, but the professors I've bumped into are fabulously friendly. They keep bringing me the most delicious cakes, and wine. I'm living on cakes and wine."

"And the house?"

"The house is so strange!" she exclaimed, and then said something I couldn't make out, a garbled sentence or two.

Oh, hell. Was I going to lose her already? "What? Alisa, I'm having trouble hearing."

Another crackly interval ensued, then I heard, "Sorry. Listen, I wanted you to know, it's not entirely safe."

My heartbeat juddered and the sun dimmed. "What?"

"Me, of course, but you, too. Anybody. I mean, I feel fine now, just a little, like, tipsy sometimes, and I did ask for it, but still, what a shock."

Books and furnishings around me shifted into focus, as if someone had twisted a lens. "Alisa, what are you talking about?"

She sounded indulgent. "Well, don't get all *worried.* Just be, you know, alert."

"I still don't know what you're talking about," I said.

She spoke again, but her sentences came out garbled. I could pick out a few words: *cloud, path*, and maybe *changing*. The music of her syllables was familiar—Alisa at her most brisk, elucidating a passage of French theory—but I could not grasp the sense. Then the tune cut out, and a dial tone buzzed. Harriet stood in the doorway. "Did you get through?"

"Yes," I said, placing the receiver in its cradle.

"Well?" Harriet pressed. "Is she all right?"

I tilted my head. "I got cut off."

"Oh, dear." Harriet's eyes glinted with suspicion, and then her face settled into a more familiar expression. "Well, I wouldn't fret. It's all new for her. It's natural for us to think of her, more than the other way around."

"Yes." I stood up. "Harriet, I'm going to take a walk. I feel sort of funny."

Harriet examined me then stepped back. She did not tolerate germs. "You look flushed. Get some air."

I grabbed my jacket and keys and burst out of the building into a breezy morning. The cool air restored me, so once I got free of the department, I slackened my pace. Should I loop campus and return to my desk? Or should I pick up that book the librarians were holding for me? While I dithered, I caught a glimpse of silver-blonde spikes as one of my American Gothic students, Anna, sped by on a heavy old bike. She waved, called out a greeting, and shot past.

I felt useless. What did my conversation with Alisa even mean?

Well, I would pick up the book, then. The wind blew a little harder, rustling leaves overhead, and I experienced a wave of déjà vu. Ignoring my unease, I veered left at the fork, accelerating toward the crosswalk leading to the library.

I heard rather than saw the accident. Tires squealed, and metal clashed.

Anna was lying in the street, her bike mangled. Another student was stepping out of his car, explaining, not very coherently, that she just burst out into the road, he didn't see her coming, he couldn't have seen her, there was no time.

Campus security must have been nearby—yes, their jeep was parked across the street. One of the guards, a guy who had worked here forever, crouched next to Anna, murmuring to her in a soothing voice. The other guard, a younger woman, was barking into a device. She must have been calling the ambulance even as she stood in the road to halt nonexistent traffic.

"I know her," I said to the crouching guard, stepping closer. "Anna. She's my student."

He blinked. "Stay near, would you?" I nodded, and he went back to whispering reassurance.

Anna was alive. Her lids fluttered, and she was trying to tell the guard something, but her legs were twisted. There was blood. I averted my eyes.

Similarly ineffectual strangers loitered not far away, a few on phones. My attention was pulled across the street, toward the library, where Fee was poised on the opposite curb, bright as a burning taper. *What curious thing will these people do next?*, her face seemed to ask as she leaned toward disaster. Our glances locked. I heard sirens.

Anna was carried off by stretcher. The Dean of Students materialized and climbed into the ambulance. They sped away. Eventually two policemen approached. I told them what I had not seen.

The security guard, the one with white whiskers, didn't require my confirmation of Anna's identity anymore. He came over when the police turned away, however, and thanked me for sticking around. He was about to move off, too, when he paused and regarded me again, eyes crinkling. "Are you all right?"

"Yes, just a little shaken up, thank you. I'm going back to my office now."

As those words came out of my mouth, I realized that returning to my building was, in fact, a reasonable plan. Before I did, I raked my eyes over the scene once more. No Fee. Perhaps she had never been there. I was not feeling secure in my powers.

Time jumped, and I was sitting in the English department describing the collision to Harriet and Camille. Both knew that my father, who had always bicycled to work, died in a hit-and-run when I was fifteen. But Anna was moving her fingers, that was good, right? They listened with kind faces, and Harriet squeezed my hand.

At one point Harriet fetched me some water and Camille asked how well I knew the student. I said Anna was a sophomore from Illinois, the one with the punk haircut. Camille nodded with recognition as Harriet handed me the glass.

"Thank you, I'm so sorry."

"What are you sorry for?" Camille said. "And do you know it's two o'clock? Have you eaten anything? Do you need me to get you a sandwich?"

No, I answered, I packed today. I walked to the kitchen in the jerky way my limbs operated now, took my salad from the fridge, and returned to my desk, closing the door behind me. I snapped open the container and regarded the wilted leaves.

College students have accidents all the time. They concuss themselves at wrestling matches and sled into trees. They fall off balconies at parties. Undergraduates die with terrible predictability in midnight drunken crashes, by suicide or overdose. So, of course, there's a protocol. The dean or the president calls the family, and eventually a public notification is emailed around, dancing between information and privacy. As her teacher, I might receive individual messages advising me, for instance, that Anna is withdrawing for the term, or if the accident wasn't as bad as it seemed, asking me to grant extensions. All I could do now was wait.

Fee had nothing to do with it. She was just standing on the other side of the street, holding some old books, thinking professorial thoughts. Or, in shock, I had imposed her image onto some stranger. This accident couldn't have been what Alisa meant by *danger*.

Maybe Alisa hadn't said *changing*. Maybe the word I had barely made out was *changeling*.

A sound issued from my throat, and then I was shuddering in long, dry sobs.

Six

Anna would recover and possibly return for spring term, after rehab. I graded her essay on "Rip Van Winkle" and buried it in my can't-throw-it-out-but-don't-know-how-to-handle-it pile. Class went on, but no one sat in Anna's chair.

A whisper of danger lingered. Sometimes I strolled by Fee's room when one of her courses was in session, listening for I didn't know what. The door's angle blocked her, but her audience seemed enchanted, leaning toward her musical voice. She had agreed to advise Royall's honors thesis; they were reading early Yeats together. When no one was around—as if someone else might get punished if I were caught—I googled "changelings," but the stories I found involved wizened freaks appearing in the cribs of missing babies. Fee remained full-grown and gorgeous. Besides, middle-aged professionals weren't easily mislaid.

A creased, water-stained postcard finally arrived from Alisa, addressed to the whole department. The picture-side showed the kind of watercolor landscape she liked, of a small lake nestled amid spiky mountains. Her message was chipper, with no hint of menace, but dated only a few days after her arrival, well before the phone call. Although a few words had smeared, I could read Alisa's amended street address clearly enough, so I posted another long letter. My emails continued to go unanswered, and I couldn't get through by phone again. I loitered by the iron telephone in my front hall, imagining my index finger turning the rotary dial, and put my right hand over my chest to regulate the flutter of skipped beats.

The iron pills for my anemia kept jumping inexplicably off the shelf, and my fingers buzzed. My new colleague was uncanny as hell. Something was happening. But none of the details added up in a way I could describe persuasively. Silvio thought my stress was triggered by hormones, new responsibilities, and a fresh wave of grief about my father. Every loss can set off echoes of the old ones.

So I got on with the work of teaching, administering the department, and, in spare hours, assembling Camille's file—her passport to the country of the tenured, or an arcane initiation rite into a more elite level of our secret society. I finally nudged Sandra into visiting Camille's Postcolonialism seminar and writing an observation letter. Both of them confided jitters beforehand, given the fascist-desk-arrangement debacle, but the observation seemed to go fine. Sandra's praise was only faintly curmudgeonly.

"You're a great teacher," I said for the hundredth time to Camille one dazzling October morning, as light poured into my office and we reviewed the file's final table of contents.

"But my enrollments are not good." Camille picked at the cast on her left wrist. She had fallen off a treadmill. "I think Royall poisoned the well."

Last year, flabbergasted by Camille's failure to recognize his genius, Royall had scooped up his final paper from the box outside Camille's office, observed the low grade and liberal splash of red ink, and stormed off to Dean Ice Maiden for redress. While any decent administrator would have uttered calming but noncommittal noises, ushered Royall out, then determined the facts—which included late submission and near-total disregard of the assignment—Barbara had, perhaps because Royall's family were big donors or perhaps because she distrusted Camille herself, told him on the spot, "Well, it certainly seems like a fine essay to me." The department rallied behind Camille, and the grade remained unchanged, but the incident shook her and reinforced the general dislike of Barbara.

I sipped my cooling tea. For a while I had avoided hot beverages at work, fearing groutfit-devastating hot flashes, but my body seemed to be appreciating the drop in temperature. Orangey-red flared in the leaves outside my office window.

The intensity of what Camille said next startled me. "No black woman was going to give *him* a D."

I went still. I hadn't seen any benefit in articulating that, even to myself, and I answered her sideways. "He certainly has the strongest sense of entitlement I've ever seen in one of our students."

Camille looked hard at me, then leaned back on my worn side chair. "Royall's behavior is what I expected here. But I didn't expect Barbara to back him."

"One could say Barbara is just completely tactless." Camille's eyebrows rose, and her mouth set. My heart did its arrhythmic caper. I tried again. "She could have brokered a conversation that would have made you feel supported while actually teaching Royall something he needed to learn." True, but not good enough, Camille's expression said. I was disappointing her but didn't quite understand how. I blurted, "You're so good. And this college has such an obvious problem. I mean, with diversity. Hiring and retaining people of. Women of. It's her job to oversee"—Christ. "She should be looking out for you, is what I'm saying, not reinforcing a punk kid's disrespect."

"Racism, you mean. Reinforcing his racism."

I nodded, recognizing, with a sick jolt, the word I had been avoiding. "Racism." The hiss of those syllables made me want to leap out of my chair and flee. Camille gazed at me steadily. "Anyway, your tenure case is really strong."

Royall, of course, might submit a vicious letter for Camille's file. I would handle him somehow. Our senior compositionist, Beth-Ann, had also made negative remarks about Camille in a recent meeting of tenured English faculty, alluding cryptically to the "limitations" of our untenured colleague. Camille didn't know this.

"We are building a persuasive narrative about your achievements, and that's all a tenure file is, a story with footnotes. Seriously, I am not worried," I lied.

Camille confirmed the list of documents we had agreed to assemble for her case. Yes, that's right, I said. And she left.

I wasn't anxious about the eventual success of Camille's case, not really. I felt a more shapeless disquiet, a jitter in my peripheral vision. I sat for a while with my eyes closed, wondering if my tendency toward camouflage and misdirection constituted a kind of power or an evasion of it. Weird energy hummed at the base of my spine. I tried to ignore that, too.

That night, after butternut soup, Rose and I headed to one of the big-box stores. I had no urgent grading, for once. Rose was wailing that none of her jeans fit.

Rose hooked up music in the car and gossiped about friends and teachers. Then in the changing room, she became grim, groaning when I brought her the same style in the next size up. "It's just your hip-bones widening. That's what's supposed to happen."

"Great, thanks," she muttered, and disappeared back into the booth. I considered telling Rose about the summer my body betrayed me and my mother kept pointing out its treachery. *Looking hippy these days, Cynthia.* But talking might make it worse.

Finally she emerged from the dressing area with two workable pairs. I bought her a shirt she coveted, too, even though it was a little sheer and probably violated her school's dress code, then we ordered ridiculous elixirs from the coffee shop, hers with syrup and whipped cream to forestall a plunge of blood-sugar. Outside the cold had become sharp. Stars glittered.

"What's gonna happen with Dad?" she asked as I merged onto the access road and pulled up to a red traffic light swinging in the wind.

"You mean his job?" The blinker kept slow time. Teddy would have been beating the dashboard in complicated syncopations.

"Yeah. I mean, one year isn't such a big deal, but we can't live in separate states forever, right?" She leaned her face against the black glass of the passenger window, which must have been icy, but Rose ran warm, like me. "Saara asked the other day if you guys were getting divorced."

I squawked and turned to her as the light changed to green. "No way, I promise!" The pickup truck behind me honked and, flustered, I steered onto the highway ramp. "That is not what this is about."

"I know. But it's hard to explain to people."

I was silent again. Truth was, Silvio and I weren't doing so hot, for reasons I didn't understand. His temporary move at first seemed like good medicine—breathing space for me, a shot at success for him—but a couple of months into the experiment, I wasn't sure. "I don't know what's going to happen either, except that we're not divorcing, and we're not living apart for more than a year or two, max." On the broad interstate, I could feel gusts buffeting the car and tightened my hands on the wheel. "He deserves a tenure-track job."

Rose nodded. "But what if they make him an offer? Would we move?"

My heart skipped a beat. I coughed. "Then we'd negotiate. Maybe an offer would give us leverage at one university or the other. I love our house, and I don't want to move, and I really don't want to relocate you and Teddy in the middle of high school, but we have to go where the jobs are."

Rose yanked a curl straight, then let it spring back. "Changing schools could be good. Ours sucks ass."

Somehow Rose's cursing didn't bother me. "It can also suck being the new person."

I thought of Camille pounding at the door of the clubhouse of the tenured, all those alarmed white people peering out the spyhole, while Fee, pale and composed, was sought after for every dinner party and quickly initiated into the ritual handshakes. I wondered if Alisa, three thousand miles away, was still being treated to cakes and wine.

Seven

I was feeling obscurely frantic, remembering Alisa's warning to *pay attention.* Was there a way to use this buzzy energy instead of trying to contain it? I shut my eyes and imagined I perceived Fee's heat signature two stories up. Next I reached east, toward where Alisa was supposed to be, and saw mountains under a damp gray sky, then a thatched cottage with a red door, standing ajar. I was hearing, very faintly, a dissonant note from a plucked string instrument.

Someone rapped on my office door, and I jumped. Then I opened my eyes and saw the medievalist. Without showing the faintest interest in why I was sitting at my desk with my eyes closed, Sandra shut the door behind her and perched on my side chair. "I found myself talking to Fee about journeys recently," she said. "I suddenly knew exactly what I wanted. It's time for me to retire."

I dropped Volume Two of a big fat American literature anthology on the floor, losing track of Charlotte Perkins Gilman's "The Yellow Wallpaper" in a crush of tissue-paper pages. "Oh, no!" I cried, smacking my cheeks with both hands. "I had no idea!"

"Your dismay is flattering." Sandra eyed me over half-moon reading glasses. "But we have to declare our intentions by November first, and I want to travel while it's still fun. I have my own pilgrimages to make, you know," she added.

"Pilgrimage" was the topic of Sandra's best-loved course. She covered everything from *Beowulf* to Donne. We were absurdly short-staffed in early British literature. Except for his first-year seminar on Chivalry, our Shakespearean wouldn't take notice of any authors before, or much after, the Bard.

"I understand. It's just the department disintegrating around me." Unexpectedly, I had to wipe my eyes. Sandra tut-tutted, handed me tissues, and patted my knee, which irritated my rash.

"Okay." I hiked in a breath. "Are you ready to write to the dean?"

She was. Moreover, with my approval, she would like to claim a year of phased retirement, teaching half-time. That was a relief, since it gave us more time to organize a search. We could keep the biggest holes in our major offerings plugged while pulling together a job description and a search committee. With the humanities under nationwide assault for their supposed impracticality, the market was terrible for literature PhDs, so we would be able to hire someone terrific, as we had with Camille. We would be okay. It was just change.

We hashed out the timing of announcements and what Sandra hoped to teach in her final semesters. When she left, I wandered into the hallway, disconsolate, with a stained and empty mug.

It was raining, and the building felt sleepy, even though classes were in session. I filled the electric kettle, tapped the button, and watched it. Then I walked over to the mailroom and gazed at Alisa's overstuffed box. Harriet was scanning and sending mail that looked important, as per Alisa's instructions, but had received no reply.

Since I had last checked my cubby, one envelope had been delivered. As soon as I touched it, I thought, *Fee*. It was that soft handmade stuff again, this time striated with gray lines, like tree bark. I saw that a couple of other boxes contained matching envelopes, but not all. I opened mine and found a slip of golden-brown paper, trimmed in the shape of an oak leaf. It read, in Fee's script:

8 pm, Saturday, October 31st

555 Lord Fairfax Street

Dress as you dream you are

Wear dancing shoes

I scurried back to my office, slammed the door, and dialed Silvio. "Sandra just marched in here and told me she's retiring and now there's so much to do and I'm freaked out. Then I go into the mailroom and find an invitation to a Halloween *dance party* at Fee's house, with *costumes.* I don't want to go!"

"Then don't go. Or hedge and decide at the last minute. You can always get a migraine." Silvio's tone was so reasonable. "You don't have to be chair on Saturday night."

Right. I paused for a beat and revved up again. "It says, *Dress as you dream you are*. What does that even mean?"

"I bet it's just a coy way of saying costumes are optional. Hold on—." Through the earpiece, I detected a shuffle, a knock, muted voices. "I have an appointment. Could I call you back?"

I sighed. "Talk to you later." I texted the kids to order a pizza because I would be an hour later than usual. By the time I left the building, the rain had cleared, and a full moon shone onto hunkering clouds.

The week blew past, shaking us down like a late fall wind strips trees. Phased retirement was fine, said the dean, but we would have to petition the administration for permission to hire a new tenure-track person in Sandra's field. Early British literature was not a priority for the college. Biology was short-staffed, she observed, and Business Administration.

This chilled us. I became a number-cruncher, gathering data on enrollments, debating how to spin them with those who could attend a last-minute meeting. Again I reflected that there was no power in my position. I was a levee trying to block power's escape.

"Let's go to the fairy ball," said Silvio over lunch on Saturday. I had told him about Ralph's Titania jokes. My own speculations after the phone conversation with Alisa, and Anna's accident—the possibility Alisa had said *changeling*, that she might have meant Fee—I kept to myself. I didn't want to hear my uncertainties mocked or, worse, endure a patient debunking.

"Rose and Teddy will be at Saara's party anyway." Silvio was loading chicken onto a slice of rye. "You should blow off steam. I'll drive, and we can come home as early or late as you want."

I licked a gob of Dijon off my finger. The leftover roast was delicious, although Teddy kept giving us horrified looks as we picked the bones clean. The night before, when I plucked the salty, crispy skin off the breast and devoured it, my tender-hearted boy had excused his long-suffering self to the bathroom.

"But we don't have anything to wear."

Teddy perked up. "Dad should be the Psychology Ninja." He made karate poses as he talked. "All in black, carrying the DSM."

Rose said, "Hey, I just saw some things in the old dress-up bin in the attic." She darted out and I heard her quick step on the stair.

"Or Pavlov's Dog," Teddy offered.

"Woof," answered Silvio, who bit into his overloaded sandwich.

"I guess we could check out the party, just to see what Fee has done to the place," I was saying when Rose returned, laden with props.

"For you," she said, hanging a woman's wig over the back of Silvio's chair. Then she turned to me, brandishing a pair of black-tipped ears and a puffy brush of a red-and-white tail. They were from one of Teddy's more provocative costumes, given that aristocrats had conducted mounted foxhunts in this area since colonial times.

I yelped. "I'm going to wear a fox costume to Lord Fairfax Street? You really think it's a good idea for a beleaguered English professor to dress like prey?"

"*Beleaguered*," Teddy repeated, shaking his head. "Who talks like that?"

Silvio flung an arm around my shoulders. "My foxy wife." This elicited gagging sounds from the children.

Affection confused me. "What about you?" I asked.

Silvio donned the long, wavy wig. "Kitty Pride."

I looked blank but Teddy started laughing. "Sort of a little sister to the X-Men," he explained. "In some versions she never graduates out of the school uniform, like they won't let her join the big kids. She changes phase, becomes, like, ghostly."

Oh.

"Tonight," Silvio announced, "I will prove my powers to the team."

Eight

I pinned the fox tail to a pair of black jeans, donned a rusty orange sweater Rose declared suited my coloring, applied lipstick and ears, and was done. It was easier than I had imagined to become someone else. Silvio's transformation was more dramatic. He dressed in gray, and the kids, working together, cut a large triangle of yellow felt and pinned it to his shirt. After he shaved, Rose applied shadow to his eyelids and mascara to his lashes. Teddy found a stuffed toy dragon—Kitty Pride had acquired this mascot on another planet, he explained with exaggerated patience—and affixed it to Silvio's shoulder like a parrot on a pirate.

I thought about seatbelts. "I'll drive on the way over."

We dropped the twins off, found a parking spot near Alisa's house, and walked through a front garden illuminated by paper lanterns. I felt a primal dread of parties, heightened by crossness about Fee's alterations to the house. Pots of chrysanthemums glowed like torches. Fee had draped Christmas lights around the door. I tapped, but the music was loud and the door ajar, so we headed through, holding a bottle of wine like a talisman.

There was an actual three-piece old-time band in the living room, now cleared of furniture. The players were locals—a woman from the farmer's market plucking a bass, an older guy with a long beard strumming a banjo, and a red-faced man sawing at a fiddle, who paused occasionally to call some phrase I couldn't translate. The house thrummed; people were dancing. When the number ended they stopped, breathless and hooting, and Fee noticed us.

She flew over, or so her diaphanous gown made it seem, her face sparkling more than her dime-store tiara. She was barefoot, although how she avoided a stomping I had no idea. "Welcome!" she cried, snatched our bottle, and wheeled away, showing off her wings. "Follow me!"

The kitchen was quieter. Fee touched my foxtail with her magic wand and said an unfamiliar word. I had the feeling she was pleased, as if she had finally pegged me. She made sure I found the punchbowl and Silvio his beer. Then she was off again.

Fee was the one person at the party to whom Silvio didn't have to explain his costume. Well, plus a guy from History who got the joke and glossed it for Camille, who may not have been listening. She was wearing a poufy white blouse and domino mask. Twirling an imaginary mustache, she remarked that Silvio looked pretty, and went off to dance.

"So Sherlock Holmes is who you dream yourself to be?" I asked the baby-faced historian, who had accessorized his three-piece tweed suit with a deerstalker hat. This question bewildered him. Eventually we figured out our invitations contained different instructions. *Wear a piece of clothing that changes you,* his oak-leaf read. A man from the German department was standing nearby and exclaimed he'd been told to *come as your favorite symbol.* I stared at him until he pointed at the little Styrofoam balls bobbing from springs attached to a hairband—antennae, apparently. "Umlaut."

I was surprised by how many attendees were half-strangers, given that I had lived in this town for twenty years. The bookstore proprietor was there, and Teddy's high school jazz band director; I met the editor of the local paper and the burly landscaper who led the local ghost tour, booked for my Gothic class the following week.

With a few more sips of flower-scented punch, it dawned on me: I liked everyone there. If Fee had escaped some otherworld in exchange for Alisa's freedom, and if she were using her liberty to attempt assassinations and trigger topical rashes, she also had her good points.

This wasn't a college-heavy crowd, although I spotted other partiers from campus. Silvio edged closer to the musicians. He had played piano, once upon a time. I wasn't surprised to glimpse him accepting a dance from the widow who owned the wine shop.

The older members of the English department were conspicuously absent, and I experienced guilty relief, too, at the nonappearance of the Writing Program Director, Beth-Ann, and her sidekick, Robin. I liked their spouses and children, but our composition specialists grated on me, Beth-Ann in particular. I wondered why Dan, sweaty on the dance floor, was dressed like a sexy priest, but I needed to cool off, so I exited to the porch.

The band director was peering at the sky through the screen. "The moon is gorgeous," she said. Fewer stars were visible here than in my velvety-dark backyard, but the moon was grand, snowy, and huge. "I was crushed when the super-bloodmoon got rained out last month."

"Yeah, me too!" What an emblem up there, shining down on middle-aged women everywhere.

Lines from Elizabeth Bishop's "Insomnia" floated into my head. I kept the verses to myself but said, "There's a poem I teach sometimes. It made me realize the moon is a mirror, the biggest one around. I mean, I guess that's obvious, it reflects the sun and doesn't shine in its own right. But the poem made me really *get* it. It's no wonder we see ourselves when we look up there."

"The man in the moon," she agreed. "Or the woman."

"The perimenopausal woman in the moon. No way that's a virgin goddess."

A pirate and Dorothy of Oz were waiting outside the downstairs toilet, so I headed for the other. From the steps I saw Silvio dancing in a crowd to a song with a frenetic pace. The cute widow was near, but they were bopping around in a tangled group. Fee and Dan, by contrast, moved like a couple. That was the way Alisa had come to suspect Sunshine, last New Year's—by watching her dance a little too close to a stranger. Sunshine always had magnetism, not so much beauty as a kind of super-aliveness. Fee, too, seemed more real than everybody around her, fully present in the moment and in Dan's arms. I prickled with the recurrent hunch that Fee flourished at Alisa's expense.

I felt my friend's absence more strongly on the second floor. As Rose said, I was afraid of mirrors, especially lately. I tsked when, washing my hands, I saw that my fox-ears were crooked, hair pulling free and clinging to my brow in sweaty curls. But in the light of the beeswax candle Fee had left burning, I didn't look so old and tired. My lipstick had gone wherever lipstick goes, but inner fires kept me pink.

I checked my phone to make sure I hadn't missed a message from the kids. It was after eleven, somehow, and I had only heard the band take one break. They switched to a sweet, slow tune, probably winding down for the night. Alisa's neighbors wouldn't tolerate the racket forever.

Movement in Alisa's bedroom caught my eye. "Sunshine?"

Alisa's ex, wearing a strawberry-blonde braid, flannel shirt, and overalls with hay sticking out of the pockets, started. Standing by a bureau covered with decorative boxes, she shoved something into a large quilted knapsack with iron buckles. Then she moved to hurry past, but I blocked her.

"What are you doing here?"

"Fee invited me." For all her boldness, Sunshine did not meet my gaze. "She eats at the restaurant all the time." That was where Sunshine's affair had started, fondling produce with a farmer who supplied her locavore café. She tried again to sidle past, muttering "excuse me."

"No," I said, as if to an actual request for forgiveness. I was still angry at how she took whatever she wanted, without considering the cost. Surprised at my own rising glow, the itch of authority in my fingers, I noticed a bare spot on the wall above the bureau. "What's in the bag, Sunshine?"

"It's mine." Her freckled face contorted into a scowl, and she clutched the knapsack to her side.

I reached for the bag, which practically leapt into my fingers. I hadn't expected her to yield. She was taller than I, and strong.

I extracted a pretty looking-glass with a frame of beaten tin that had obviously hung from that exposed nail a few moments ago. "I bought that in Mexico," Sunshine snapped, and added when I pulled out two miniature watercolors, British landscapes that used to hang downstairs, "Those were birthday presents. To me." At the bottom of the sack, two fancy pottery mugs, recognizably from a nearby gallery, were wreathed in Alisa's scarves.

Nothing valuable, as far as I knew. Still, my outrage began to reach white heat. I had known Sunshine for years and years, sharing long evenings over food and wine, watching her feed treats to my cats and tickle my little children on sofa cushions. Why had it taken me so long to see her for what she was? And why would Fee invite Alisa's ex over, anyway, to rummage through the few artifacts that still spoke of my friend?

Was Fee preventing Alisa's return, so that she could stay?

I dumped the rest of the purse's contents onto the bedspread and handed the bag back to Sunshine. "Get out."

She snatched her wallet and keys and ran. Feeling sick, I placed the mirror back on its bent nail and avoided my own glance. Heaven knew where the other items belonged. After an indecisive wobble, I left the mugs, miniatures, and scarves scattered over the quilt and clicked the door shut behind me. Descending the stairs into music, I felt madder and madder. My fingers burned.

Fee hadn't broken up Sunshine and Alisa, some part of me understood, yet Fee's interloping presence marked the catastrophe. Like an umlaut. Alisa left, Silvio left, yet the queen of the fairies gets a job in my own damn building and is universally worshipped.

There she was, slow-dancing with handsome Dan who had been Barbara's secret honey until two months ago. Fee's eyes were closed, her tiara rested just below his clerical collar, and they looked *happy*.

I wanted to wreck it. I wished for the celebration to end, for everyone—no, for Fee—to hurt like I did, having lost so much I used to like about my life. She needed to feel vulnerable, too.

Sweaty with resentment, hardly knowing what I was doing or why I thought I could do it, I summoned trouble. I raised up a curse against the charmed luck of the interloper; the energy beneath my skin knew where to go.

The front door flew open and in walked the Ice Maiden. She was always exquisite in pastel blouses clinging to her bust, in pencil skirts and patent-leather heels and frosty blondness, and tonight was no exception. Now, however, she communicated a wild sorrow. I gazed down from the steps and felt sympathy for Barbara. Then her lips twisted as if she were summoning some ugliness of her own.

Dan froze, the oversized crucifix he wore on a chain swinging like a pendulum. His dance partner opened her eyes and stared right at the dean. Still as a listening deer, Fee didn't look penitent. She shone, instead, with her own magic, a stronger force than I might ever be able to match.

Could Barbara freeze Fee out of our territory?

Barbara held Fee's gaze while the last note reverberated, the fiddler now dangling his instrument by its neck, members of the party crowd moving more and more slowly, like molecules in a chilled solution. Then, without saying a word, the Ice Maiden pivoted and strode back to the door. Her heels clacked against the oak floor and the front steps as she exited, a not-yet-exploded bomb. Tick, tick, tick.

Nine

"I know, in the scale of things, this isn't trouble," I said, sitting up in bed Monday morning. It was only six a.m., and I was no early riser, but I couldn't shake a weird dream. Plus, my period was back with a vengeance.

Silvio had already showered and was tossing his shaving kit into a duffel bag as I added, "I mean, school shootings in Oregon, Arizona, Texas. People are dying. We just have a pissed-off, jilted dean."

Silvio grunted, standing there in underpants and buttoning a shirt. His hair glistened in the lamplight, dark from water. How mysterious people were, even when you shared their bed for decades. "What do you think she'll do?"

"I don't know." I punched the pillow and lay on my side watching him pull up corduroys. They made a scraping sound against his dry calves, which bulged from jogging. "But I feel a sense of doom."

"Is Dan going to get a smaller raise this year or lose out on conference funding?"

"You know, I don't think of Barbara as an especially intelligent person, but she does know the rules. She had a secret thing with a guy she supervises, so she can't dock his pay. Then he'd have a legal case for retaliation. But I'm glad he's tenured." With a nauseating flush of warmth, I realized that if Barbara's fury included me, this would be a terrible year to try to leverage a tenure-track job for Silvio in the psychology department.

Silvio zipped the duffel, delivered a cool kiss goodbye, and promised to call when he arrived.

I stayed in my cocoon, wiggling my toes and remembering what had seemed like magic flashing around Alisa's house. That must have been the surreal thought-process of a buzzed masquerader. My confrontation with Sunshine was proof I hadn't been myself. I didn't boldly wield eerie abilities. I didn't act at all, not when my best friend disappeared, not even when my marriage was starting to fail.

As I unpacked my satchel and booted up my office computer, a meeting request pinged in from the dean for eleven a.m. *today.* Dread rolled through me, like the opposite of a hot flash.

When, cramping sharply but fortified by coffee, I arrived at the dean's headquarters, the administrative assistant greeted me in a chipper voice. I hung my jacket on the coat rack and sat down to wait. It wasn't long. A furtive-looking sociology professor reeled out of the Ice Maiden's office, and Barbara came out, smiling. "Cynthia," she said and gestured for me to follow.

Some occult *feng shui* governed the arrangement of chairs and loveseats in her office. Where would the strongest person sit? I plumped myself down on a sofa. Barbara sat in a chair that was, of course, the real seat of authority.

She was a woman studying power. You could see it in her body language, her outfits. Male administrators tended to all look the same: sun-starved complexions, neutral suits, bristly gray haircuts. Women in these positions—not that there had been many—demonstrated a wider range of expression. We'd had a female president briefly, a square-shaped woman who played herself as outdoorsy even in pinstriped skirt-suits. Her heels were low, her hair short and tidy, her tone no-nonsense, and she hunted and fished. That was one path to authority: trick men into thinking of you as another old boy. That president had given me a book once, on women leaders in academe. Instead of reading it, I left it on my desk for a month, untouched, then returned it through campus mail. I would not acquiesce to that particular magic.

I had seen ampler, gentler women in elevated ranks code themselves as maternal with soft hairdos and flowy blouses. They didn't rise as high. Barbara's professionalism was feminine, too, but of a sexy kind. Today her skirt and blazer were tweed, her blouse pale coral, heels a color marketed as "nude." A string of pearls nestled against fair skin. She was good-looking but had already crossed to my side of forty. I wondered how this persona would wear over the years.

For now, it exerted force. "Sandra's retirement," she began, "gives us an opportunity to reconsider the shape of the department."

My eyes widened, but I kept my mouth shut. It was never good when an administrator wanted to micromanage your staffing, but sometimes you had to play along to get what you actually needed.

"Surely you have considered long-term enrollment trends away from literature, toward writing."

"Creative writing," I qualified, not liking where this was heading.

"And composition. The first-year writing courses are always full, and Beth-Ann's advanced composition course is doing well. Writing is the skill your alumni value most highly, according to exit surveys. Since literature's relevance is much narrower, it may be time to restructure."

Oh my god. She had been reading the anti-humanities playbook. I tried not to choke. "Writing instruction is very important to all of us. But we can't stop teaching *literature.* The mission of a liberal arts college is to produce well-rounded—"

Barbara waved my noun away with a manicured hand. "Being 'well-rounded' is a luxury. The economy and the educational climate have changed. But of course your department will have to discuss this." She kept avoiding the word "English," with its literary taint. Holy hostile takeover.

Be respectful, Cyn. "What exactly do you want us to consider?"

Touching her pearls, the Ice Maiden revealed how far the seas had already risen. "Beth-Ann and I have had some exploratory conversations, and this weekend she emailed me a proposal for a Writing Major. I'll send it over to your department, but in short, it preserves Literary Studies as one track among three. The others would be Creative Writing and Strategic Communications. All three tracks build on a yearlong foundation of composition courses."

"First-year seminars?" I croaked.

"Existing introductory courses would be abolished in favor of more cutting-edge pedagogy. All teachers of the new courses would adhere to syllabi devised by Beth-Ann."

The phrase "cutting-edge" drew blood. If she used the phrase "outside the box" next, I would...what? Wish her inside one, with a horrible, mean monster sporting ash-blonde highlights? "The way we currently run our first-year seminars is wildly successful."

The set of Barbara's mouth was becoming smug. "Yes, they are delightfully quirky. But is it the best possible use of classroom time? Are students learning how to function effectively in a global marketplace?" She rose onto her spikes, radiating vitality, towering over my depression in the soft couch. This was a tacit dismissal, so although light-headed, I struggled up, too.

"Call a meeting and talk it over," she said. It was a command. "But it's a very good proposal. With implications for future staffing, of course, which is why these discussions have urgency. It would be much easier to make a case for, say, an expert in technical writing than an Early British specialist." Beth-Ann's crony Robin specialized in technical writing.

Staffing was the way to control the department's decision. Better a second composition professor, even if he had no interest in literature at all, than to lose the permanent position—or so Barbara hoped we would decide.

Had Beth-Ann been trying to create a tenure-track line for Robin at Camille's expense, before Sandra had announced retirement? In a recent meeting, the senior compositionist had disparaged Camille's file. *This essay is gussied up in theory*, she said, *but it's a superficial treatment of minor works. And Camille is too...political. The students hate that.* I had suspected she was trying to stir up trouble, but I hadn't known why.

The last of my feisty heat drained away, and I skulked out of Barbara's office, resembling, I was sure, that furtive sociology professor.

Since every forty-five-minute interval in my life required a stop in the bathroom, Beth-Ann's proposal arrived by email from the dean before I reentered my office. I forwarded it to the English faculty. Howling and rending of flesh ensued, but I couldn't find a meeting time until late afternoon Thursday. Harriet booked a room and warned everyone to be there, contingent professors too, if they wanted a voice.

Thursday morning, wan with sleep deprivation, I met the honors thesis students in the Main Street coffee shop. This group included three creative writers; a woman studying medieval women mystics with Sandra; and Royall, who was now obsessed with Yeats and Fee. I arrived with time to place an order for a flat white. I needed energy from somewhere.

Three students were already chattering at a large table in the back room, and a fourth arrived just after me. Sandra had announced her retirement in class yesterday, and her ascetic, frizzy-maned thesis advisee was *verklempt*. They didn't know about Beth-Ann's proposal, which had already dwarfed Sandra's retirement among my anxieties.

"Will English be running a search for her replacement?" said one of Dan's protégés. Her eyes were watchful, her fiction satirical. As a sophomore she had participated in a sample class that had led to Robin's hire on a three-year contract, so she knew the drill.

I framed my reply carefully. "Not this academic year. We need time to work up the job description. And before we even get that far, we have to petition for the return of the line."

Royall slid in last, ducking into the empty chair with hair still damp, but he picked up the gist. "The line?"

I was impressed despite myself by Royall's metamorphosis. This was not the stoned narcissist of yesteryear. As I distributed handouts, I explained that the college had a fixed number of tenure-track slots, so when people retired, all departments fought for the position. I was preparing a case for English.

The women-mystics researcher looked as pained as a saint. "But we need Chaucer! There's no one else who teaches medieval stuff at all!"

"I agree. We wouldn't be much of an English Department without Chaucer."

Royall had been staring into his coffee foam. "Is there any chance of Professor Ellis becoming tenure track?"

My suspicion that Fee was manipulating us all from behind the scenes resurfaced. "Not really. Her field is too close to Alisa—I mean, Professor Humaran's. We're a small department, so we can't afford a ton of overlap."

"Professor Ellis is also a poet," Royall observed. The boy was besotted. "We don't have a tenure-track poetry writer, do we?"

"No, that's true. It would be good to have another tenured creative writer, in addition to Professor Kuo, that is." I glanced at my watch.

Royall persisted, his cheeks still chapped by early morning cold. "Is Professor Humaran definitely coming back?"

"Yes. At the end of this year. She's *definitely* coming back."

The only meeting space Harriet had been able to reserve was in enemy territory: the dean's conference suite, a still-unseized "naming opportunity," according to Development. When I entered, Beth-Ann was holding court at one end of the shiny oval table. A neat stack of documents sat before her, next to a steel water bottle. She was an alchemist, prepared to transform our unhappiness into her gold. The chair to Beth-Ann's left was conspicuously empty, but her junior ally perched at her right hand, laptop open, with his timid poet-spouse on his other side, braiding the tassels of her scarf. Fee and Dan were conversing over steaming mugs—the handsome ceramics I'd rescued from Sunshine. Their body language suggested a team of two, not yet allied with either of the department's other factions. Camille was clicking laptop keys. Ralph and Sandra sat together, straight-backed, and Sandra held a textbook in her lap. The seat directly opposite Beth-Ann remained empty so I sat there, trying not to feel defensive. I missed Alisa, a better warrior than I would ever be.

After setting up my own laptop and taking a deep breath, I called everyone to order with a reminder to remain civil. "We've all read Beth-Ann's proposal, so we need to hash out pros and cons. Let's start with each person speaking for three minutes, no interruptions allowed, beginning with Beth-Ann, then moving around the circle. Once everyone says his or her piece, we'll see where we stand."

Beth-Ann, larger-than-life, spoke with a confident Texas drawl, but she muted it slightly as she began to sling lingo. Her terms reflected an odd mix of conservatism and trendiness—"digital rhetorics," for instance—probably meant to appease different biases but alienating everyone at the table. When she said "outside the box" and followed it with "impactful," another bit of corporate-speak, I smiled blandly. I had asked Dan to monitor us with the stopwatch on his phone, and he called time exactly as the final syllable of Beth-Ann's practiced speech rolled from her mouth.

"My turn?" Sandra demanded, and I nodded. She lifted the book from her lap and slammed it onto the table. We all twitched. "Has anyone else read the textbook Beth-Ann wants us to adopt for these up-to-the-minute composition courses?" Robin opened his mouth then shut it again. "No? Well, I did, and it's utter, unredeemable trash."

Beth-Ann framed a syllable but, with a glance at me, swallowed it. She flushed scarlet, not with embarrassment but fury.

"Criticism without evidence doesn't help us," I warned Sandra.

"Cynthia, dear, you're only urging moderation because you haven't read the atrocious thing. There's not a word of literature in it. It's bad enough for a talented department to become a bunch of robots, all teaching watered-down exercises from the same tiresome manual, but what she proposes is *no more literature.* There's a whole school of compositionists advocating this now, and Beth-Ann has joined the cult."

Beth-Ann sat still, but Robin fidgeted. I hardly ever called him by name, because it felt like making fun of him as protégé to the black-clad compositionist-superheroine. Robin's wife stopped knotting her scarf-fringe and gawked.

"This book contains no short stories or poems. There aren't even any autobiographical essays. All the writing samples are *essays about composition by composition specialists.* They could not be duller or more crushing to the spirit. This whole movement is a universal employment bid by and for comp-rhet true believers."

Camille uttered a tortured sound, half laugh and half gasp, then clapped her hand over her mouth. Her eyes flickered from face to face.

"God forbid writing students be exposed to any good writing. This whole proposal is a disaster from beginning to end. The quality of our teaching would disintegrate. Our majors would either transfer allegiance to real disciplines or end up with a degree not worth the paper it's printed on."

"Time," Dan whispered.

"I'm done," Sandra replied, her voice now shaking. "I mean I'm really done. This is an *English* major, goddammit. We teach books. The department implements this proposal over my dead body."

The silence stretched. Light-headed, I was suddenly aware of Sandra's skull, a death's-head pressing against papery skin. "Well," I said. "Ralph."

Looking stormy, the Shakespearean answered, "Of course Sandra is completely right. I agree with every word she said. I was a little alarmed when we hired a creative writer."

Here Dan exhaled and rested his elbows on the conference table, brow thumping into his hands. I glimpsed Fee's expression—could that be glee?—but she spotted my glance and composed herself. Dan peeked out again at the curmudgeon's next words.

"But that worked out all right," Ralph conceded. "Creative writers care about literature. In their own way. They are book people. I was wrong about Dan, but completely right about Beth-Ann *and* her sidekick. They do not belong here."

"Ralph." My voice had an admonishing edge, but a squint at Beth-Ann told me it was too late, or hopeless to begin with.

Ralph's closing speech was hurried. "Anyway, terrible idea. Nothing more to say."

Beth-Ann erupted out of her chair and grabbed her things. “Beth-Ann,” I said, “Ralph was too harsh. This proposal just blindsided everybody. Stay, and let’s keep talking.”

She exited in a whirl of rage and paper, Robin behind her, and his wife the poet trailing behind Robin, mouthing, *Sorry.* She dropped her scarf in the rush. It lay on the floor in a silvery puddle.

Ten

I banged into my house, yanked vegetables and leftover rice from the fridge, and got out the wok. Silvio was still down south, attending a dinner and an evening lecture.

I took satisfaction in diminishing hairy carrots to clean orange disks; slicing green onions on the bias; dicing a slippery lump of pressed bean curd into well-behaved cubes. Rose sidled up when I was ready to combine it all in sesame sauce.

"Not tofu," she groaned.

"Your brother likes tofu! I like tofu! You will eat it without complaint or you will organize and cook your own nutritious meal, also without complaint!"

Rose held up her hands, backed away, and set the table. As my carnivore folded the napkins with extra care and hunted out chopsticks, Teddy jutted his head around the kitchen door. "Um, everything okay in here?"

I banged three bowls onto the island and dished a heap of stir-fry into each. As if in defiance, I sprinkled flecks of cilantro on each mound and tucked wedges of lime at the rims.

Rose served milk for Teddy, tap water for herself, seltzer for me, then helped carry bowls to the table. Teddy was lighting a candle. The one good thing about daylight savings was closing the curtains against my stupid day and eating by candlelight.

"Mmm," said Rose, with a full mouth. "Good tofu."

I cracked up, although the laughter became a moan. I dragged my hands down my face in a way my mother taught me not to, because it stretched the delicate skin around the eyes and promoted early wrinkling.

"So what happened?" Rose asked, squeezing lime over her dinner.

I told them, realizing too late that I had sworn my colleagues to confidentiality. Oh, well.

"Sounds like Beth-Ann deserved the old-lady tirade." Teddy shook his head. "That was sneaky of her, going to the dean behind your back."

My Monday morning dream popped into my head, so I told them about that, too. I had been hosting a party, not here but in some other lamp-lit house. I never got a clear view of any guest's face. It was supposed to be for turning fifty, although that birthday remained a year and a half away. Mostly my dream-self watched a shadow sliding around people's legs among their dress shoes.

"That's Pluto," Teddy said.

"Like him, yeah. But in the dream, it was a long-haired black fox with writing on its back, characters in flaming red that were supposed to be a message for me but that I couldn't read. Then someone opened the door. I tried to follow, but it was gone."

"Even more like Pluto," Rose said.

"I'm sure that's why I dreamed it. But when you called Beth-Ann sneaky, I thought of how sly foxes are supposed to be."

"Beth-Ann's the giant one, obnoxious, dresses in black?" Rose asked. I snorted and rose to clear the bowls.

"No, Mom, sit." Teddy took the dish out of my hand and stacked it on top of his and Rose's. "Or pour yourself a glass of wine."

"You just want me sedated." I went to the fridge, sure a bottle of sauvignon blanc was open, but it had disappeared. I cracked a beer instead.

While Rose blew out the candle and Teddy heated tap water, both of them whispering, I wandered with my microbrew to the dark living room and gazed out the window. Pluto, sitting on the sill, purred as I approached. I scratched him between the ears, missing Alisa, missing the fizz of power I was not allowing myself to believe in.

I read for a while and checked my email around nine, wondering if any additional fecal matter had hit any rotating blades. The only interesting message was from Dan. Cc'ing Camille, he asked if we could meet at Fee's tomorrow to share a glass of wine and talk.

The compositionists would be visiting a regional writing conference all day, so it wasn't as if I could reconvene the whole department anyway.

Yes, I typed to Dan. I'll be there.

The next morning in Harriet's office, I gave her the gist. Then we admired new pictures of her grandbaby.

"You know how I feel about Beth-Ann," Harriet said. Beth-Ann only spoke to her to conduct swift transactions—fifty copies, please—then departed without a how-do-you-do.

"She doesn't understand how mighty you are," I said, and Harriet laughed.

As I moved to leave, insight made me reel. Harriet was black. Beth-Ann, scion of a wealthy white Dallas clan, treated her as unimportant.

Harriet looked at me and waved. Her expression reminded me of how I felt when a student was being slow, but I had to keep my mouth shut and let him figure things out.

I waved back and teetered out. Beth-Ann had been slyly dismissive of Camille, our one African American professor—hell, she had tried to undermine Alisa and Dan, too, both of whom were children of immigrants. I remembered Camille sitting in my office, trying to get me to say the word *racism.* As in my dream, the writing was on fire, but I hadn't been able to read it.

Pay attention, Cyn.

Nauseated, I settled at my desk. What could I do with all this hot shame, my scanty power? I needed to spend it now, on something unambiguously good. I decided on reference letters and tried to infuse them with uncanny persuasion.

A half-hour before Silvio swung by, fresh from the highway, to meet me for a late lunch, my desk phone rang. Absorbed in the intricacies of a particularly annoying online submission system, I picked it up without checking caller ID.

"Hello, Cynthia?" my mother said. Oh, god. "So you're at the office. Are you working?"

She always seemed surprised I wasn't at home like all the other lazy so-called professors who taught for a few hours a week then put their feet up to peruse *The Communist Manifesto* while munching artisanal seaweed crackers. "Sure, but I can talk for a minute. What's up?"

"I hear Andreas is visiting you for Thanksgiving."

Busted. "Yes, with his new girlfriend." The younger of my two brothers was recently divorced, and his ex was taking the kids to Florida, so he was driving up from Atlanta to see us. "And we don't want to travel this year, given how many hours Silvio spends on the road already."

"Oh, yes, so tragic, leaving you and the kids all alone." My mother sounded blithe. *Please, no*—but already she was delivering her news. "That's why I'm coming to you. I just booked a train ticket. You can pick me up at the station on the Wednesday."

"Let me write down the details," I said, fishing for scrap paper in my desk, considering carving the appointed hour in bloody letters on my still-itchy arm.

I griped to Silvio about the impending visit all the way to the café and through the placement of our orders. Then I carped about Beth-Ann's proposal.

"Dan's invitation to drinks at Fee's is interesting," he said, stirring his iced tea. We had scored a window table and the tea, with its wedge of lemon, shone like a pane of stained glass. Reflected sunshine played across his features.

"Worth a try." I regarded his face. His expression was neutral, contained, and un-Silvio. "What's wrong?"

He shrugged. "Nothing. Broome State is good. Classes are good. My colleagues are great."

"Seems like you all go out a lot."

Silvio tensed. "What does that mean?"

"You all socialize after work at least once a week, right? That kind of friendliness is not so common."

His shoulders relaxed. "No, it's not common. But it's nice."

I paused, seeking the right words. "So, this was a good decision?" I heard the quaver in my voice. "You're happy?"

Again, his face seemed closed under the dancing lights. "Sure, I'm happy." He smiled at the waiter as he approached with two plates, and Silvio leaned back into shadow.

I turned to the window and watched a starling perched on a bike rack outside, grooming itself. The bird cocked its iridescent head, as if listening, then whirred up and flew right at me, smashing against the glass.

Adrenaline from the bistro dive-bombing sharpened my afternoon. I disposed quickly of tasks I had been dithering over and cleaned out my inbox. Near five, when I met Camille to walk to Fee's, I realized my lethargy had dissipated and that it was a lovely evening, the heavens streaked with unlikely hues. Fresh from a conversation with my students about literary realism, I thought for the millionth time: reality and realism are conflicting phenomena. Realism requires fantastic levels of artifice, while what passes for ordinary life is unrepresentably strange. In what sense was that psychedelic sky plausible?

We didn't talk about the awful departmental meeting on the way over. I asked Camille about the guy she was dating, and she grew animated. She was wearing his oversized jacket because her own wouldn't slide past the cast on her wrist. Camille had been lonely, and this boyfriend seemed good for her. Best of all, he practiced law half an hour away, in a larger town, closer to DC. More worried that Camille might find another job than about her tenure case, I was rooting for local entanglements.

Dan greeted us at the door. I remembered Halloween's weirdness but tried to act normal: shuffling off my coat, admiring the fire in the living room grate, handing Fee a box from the chocolatier. She accepted with delight then receded by some sleight-of-hand into the background. It was difficult for a beautiful woman to become invisible, but she nearly pulled it off. I kept glancing at her, wondering about her stake in all this. None of our politics should matter to a visiting professor.

In the living room, which seemed rearranged although I couldn't have said how, a couple of wine bottles were set out, as well as single-malt scotch and a silver bowl of almonds. I didn't see the miniature landscape paintings.

When everyone was settled with a glass in hand, Dan leaned forward to rest his arms on his knees. Hair fell into his eyes with cinematic panache. "So," he began, "Sandra and Ralph were totally out of control."

I choked on nut fragments. Camille said, "I couldn't believe Ralph. He basically said he hadn't wanted to hire any of us. But Dan, *you* turned out all right."

I picked up a napkin and tried to act calmly authoritative, like a department chair. "Ralph got called in to speak with university lawyers today about breaching search confidentiality, so I want to be careful here. But Ralph didn't kick up the fuss he implied about any recent hires. He was enormously impressed with your tenure file, Dan."

Dan held his whiskey up to the firelight. "People just get freaked out about change."

"Old people," Camille said.

I reached for another almond, folding one stockinged foot up on the leather chair and remembering Dan's predecessor, not a fiction writer but an eighteenth-century literature expert and master of a wide spectrum of snobberies. "When I was hired, back in the Stone Age, one of the guys judging my tenure file thought American Literature was a newfangled area of study."

"I know people who think that way," Fee said from her dusky corner, moving so lamplight revealed her amusement. "They believe nothing worth noticing has happened for hundreds of years." Hmm. I had been referring to an Episcopalian from Birmingham with a Jonathan Swift obsession.

The changeling or European or whatever she was still wore green, blue, and white. Tonight she sported a soft wool sweater in a mossy hue as well as splendid leather boots. Although I still found her uncanny—too perfect—Fee looked comfortable here, in this town, this house. In her body.

"Same dude who thought Presbyterians were stupid, I bet," Camille answered me, as if she hadn't heard Fee.

"You got it," I flashed back. Camille never forgot a story. "I guess you have to be Episcopalian to understand."

"Anyway." Camille had business to conduct, and scotch would not be slowing her down. "So there was crazy talk, but it wasn't all crazy. I went to Sandra's office today to borrow that book." Interesting—those two were friendly again. "Just like she said, it was bad. The whole proposal's bad. It's just a power grab."

"Agreed," said Dan. A new coalition?

Fee retrieved a board from a side table and began slicing a wedge of Manchego into neat arrows. Magic was wafting from her, wasn't it? Yet she hardly uttered a word.

"So," I asked, "what next?"

"I want the proposal to go away, but it's not that simple." Dan rumpled his hair, making an elf-lock stand straight up. "Barbara loves it. She loves Beth-Ann." His grimace conveyed embarrassment. "I, uh, heard something about this idea weeks ago, separately, from both of them. I thought Beth-Ann was just tossing around possibilities, seeing if I'd be on board with the Creative Writing part. I said I wasn't sure but it would be worth discussion. I didn't realize how far planning had gone, but I should have mentioned it, Cyn."

I looked up from my wine into his apologetic face. The playboy thing had always put me off, but Dan was a good colleague, smart except where Fee was concerned. "So. What *do* you think about a Creative Writing track through the major?"

"I wouldn't push it if no one else wanted it." He spoke slowly, and I felt Fee's focus pouring into him as he continued, "Some of our current majors might have chosen Creative Writing instead of Literature, if it were an option."

Camille nodded. Reassured, Dan went on. "I don't want to hurt enrollments or jeopardize any of our existing fields. I actually want my workshop students to read *more* good literature, from more periods. About more composition courses, however, I could not give a flying fuck."

"A flying fuck!" Fee echoed, delighted by Dan's aerial imagination. She finished slicing the cheese, and all of us lunged for pieces.

My cheesy arrow pointed right at my mouth, so I nibbled it to bluntness.

Positioning hers on a cracker, having mastered pincer movements despite the awkward cast, Camille said, "If the dean wants a proposal, we could write one of our own. Two tracks. Literature and Creative Writing, study and practice of the same art. Fancy it all up by drafting new learning outcomes including digital methodologies or some such shit."

I couldn't keep quiet anymore. "I've been wondering what Barbara does want. Is she on the market? Does she need to take credit for splashy changes in the curriculum?"

Dan replied, "Last I heard she was watching advertisements, but not urgently. This is her fourth year as dean, so it would be a logical moment to step up the ladder somewhere. But she's not desperate."

Right.

"She could be plotting a long-term exit strategy." Camille was tearing apart a dried fig.

"Or she could simply want revenge. To replace people she perceives as enemies with people she perceives as allies. And I don't just mean she's pissed at Dan," I said. Dan leaned back to put a hand on Fee's knee, while Fee smiled with serene self-possession. "She thinks we're elitists looking down our noses at her Business PhD. She's never liked English, and most of us don't like her."

"Truth!" Camille hoisted another Manchego slice like a flag. She and Fee were laughing. I wasn't sure why, but I could feel common cause building and narrowed my eyes at Fee. "So what if we wrote a counter-proposal?" Camille asked. "Appeasing the dean, our own way?"

I nodded. I didn't understand how this played into Fee's hands, but she smiled and smiled.

Well, damn, they were excited. We hashed out details for a while, layering notion onto exuberant notion, then divided up tasks. Camille had to rendezvous with her boyfriend. I waved her off as I unhooked my jacket from a peg.

Dan was carrying glasses back to the kitchen as I paused at the lintel, experiencing a pang of compunction. My paranoia had turned me into a lousy host. "Fee, I neglected to ask you about Thanksgiving. Do you have plans? I'm cooking for relatives, and we'd be happy to include you."

"Dan is taking me to Northern California," Fee said. "I will meet his family, and see redwoods, and taste wine, and ride horses!" She flung her arms wide. I didn't understand how this buoyant spirit could inhabit the same body as secretive Fee, the visitor about whom I still knew almost nothing. Or the version of Fee who glinted with spite.

As I strolled down the front path toward the sidewalk, I imagined titrating a dose of Fee into three days with my mother and watching the reaction. My mother spewed toxins, but if anyone could bind and neutralize her venom, I had a feeling it would be Fee.

Eleven

Tory—one of several girlfriends since Andy's divorce, but the first he had brought to a family gathering—dabbed sweat from her hairline as my mother, seated near her at the kitchen table, pried into her job, religion, and politics. Andy drank coffee without speaking. While I chopped celery at the counter and weak sunlight streamed in, Pluto marched back and forth, keeping watch over the interrogations.

Giving him the eye, Ariadne, my mother, paused. "What a hairy beast. Tell me again why you named him after the god of the dead?"

He's named after a cat in a story, Teddy said, by Edgar Allan Poe. Shifting my weight from foot to foot, tired of standing but glad of my distance from the table, I concentrated on the clean, salty smell, stripping away long fibers from each stalk. I didn't notice Teddy's proximity to a sore subject until my mother was expounding on the roots of "Andreas" and "Cynthia" in family tradition and, why not, Greek history.

"Cynthia refers to Mount Cynthus on the island of Delos, sacred to Apollo. The Pythian priestesses told prophecies to pilgrims there for thousands of years," Ariadne said, then spun a few examples. I wasn't convinced her facts were trustworthy but didn't intend to contradict her while onions were frying so fragrantly in butter. It was late morning after a light breakfast, and Ariadne would fast until dinner; the longer she smelled good food and refused to eat, the angrier she became.

She hated my nickname, Andy's too, and began lamenting them as I stirred diced celery into the onions and handed a colander of golden potatoes to Silvio. He set up a paper bag between his knees and began peeling them. I ran water into a large pot, and the noise washed out the details of a familiar tirade.

As I turned off the tap, Ariadne pointed at the twins, who were required to spend time with their grandmother without headphones. Both hid behind their hair, which she had already informed them needed to be cut, and their phones, which incited comments about hunched necks and bad posture. "And you two, Rose, Theodore. Why your Italian father and your Greek mother gave you such waspy names, I will never understand."

"Silvio *and* his parents were born in this country, ma, as were you. And Dad was French-Canadian. And your parents, the real Greeks, died before I was born. We're American."

"Such a terrible thing, loss of heritage." Ariadne clasped her bony hands together and bowed her dyed-brown head. "I will always regret it." Then she perked up. "I was thinking, Cynthia, that you're old enough now to serve as Pythia."

"Not quite fifty yet," I answered, using the sibylline authority of my glance to warn that her age, too, was a plausible topic of discussion. The eerie energy that had ebbed from me for a while was rising again.

"You're practically fifty. But the position is now closed, I hear." She giggled then turned to ask Tory her age, evidently younger than mine although Andy was eight years my senior. I cast my brother a sympathetic look, though not too sympathetic. It's not like he rescued me, ever.

That evening, when we helped ourselves to seconds of whatever we loved best—dark meat and sweet potatoes for Rose, mashed potatoes and buttery rolls for Teddy—I poured mushroom gravy over my challah-bread stuffing and scanned the table. Andy was sitting next to Silvio and talking sports, screw them both. I wished with all of my malfunctioning heart for just one sibling, or even one parent, with whom I shared enough common ground to banter until hours melted away. Yet I was relieved to have pulled off another Thanksgiving and to be off my aching feet. Silvio and the kids, I knew, would leap to help each other with the dishes, if only to escape the boozy intensification of my mother's attention.

Tory complimented the meal but refused seconds of everything except wine. Ariadne beamed at her. "Such a delicate eater. That's why you're so slim, Tory." My mother raised her eyebrows at me, or rather what was left of her eyebrows after decades of plucking and penciling. "You've put on some weight, Cynthia, honey. Must be because you're such a good cook."

I lowered my wine glass while, in synchrony, Rose dropped a forkful of yams. Across the table, Silvio stopped mid-gesture. Heat fizzed in my fingers.

Was it worth engaging? Didn't I feel better when I took the high road? "You're looking too thin, actually, mom. Put a little meat on your bones, and you'll live longer." Oh, crap.

Ariadne's laughter tinkled again. "You can never be too rich or too thin, can you, Tory?" The poor woman blushed to the roots of her hair and tore into a dinner roll.

My mother ignored that. "But you've always been different from me, Cynthia, so different, focused on your career rather than your family. Not self-conscious about looks, either, which is such a blessing."

"I feel focused on," Rose said. "As in, laser-beam attention."

"We're proud of Mom," Teddy said.

"Yes." Ariadne looked from my lanky son in the wrinkled tee-shirt to my blue-jeaned daughter with the stubborn mouth. "You both take after her."

"They do take after Cyn, and amen," said Silvio. I tried to smile at him. He began to collect plates, but Ariadne could not be deflected.

"Neither you nor Rose resembles me at all," she went on, although that wasn't true. My hair was lighter than my mother's natural color, and my features were my father's—I missed his funny, pointy face. Yet my build was hers, just more generously fleshed, and, though an inch taller, Rose was cut from a similar pattern. Ariadne was short, like a wolverine.

"I sometimes wonder," Ariadne said, "if your sister had lived, would she have taken after me."

Andy put his napkin down and opened his mouth, but nothing came out.

"My sister?" I glanced at my mother and then at my brother as I strove to understand. "What are you talking about?"

"Didn't I ever tell you? I couldn't stand to talk about it, not for years and years." As she spoke, my mother shrank before my eyes, becoming less demonic, frailer, worn to translucence. I couldn't recall meeting this small mother before. "I bet Andreas barely remembers."

"I remember a little," he said. His dark eyes turned first to me, and then to Ariadne. "I was four, right?" My mother nodded. Andy's voice was hesitant: my mother doted on her sons, but the price of her worship was their obedience. "She was a tiny baby, impossibly fragile it seemed to me. I was afraid to touch her. Then she died, and you"—he stared at Ariadne—"you fell to pieces. For a long time. When one day you walked downstairs in your normal clothes again, cooking breakfast like you used to, Dad said we were never to mention the baby. And Cynthia came along."

"That's right."

My birth had followed the death of a sister, a sister who, in some vital way, hadn't existed until five minutes ago.

"Poor little kitten was just nine weeks old," she whispered. "Well, that was fifty years ago, water under the bridge, as they say. But it changed me, all right."

I felt that metamorphosis sending out its ripples even now, from the shadows under the bridge, right down the generations. Sister Fox shimmered in the air.

"Sorry," said Andy in soft tones after pie, as he and Tory and my tired old new mother prepared to return to the hotel. Ariadne was in the bathroom, and Tory standing near us in a dim, clean kitchen while Silvio dried dish after dish, returning rarely used bowls to their high shelves. "The subject was taboo for so long, and then it was just weird to bring it up. Mom isn't wrong that I barely remember. I thought about it when my daughter was born, but it seemed like a dream."

"I'm glad to know now, anyway. It explains a lot."

"A secret grief," said Tory, and I nodded and hugged her. She looked surprised.

"I don't think I ever told you, Andy." I turned to my much taller brother, already holding a heavy winter coat. Those Atlantans acted like it was freezing up here. "I had two miscarriages before conceiving the twins."

"I'm so sorry, Cyn." His face was lined, I imagined, with his own sorrows, the experiences that, by middle age, could be etched visibly on our bodies. Maybe, however—I thought of Ariadne—one had to immerse oneself in the language before deciphering the script.

"I didn't tell Mom, either, because it made me feel weak. I had this idea," I said, shaking my head, "that being an intellectual person meant I would never be able to carry a child to term."

Andy cracked a grin. "And instead you carried two at once, like some kind of superhero."

I belly-flopped into sleep, as though crashing down into water, and surfaced at three, wide-awake. When insomnia plagued me in Silvio's absence, I could get spooked, thinking about what mirrors reflected in the dark. (They reflect darkness. In the wee hours, this is not a satisfying answer.) Silvio was here, however, and had rolled onto his back. He was gently snoring.

In the bathroom I discovered I was menstruating again, too soon. I sorted myself out, took pills against headache, and tiptoed downstairs to eat a banana. Standing in a kitchen illuminated only by green clock displays, with Pluto purring around my ankles, I gazed at the starlit backyard.

I had been wishing for a sister and, in the saddest way, my mother delivered one. My ill-framed petition brought no luck, or not the luck I wanted.

I did feel more compassion for Ariadne now. Her rage, long predating my father's death, seemed less baffling.

Able to consider frightening ideas only at night, I cast back to September. If my desire had diverted the car aimed at Teddy—which was impossible—that had been a wholly successful wish with no harmful consequences, neatly baffling forces of destruction.

What about wishing broken-hearted Alisa out of my hair, or mopey Silvio? Or standing on Alisa's staircase in my foxtail, longing for Fee's comeuppance? Or even calling to the starling from inside the bistro, the one that crashed a few beats later into the window? If any of those had been acts of will, the kind of magic my childhood self once tried to perform, they had all gone bad. Alisa muttered of danger over a phone call I had forced, then a student got hurt, and my friend fell silent. Silvio seemed all too happy without me, and I felt moodier than ever. Fee was settling into my department and my town; stopping Sunshine's theft hadn't fixed the deeper problem. Plus, as if all the women in my life were working counter-spells, trouble had redounded on me through Beth-Ann's plotting with Barbara. Those two were suffering—clutching power desperately now that an important ally, Dan, had changed teams—but Fee, target of my frustration, seemed cheery.

Fee was, I realized, the beneficiary of our departmental meltdown, better-woven into the team now, enjoying weekend adventures with her handsome boyfriend. Her weird presence was becoming *normal.* What I had come to think of as my allergic reaction to Fee, that persistent rash, had calmed.

I regarded the faint spill of light from our house onto dormant grass and whiskey-brown leaves clinging to an oak. It was irrational to imagine I had influenced others' actions, much less automotive physics, by force of will. It was even crazier to wonder if Fee were a changeling, working powerful glamors, or if Barbara exerted some witchy ice-magic. The world worked otherwise.

Yet some part of me, insomniac and shivering, suspected my wishes had consequences. Maybe I could pretend I believed in magic and see what happened. On the odd chance I was developing an ability to influence events via the mythic transformation of perimenopause, I would have to be careful, anticipating how desires get bent. How other yearning people around me might be sending out their own wishes and interfering with mine.

I bent to stroke Pluto's fur. He was a materialization of darkness, vibrating.

If I had three wishes, what would they be?

Twelve

For one thing, I wished Beth-Ann's proposal would go down in flames.

During my Monday morning email triage, a text from Camille flashed across my cell. *BATMAN AND ROBIN HAVE BEEN HAVING AN AFFAIR*. I had revealed my private nickname for Beth-Ann to Camille, who now used it indiscreetly.

Camille's next alert: Robin's wife, the poet, was walking down from Camille's office to mine. Sweet Jesus. No more tears! Before I could do more than panic, a less-timid-than-usual knock sounded on my door.

The poet, however, was calm. With no extra verbiage, never mind weeping or expletives, she described how she had suspected a relationship between Beth-Ann and her husband for months. "So I started looking for a job," she told me, as I tried to match her composure. She had just been hired at a nonprofit near DC.

"Not a lot of money. But I never liked teaching, really," she confessed. "I'm glad to start something new. I'm just sorry to leave you in the lurch with those workshops I was booked to do—I have to move north by January."

I wished her well, sincerely, even as I was turning over possibilities for replacing her—registration was over, her classes full. After she left my office, I cross-checked schedules to see if my notion would work. It did. I dialed a number.

Yes, Fee said, she would love to take over the poet's two spring-term workshops, if the dean approved. If my scheme succeeded, Fee would keep her seminar on twentieth-century British and Irish poetry—but for her lower-level literature courses, also well-enrolled, I would try to hire the partner of a new engineering professor, a youngish guy who had just finished a PhD in Comparative Literature. His expertise was similar enough.

The dean was pleased, wanting to keep the engineering professor happy. She worried about retaining *some* junior faculty, apparently.

And oh, Fee said, when I called her back to confirm, she'd recently had a few poems accepted by American literary magazines, as well as a creative nonfiction piece. She flashed prestigious journal names at me like fairy bling.

When the department met later that week, Beth-Ann wore unrelieved black and an air of hauteur. Robin, his nerve depleted, kept his mouth shut. The poet didn't appear.

Dan's proposed Creative Writing track included a lot of literature courses, and Camille and I had added a few upgrades to the Literature track that bemused Ralph. We achieved a quick endorsement, with two dissenting votes from the obvious quarter. I would present our curricular recommendations to the dean and arrange for her to meet with the department.

The dean's assistant and Harriet couldn't work out a mutually agreeable time until the new year. "I sense stalling," Harriet said, her eyes brilliant amid a web of laugh-lines.

How could any of this have resulted from wishing? Our counter-proposal had been a collaborative effort involving many hours of work. Batman and Robin's affair, and even the poet's awareness of it, had preceded the dean's attempted coup. If my overblown sense of crisis had influenced the course of events, I felt sorry for the dynamic duo's children and spouses—or, mostly sorry. The poet had rough transitions ahead, but she was free of the treacherous Boy Wonder.

My second desire was to discover what in hell the twins were up to.

Our guests left the Saturday after Thanksgiving, liberating Rose and Teddy from the obligation to sit still and get criticized. They wanted to go to a party with friends we didn't know, so I drove them to an enormous house in the county with a Ted Cruz sign on the lawn and made sure I got a wave from the parents. Silvio planned to pick them up at eleven, an hour that infuriated Teddy. A senior from jazz band, he kept protesting, could drive them home later. On dark country roads at one in the morning in some teenager's truck? No way, I countered. Teddy was muttering angrily when he slammed out of my car.

When, a few hours later, Silvio drove off to retrieve them, I went to bed and slept heavily, so I didn't hear about the drama until morning. I trudged downstairs in my pajamas as Silvio was grinding coffee beans. He described how he had arrived just after eleven to find Rose on the stoop. When he stepped inside, Teddy burst through the patio doors stinking of cannabis smoke.

"He was high?"

Silvio poured coffee into two mugs; unhappy creases crinkled his brow. "Someone was definitely smoking weed, and Teddy's eyes were red, but I was too angry for a real conversation. When they get up, we have to talk."

When the morning got so late it was obvious the twins were starving in hiding, we called them down and sat them on the sofa. Both admitted to drinking beer.

"Which was nasty, so I poured mine down the toilet," Rose said. Teddy stayed silent.

Silvio inspected one face, then the other. "Did you smoke?" he asked.

"No." Rose met Silvio's eyes steadily.

After a fidgety interval, Teddy spoke with his eyes cast down. "There were kids smoking pot in the backyard. But I was just out there talking to them. I swear."

God, they were obvious. Well, Teddy was. I was less confident I could see into Rose.

Silvio launched his too-young-to-drink-or-smoke speech: there was nothing immoral about a beer or a joint, but imbibing intoxicating chemicals at a young age biochemically primed the brain for addiction. He possessed excellent professional credentials on the subject, so I always let him handle it.

I had a more specific story about getting drunk at sixteen, not long after my father was killed by a speeding driver. I passed out in someone's guest room and came to consciousness as the boy I had a crush on was raping my inert body. I didn't tell anyone until Silvio, years later, and I wasn't sure how to tell my children now.

When Silvio paused, I added, "Plus teenagers who get drunk or high can hurt people they care about, or people can hurt them. Parties are not safe." Rose leaned forward to scrutinize me. Silvio just said *right* and resumed his teenaged-brain-on-drugs lecture.

Teddy maintained an earnest expression, nodding appropriately, murmuring *I know* at decent intervals. Gray light washed over his features. In the window above his head, rows of clouds arranged themselves in foaming breakers, bright but opaque.

Sharing the same couch, stubborn Rose lurked, mostly, in shadow, although I sensed she hadn't wanted to attend that party in the first place. Repeatedly she bent down to stroke Pluto, who sat at her feet purring and staring at me. Whatever insight he was beaming in my direction, I could not translate it.

The next morning, when I was sure the twins had caught the school bus and wouldn't be returning with hangdog expressions, I searched Teddy's bedroom. No condoms, no roaches. My eye lingered on his cheap laptop, which overheated constantly, but it was password-protected.

I also pawed through Rose's things. I found nothing but an actual paper diary in her sock drawer. I held it with both hands for a minute, running my thumb over the embroidered silk cover. I did not open it.

Teddy became the soul of reasonableness, helping with chores, practicing the trumpet without reminders, once even making his bed. Rose's criticism, meanwhile, wore me repeatedly to the snapping point, and then she criticized my bad temper.

"It's like you're possessed," she hollered on Tuesday night. "No wonder Dad left."

She slammed her bedroom door. I stood there open-mouthed. The twins were already grounded, and I had confiscated Rose's phone after fighting about chores. If there was any other privilege I could strip away, any punishment Rose actually cared about, I didn't know it.

Late on Wednesday, the day I ran a successful vote to overhaul the major, I rolled the kink out of my shoulders and knocked on Rose's bedroom door. "What?" her muffled voice demanded.

"May I come in?"

I heard shuffling sounds, then, with an excess of patience, Rose answered, "Yes."

She had removed only one of the ear buds connecting her to the laptop. The other dangled, emitting tinny music. I sat on the edge of her bed, rubbing a frayed spot of the bedspread, trying to put genuine openness into my question.

"Rose, will you tell me what the matter is?"

"What do you mean? Nothing." Her pointy chin jutted a fraction more.

"Is there trouble between you and Teddy?"

This disconcerted her; one hand froze in the act of pushing curls behind an ear. "Teddy?"

"I just have this feeling," I said. "The way you've been looking at each other since that party. Did something else happen?"

"No!" Rose looked even angrier. "We told you, we didn't do anything worse than one beer that night, and I didn't even finish mine. You laid down the law, no more parties in the county, and I get it. There is no trouble except this paper I *have* to finish. Can I please just do my homework?"

A hot flash prickled, radiating out from a spot deep in my rib cage, then was extinguished in the sea of my daughter's stare. She wielded her own force, and it was stronger than mine.

Silvio returned late Thursday for a weekend of shopping and Christmas decorations, since he would be staying in North Carolina the following weekend. We wedged a real tree into its plastic stand on Saturday. We decorated it while carols played on the stereo, although the twins spent several minutes texting for every ornament they placed, and I redid much of their work, moving the lamest old decorations deep in the needles and trying to camouflage a patch of bare branches. As usual, we had chosen a blighted specimen, one that leaned drunkenly.

I kept the atmosphere light by describing my American Gothic class. "They made this awesome campus ghost tour. I mean, I was kind of hoping they would have noticed all the massacres and enslavement in the area, which most of them didn't want to talk about, but they did uncover some wild stories. Julene interviewed the president's wife and had this tale about their basement." I paused dramatically, looking around, but the kids were ignoring me. Only Silvio asked, so I recounted the narrative with few extra flourishes, waiting in vain for one of the twins to show interest.

When Julene and Persis had delivered their presentation, the president and his wife stood rapt on their front porch. Now even Silvio gave a distracted response. He, too, was concealing the tree's dead spots with ornaments, but whenever he straightened to fish another decoration out of dusty boxes, Pluto would dash in, knock the latest silver ball out of the branches, and chase it across the floor.

"Can we go?" Teddy asked, and I waved them off in disgust. Both kids pounded upstairs as Silvio collapsed at the kitchen table and blew out a sigh.

I sat down, too. "Ho, ho, ho."

"I almost screamed at them to cheer the hell up."

I put my feet on his lap, but he didn't get the hint about how much they needed rubbing.

"So," my conflict-avoidant husband said, meeting my eyes. He was wearing a reindeer sweater, a holiday standard, threadbare now. "Something happened to me, Thursday, too. Nothing bad! I just haven't quite wanted to say it out loud."

I waited, feeling hot and anxious again, as he grabbed my big toe. This was the third wish: for Silvio to come back and be happy here, somehow. Whatever it took.

"My chair, Ross, came to see me. He said I was doing a great job, he's been hearing raves from my students, and everyone was really impressed with my colloquium presentation before Thanksgiving."

"That's wonderful!" I said. But I felt paralyzed.

Silvio grimaced as multicolored lights twinkled among rapidly drying needles. "He also said Broome State would love to keep me. They haven't managed to secure the tenure-track line yet, but he could definitely offer me another full-time year, and he hopes I'll hang on while they try to convert the position."

I inhaled a deep breath of festive pine scent. "Okay. So now what?"

"He doesn't need an answer right away. But I should get in touch with the Psych Department here, let them know, and ask what they can offer me, if anything." The local head of Psychology was not, we thought, an ally of Silvio's.

Our decrepit multi-change CD player, set on random, whirred as the carriage rotated to play another disk. The first notes sounded of Elvis Presley's "Blue Christmas."

Silvio and I chopped vegetables for soup. Our conversation was interspersed with long silences, and his knife-hand trembled as if he feared to cut the leaf-end from the parsnip. When I turned the bubbling pot to low, the phone rang.

It was Sandra, my retiring medievalist. She'd had lunch that day with her old friend, the developmental psychology specialist whose field overlapped with Silvio's. The psychologist had been diagnosed with leukemia, one of the acute kinds, and the prognosis was not good. Nor was treatment likely to buy her much time. Six months, the doctors thought, maybe a bit more, although it was never easy to predict. Sandra's friend planned to teach her scheduled spring courses, but after that, who knew.

Sandra was upset. Her friend was just shy of sixty, a beloved teacher. Yet she called not out of grief but because the news foreboded a job opening that would be perfect for Silvio.

Third, most dreadful wish.

Thirteen

The rest of December was beautiful but wrong. Before Silvio could figure out a tactful way to contact our psychology department, the chair wrote to him, wanting to determine his teaching availability for next fall.

The office hallways resonated with Ralph's off-key whistling of Christmas carols. He had a limp now—what was that about? Beth-Ann exuded superiority in high heels, even as she thinned down to the musculature of a distance cyclist. Her face was all disdainful eyes and aristocratic bones, while Robin's sagged in premature wrinkles.

Even the weather was inverted, a mirror-image of the proper season. The days were balmy. Instead of snow, frilly blossoms clung to apple branches.

The weekend after classes ended, I baked a few trays of cookies, the main ingredient of which was resentment. Rose prowled the property in an infectious bad temper, Teddy fled to a friend's house to finish a school project, and I graded and shopped and seethed.

I even begrudged my own diligence. Why was I working so hard to care for people oblivious to my labor? Why not, instead, get a jump on my Christmas break research plans—ugh—or lie on the couch with a novel?

I jammed melty broken chocolate crumbles into my mouth while loading up cookies for the freezer—the kids could eat sweets when I liked them again—and arranging others in tins. I yelled to Rose that I was off to do errands and slammed out to the car. Pluto, on the windowsill, watched me back into the road.

After a run to the butcher's and the wine shop and the food co-op—how did my life now require so many separate errands?—I dropped cookies off with the chess tutor and an older woman who used to babysit the twins. Then I parked near Fee's house. Alisa's house. I carried a festive tin up the slate walkway, like the homemaker my mother trained me to be. Those lights Fee had strung around the entrance for Halloween still twinkled, and a fragrant brush of pine adorned the door.

Fee answered in leggings and a creamy tunic with the sleeves pushed up. Her hair was coiled at her nape, and she held a pen. Evidence of actual human effort, and on a Saturday! Months after meeting her, and sending Alisa to Wales in her place, I was still uncertain about Fee. Her strangeness could be a changeling tale I spun to distract my lonely self.

Like a normal person, Fee greeted me with a show of friendliness and led me back to the kitchen, past a dining table stacked with student papers. "Stay a minute. I was just about to brew more tea."

Trying out affability, I sat at the counter. She hadn't put up a Christmas tree, but as I walked in, I'd glimpsed cut greenery on the mantel. In the kitchen, Fee was shaping a wreath of fir, holly, mistletoe, and sprigs of acorns. I complimented her work and, with a few deft twists, she completed the circle as the kettle heated. "It's for you," she said.

I protested ritually then accepted the lovely thing.

"I like making them," Fee said as she poured boiling water into a teapot over a concoction of loose buds, leaves, and twigs. "Bringing wildness indoors."

"This wildness will have to go on an exterior hook. Pluto is a marauder. Last night he tore my dining room centerpiece apart—I keep finding holly berries everywhere."

"How does the fair family celebrate the holidays?" She placed a few of my jelly thumbprint cookies on a saucer; the raspberry and apricot centers caught the late afternoon light. I watched Fee wait and realized that if I were Fee, I would be swirling that teapot around, pouring a little water prematurely, impatient for the brew. But Fee leaned against the counter without any appearance of considering time at all.

We would have presents and Christmas breakfast at home, I explained, then drive to upstate New York for a long weekend, where Silvio's noisy, sociable clan lived. "The twins have lots of teenage cousins on that side, so they love to visit," I added, as I finally succumbed to the lure of my own buttery cookies.

She told me of her plans to fly to Miami with Dan, drive along the Gulf Coast in a rented car, and spend a few days in New Orleans. "I have always wanted to see the Big Easy," she said. "Pick up some voodoo charms."

I presumed, after her fairy costume at Halloween, Fee knew Ralph referred to her as Titania. I was less sure about whether she intuited enough about my fears to be taking sly digs at me.

Whatever her resemblance to elven royalty, Fee had been a good colleague so far. More of a constructive force than I had feared, whatever her motives. I sipped her homemade tea, strong and floral, almost minty.

"I saw Teddy downtown today." She fished a stray twig out of her china cup with a finger impervious to heat. "With his girlfriend. Such a good-looking couple."

I cocked my head, remembering Teddy's painstaking account of study group plans, the challenge in his eye as he made certain I was paying attention. He said he would be at Emmett's. Now I considered how to probe Fee's remark with an appearance of casualness. "He has female friends, but not a girlfriend, exactly. What did she look like?"

Fee smiled. "Long dark hair, olive-skinned, pretty. They were holding hands on a bench in that little downtown park while she finished a cigarette." She took an innocent sip, her eyes cast down at the teacup.

Great.

"Don't worry if he hasn't told you." Fee looked up, her thick lashes flicking. "Teenagers like their secrets, and love is the best kind of secret. Harmless."

I thought of pregnancy, rape, disease, Robin's ruined life.

Fee laughed as if she could detect those words scrolling across my forehead like a CNN crawl. "You don't keep secrets very well, do you? Except one."

I placed my nearly empty cup down on the china saucer, trying not to see omens in the loose foliage clumped at the bottom of the cup. "What do you mean?" I rose to get out of there, swaying in my boots.

Having avoided looking into the tea leaves, I read my fortune instead in Fee's green eyes. "The secret you keep from yourself. That you are unhappy."

I ventured into the early winter twilight holding my wreath. Was I unhappy? Had it been a secret?

Mr. Mukherjee's placid yellow lab, paws against the fence, barked and barked—at me.

As I walked, not watching where I was going, a jagged charge ran up my leg. I looked down and saw that I had veered off the curving walkway onto the springy turf under an oak. The branches were bare but the grass underneath, dotted with moss, remained green. I had trodden on a sprinkling of mushrooms. No, on an uneven line of them. Oh, holy smoke, a *ring* of toadstools brushing the knobby roots of a grand old oak on a grand old street in central Virginia. I was half inside a fairy ring.

With a shudder of desire, I brought my other foot forward, too. Is this what unhappy people do, walk into fairy rings?

Once I stood inside the circle, the dog's bark was muffled, then melted away. I heard a trickling stream but couldn't see it. The light changed, not darkening exactly, but turning greenish, the hue Midwesterners say precedes a tornado. Yet there would be no storm here, just a watery peace.

I dropped my coat and purse but held onto Fee's wreath. No more burdens. Inhaling piney air, I realized the aches in my shoulders, hips, and temples had vanished. I hadn't been conscious of pain until it released me.

Had I really spent three wishes on Silvio, the twins, on my fucking *department*? Man, I was so far gone.

It came to me I was dreading Christmas not just for the chores, the anxiety of choosing presents and cooking meals and never being sure I would meet everyone's expectations. I was also balking at the two weeks after Christmas, before the new term commenced, in which I had promised myself, following Alisa's example, to implement some article revisions, write a grant proposal, and lay groundwork for next summer's research. My writing projects were difficult, finicky, and ultimately subject to the difficult, finicky demands of editors and reviewers, and the work bored me. I had been promoted to full professor, had no more hoops to clear, and could no longer see my weary industry doing anyone any good.

Little currents still fizzed up through my limbs, but not unpleasantly. The warmth felt normal and right.

Was I bored with my job? I asked myself, and the answer followed: no, not all of it. I liked helping my students. I loved class discussion, turning the novel or poem over in our hands, passing it around, asking questions as if it were a Magic 8-Ball, and reasoning through the consequences of the answers.

So: I wanted to teach, but I did not want to write articles and grant proposals.

For the short winter break, avoiding writing projects would be easy enough, but eventually summer would come. If I put aside writing forever, what would I do with the hours?

All these months, years maybe, I had thought I feared change. I fought to keep my department intact, my husband his cheerful old self, my kids young—everything the same.

Maybe, instead, I desired transformation. The air swirled around me, breezeless yet alive. The trees, the dirt, my body all hummed with vitality.

"Cynthia."

I realized that for a while now I had been hearing a low feminine voice call my name. I rotated, scanning for the source, but saw only a green glade illuminated by indirect sun. The world's glow was filtered by clouds, leaves, and something else. I felt a pull in my hands, however, as if through the wreath, and allowed myself to be drawn. "Cynthia."

I stumbled into Alisa's front yard. Fee stood there, at the edge of the path, looking resigned. The night was fully black, mist blocking the stars, but a hazy moon made a bright spot above the houses.

"You were in your own world," she said.

Looking over my shoulder, I couldn't see the toadstools in the grass, but my rumpled coat and purse were strewn there. I was about to walk back for them when Fee huffed.

"Let me," she said, blurring with sudden movement as she dashed forward then returned to drape my cold belongings over one arm.

"I'm glad you gave me the wreath." My voice sounded strange, as if it came from a distance.

"Yes, that was lucky." She examined me, tense about something, then seemed to give up. "You probably want to go home now, Cynthia."

I glanced at her in surprise. "Yes, I do. Thank you for the tea."

"And thank you for the cookies." Fee walked me to my car, saw me in, coaxed me to put the wreath down on the passenger seat, and shut the door. She waved that I should just go, already. I started the engine. She shook her head and walked back to the house.

Shallow scrapes on my ankles were throbbing as I released the emergency break and put the car in gear. I glanced into the rearview mirror. Petals dotted my hair.

Rose and Teddy crowded into the doorway, faces dark, haloed by light. Teddy snatched Pluto as he tried to charge out and flipped the cat upside down in his arms like an evil, toothy baby. I climbed our front steps, bemused.

"Are you okay, Mom? What's going on? Where were you?"

"What time is it?" I asked, shaking off bits of blossom before I squeezed past them into the house.

"Nearly ten!" Rose, usually as rational as her father, looked flushed, almost teary. "We've been freaking out. Why didn't you answer your phone?"

"My phone never rang." I slotted Fee's wreath onto an empty hook before I pushed the front door shut behind me. After a moment, I twisted the lock.

Teddy dumped the cat onto the rug, took the grocery bags from me, and thudded back to the kitchen. Pluto, playing one of his obscure games, jumped to slap his paws against my thigh and galloped after Teddy.

Rose snatched the cell from my purse, thumbed in my passcode, and scrolled through messages. Her brow creased. "The calls and texts didn't go through. God, mom, you're way behind on updates. I'm going to fix this, and call Dad on my phone to let him know you're okay."

Still clumsy, I hung my jacket in the hall closet with excessive care. This is what a person does when she comes home for the night. I removed my shoes and paired them, one by one, under the bench. In the bright kitchen, I squinted, gathering from the pot in the sink that the twins had fixed themselves macaroni and cheese. I registered the murmur of Rose's phone call from the other room.

As Teddy finished putting away the groceries, I wondered when I had last really looked at him. His shoulders filled out his hoodie, and his clothes seemed less wrinkly. Most of his dark blond hair was gathered into a stubby ponytail, but one green lock grazed his jaw, which appeared to have widened, too. Was that fuzz on his chin? His eyes were shifty, avoiding mine, but at least they weren't veined with red. I took another step towards him and inhaled.

Teddy jumped. "Are you sniffing me?"

I caught a whiff of cigarette smoke, acrid and stale. Nothing, shall we say, herbal.

"Where were you today, really?"

His shoulders slumped, and when he answered, there was an accusatory note in his voice. "Rose told you."

"Rose has hardly said two words to me lately." My eyes, which burned as though I had been awake for days, followed Teddy as he headed for the rumpled couch. "I was with Gina."

I still felt unable to integrate my body with my thoughts, as if some part of my awareness were hovering up to the left somewhere, near the ceiling fan. Pluto stared up at the fixture with round eyes.

"Tell me."

Rose padded in and sat in one of the wooden chairs as Teddy told me about the dark-haired girl from jazz band, a double-bass player whom he might or might not be dating, exactly. The smoker. I remembered her from a school concert. I'd thought it was cute how the huge instrument dwarfed her.

"This relationship started around Thanksgiving. Gina was at that party." Listen to me, the oracle.

Teddy acknowledged my omniscience. "Yeah."

I sat down, like Rose, in a wooden chair. "You've been lying about seeing her. Have you been lying about alcohol and cigarettes? Did you lie about smoking pot?"

At this my pliant child set his mouth. When he added folded arms to the pose, I was reminded of his tantrums as a toddler. He had looked so adorable in rage.

"You might as well tell her everything," Rose said. "Seems like she knows already." Her own jaw, though more delicate, was set as firmly as her brother's. Teddy, wanting to escape, said, "Ma, just a couple of hits at that one party. Gina smokes, but I don't."

I eyed him.

"And?" Rose prompted. Now that I had finally caught on, Rose wasn't letting her brother off easy.

Teddy stared at his twin for what felt like half a minute. "She's eighteen. A senior."

Ah.

My freshman son was seeing a sexy, cannabis-smoking high-school senior who had a driver's license. I asked, "Is that all you have to tell me?"

Teddy lowered his pretty-boy lashes. "Yeah."

"Okay. One of you wash that pan. Teddy, you're grounded again until I talk to your father."

Even after they'd both gone upstairs, I continued to sit in that chair for a good, long while.

Fourteen

Warm rain fell just before Christmas, and again I bled in floods. Under the tree Christmas morning, I found scarlet gift bags containing two red sweaters, one claret and the other fire-engine-bright. Smaller packages yielded a scarf patterned in colors from maroon to fuchsia, a crimson blouse, and a fiery array of socks. In my stocking, Silvio had tucked cranberry tights and cherry chocolates.

Not-myself had a better-than-usual holiday: cooking less, daydreaming more, sleeping soundly even in a New York motel. And not-myself managed Silvio's rambunctious family cheerfully while consuming moderate doses of eggnog. She did not pursue professional or domestic projects that bored or annoyed her. She was, on the whole, an improvement.

The day after we returned from upstate, after hours of radio about floods and tornados worldwide, we lit a fire, and I, lying on the couch, fell into winter dreaminess. Nearby, Silvio tapped on a keyboard, and upstairs, Teddy practiced the trumpet. Rose reclined in her favorite overstuffed chair, legs thrown over one of its arms, reading a Christmas book about Japanese folklore. Rose liked math and science courses best but was attracted to all things Japanese. She talked about signing up for an online language course.

I asked her, remembering a student tale from the first day of American Gothic, if there was anything about a ghost girl and a haunted bathroom.

"Yeah! Hold on—." Rose riffled through pages, finding one she had dog-eared. "I love this. It's a newer legend, apparently. Hanako of the toilet. Here we go. *Details differ from school to school, but typically it is said that if you go to the girl's bathroom on the third floor and knock three times on the door of the third toilet stall, a girl's voice will answer. In some versions, the door swings open but nobody is there.* Wait a sec. ...*and in some versions, Hanako does appear: a little girl with a bob haircut, dressed in a white blouse and red skirt.*"

I gazed at my daughter, pink and laughing in yoga pants, swinging a calf idly.

She continued skimming the entry. "And, whoa, in some versions, a white hand reaches out of the toilet bowl! Oh, and this sentence is why I marked the page. *Moreover, a toilet—with its hole leading to somewhere else—can be thought of as a kind of portal to another world.* That makes total sense."

"Like crossing water to get to the afterlife."

"Yeah, or you could just look down the toilet. It's awesome."

I draped my hand to graze Pluto's head as he paced by, purring. I could barely reach him, but he enjoyed the spirit of attention more than the reality. "And a bunch of horror tales are about bathrooms. *Psycho* and the shower scene."

"And Bloody Mary," Rose added.

"I thought you were supposed to call on her while you were walking up the stairs backwards?"

Rose shrugged. "We always did it in the bathroom mirror."

I squawked. "Not in our bathroom!"

"At least once. Calling Bloody Mary is like this thing you have to do at all middle-school sleepovers."

I settled my head on a pillow, grumbling that I didn't like séances in my own house, not one bit, and Rose became absorbed in her book again. I picked up the travel section of the paper, leafed through it, and tossed it into my discard pile. We wouldn't have funds or time this year for any vacation more exciting than a few days at the beach.

After a while, Rose spoke again, asking if I had ever heard of *kitsune*.

"The word sounds familiar."

She explained about the shape-shifting fox, sometimes appearing as a seductive woman, occasionally maintaining human form long enough to marry a man and bear him children. I remembered Fee at the Halloween party admiring my lame fox costume and mouthing a word I hadn't quite caught.

"They're tricksters?"

"Sort of. Messengers. And they can bewitch or possess people."

Alisa had once given me a book about Bridget Cleary, an Irish woman allegedly possessed by fairies, who was beaten and burned to death by her suspicious husband in the late eighteen-hundreds. We were both fascinated by that hinge of history between folk beliefs and a scientific world order. "How do you recognize *kitsune* possession?"

Rose scanned the chapter. "I guess some people run around naked or eat gravel. Or they have seizures."

Nothing I had done lately. "Maybe it's a way of explaining epilepsy, then."

"Misbehavior, too, like adultery or running away." Rose waved vaguely.

It was getting dark again already. "How do you exorcise *kitsune*?"

"Same-old. You chant spells. Or feed them rice cakes instead of communion wafers." Rose reached to the coffee table for her water glass and a handful of sugared almonds. "Or you sic dogs on them. Dogs always know a fox when they smell one."

Our family practiced an annual ritual sometime around the new year. We opened a colorful box stashed in the attic with Christmas decorations, read out previous lists of resolutions, then each wrote a new set.

I had read about this family togetherness activity in a parenting magazine when the twins were four—in a doctor's waiting room, probably. In those days, whenever I got lost in a book, I was liable to emerge to find Rose drawing whiskers on Teddy's face in permanent marker, or both of them giving a frightened cat a haircut.

What a vision I had entertained when I read that article: annual musings about self-improvement, devoted parents leaning on their elbows to listen, children growing wiser with each soul-baring iteration. Usually the twins would snort at the goals of previous years, especially from the oldest lists. *Be good so I get a hamster. Learn to speak robot. Unlock every guy on Super Smash Bros. Eat a whole pizza by myself. Find Minecraft log-in. Improove spelling.*

I insisted every year that resolutions must focus on *self*-improvement, because otherwise the ritual became an occasion for pointers. From Teddy, a couple of years ago: *Get Rose to take a chill pill.* From Rose: *Make mom stop nagging me to floss.*

Not-myself now read a decade of her own lists, sweating. Every single one began with revulsion at a thickening body: *Lose weight, eat less sugar, drink less wine, exercise more.* Those are not bad practices, but their consistency was joyless.

Maybe joylessness was latent in the exercise, a sense of being sinful creatures who must strive to scrub away stains. I had read too many Jonathan Edwards sermons. The kids never approached their own lists so grimly. Silvio attacked the exercise in a practical manner, generating annual to-do lists of professional goals and domestic chores he'd tick off the following year. Done, done, done. His mental clarity enraged me.

The self-loathing, the commitment to endless futile struggle and doomed regimes, appeared to be mine alone. I sat at the Christmas tablecloth, listening to Teddy's pencil scratching, the clock ticking, and slant rain smacking the window screens. Rose was snickering as she wrote. Silvio leaned back in his chair with eyes closed, scratching his scalp under a cheap Santa hat. We had cleared our bowls of hoppin' john and tidied the kitchen. Night surrounded the house, pressing in on our lamps and candle flames. Pluto sprawled on the floor nearby in his stone lion pose, squinting and purring, pretending not to guard the stray black-eyed pea between his front paws.

I tried to reason with myself. If I had wishes, it was fine to spend some on my loved ones. Silvio, the kids, and my friends all deserved to thrive on their own terms, regardless of how I wanted my life to work out. Even reckoning selfishly, their happiness would increase my own. We were entangled.

But ignoring my own desires was no way to start a new year. Whoever I was, what did I want for myself this year? The tea-drugged stranger who stepped out of the fairy ring, what were her plans?

Stop losing time, I wrote. *Make sure Alisa is where she wants to be.*

I dreamed that night of trudging up to the third-floor bathroom in the English building. In waking life this was a single unisex closet, but in my dream the women's room was large and elegantly appointed, with four stalls and candles flickering in sconces. I knocked on the carved third door. Unlocked, it swung open.

Another me was standing before the toilet in a gray cotton dress and practical sandals. I looked down at the body I was wearing, its garb of rusty red knitwear and snug black jeans—my Halloween outfit. I felt for my tailbone. Instead of costume fur, real brushy appendages were growing there, sending awareness to my brain through a host of bristles. Three foxtails: I couldn't see much, but I could count them with groping fingers. They counted my fingers right back.

I stepped toward the other me, into her, and we merged with a click. My foxtails vanished but I could sense a vestigial sensitivity, a deeper balance.

Fifteen

Magic, I typed into the search engine, and more than a billion results popped up. *Blood magic* yielded only half a million hits, and aside from Minecraft sites, the first twenty looked sketchy. I considered searching for *fairy professor,* then thought, maybe not on my office computer.

In the mailroom I found Camille pulling a hot stack of pages from the printer and fanning through them. She was cast-free.

"Finalizing syllabi already?"

"The first day of classes is less than a week away," she said. I asked about her break, and though she didn't give much detail, her posture was relaxed and a half-smile came to her lips.

I began copying an article I needed for the essay I, clear-headed at last, had decided to finish revising. I didn't know yet what needed to come after that. The future was incomprehensible but here anyway, blank as mist, bare as a small town without students or tourists.

"Silvio's break is a week longer than ours."

"Damn that handsome man."

I grinned. Camille was definitely happier; Christmas with the lawyer-boyfriend must have gone well. "Yeah. But it keeps him home longer." I kept turning pages and positioning the volume, trying not to stare at the brilliant bar of light sweeping over the leaves, memorizing them by some hoodoo, spitting out likenesses.

"Do you go down to visit him sometimes, or does he always drive up?" Camille watched me with an absent expression, rocking the heel of one boot sideways.

"Well, mostly Silvio drives up." The rhythm of slide, close, press, turn, slide was mesmerizing. "I'm trapped here because one kid or the other always has a Saturday mock-UN meet or a chess tournament or whatever. But my spring break lines up for once with the kids', and Silvio's is different, so the three of us are planning to visit him in March."

"What's going to happen with Silvio?"

"You mean, will he come back?"

"Or if he stays in North Carolina, do you think about finding work down there?"

I pulled pages out of the copy tray and pretended to check them. "It's hard to imagine teaching anywhere else. What about you?"

"I imagine it," she said, then pulled herself up, planting her boot heels. "Well, I mean, you have to go into a tenure decision with a back-up plan."

I was about to ask more when I heard Harriet hurrying down the hall. "Cynthia." Her expression made me sick with fear. "It's Sunshine. My friend at the newspaper just called. Sunshine passed away of an aneurysm. Died in her sleep, bless her heart."

Harriet was teary, and I hugged her; my own eyes stung. Camille hadn't known Sunshine well, and Ralph, unnerved to discover a weepy scene in the mailroom, hardly at all. But Harriet and I had known Sunshine for years and fussed together when she left Alisa. Comparing the signs we missed about Sunshine's scheming side, we had lamented falling for her charm.

Harriet pulled a hankie from her sweater pocket. "Do you think anyone has told Alisa?"

I said, "Sunshine wasn't on speaking terms with Alisa's family, and all their friends pretty much chose sides, like I did. I don't know who would have contacted Alisa. Or how."

Harriet was staring at me somberly. I sighed and nodded.

I had those long Welsh numbers practically memorized, but had never made them work after that one day in September. I tried them both for the millionth time, but the office number wouldn't connect and Alisa's cell told me her mailbox was full. I did more searching, found a number for the Dean of the School of Arts and Humanities, and reached an answering machine. I left a message explaining the situation.

Email, text? I listened to my watch tick for a while and composed a brief message. *Important. Call me.*

In the main office, Sandra sat murmuring with Harriet about the news. They looked at me, expectant. I shook my head.

"Well, hell," Sandra said. "We've seen so many omens of apocalypse, I've lost count."

I leaned against the wall, remembering a conversation in this same room months ago, after the collision that injured my student Anna.

"I had a cousin who went like that, from an aneurysm," Harriet said, sliding her pendant back and forth across its chain. "There are worse ways. But it's a terrible shame, a young person passing all of a sudden."

"All her sins unshriven." Sandra had obviously taken sides, too. She sounded as bitter as I felt.

I'm bitter and shocked, but not grieving, I thought, walking back to my office. Sunshine had been selfish, trying to take as much from Alisa as she could, even after the affair was exposed. Her death seemed terrible, but I was not mourning in a personal way.

What I felt was dread. An unnamable danger had crept closer to my circle of safety. This was the first fatality, although casualties were mounting. I had to figure out how to put my world to rights, and soon.

I sat down at my desk, at a loss for what to do. I checked messages, not really expecting to hear from Alisa. As I clicked on an email from an unfamiliar address, I reddened. I had won a state teaching award, a prize for which few professors at my tiny college had ever been selected. Please don't publicize this until the press release in two weeks, the note said, but you may alert university administrators now.

Sandra's friend in Psychology won it maybe five years ago, the woman with terminal cancer. The woman upon whom I had definitely not wished terminal cancer, because I was not a monster sacrificing other people to my own greedy ends.

Telling Silvio and the kids about Sunshine was miserable. And by the way, guys, I won a prize!

Alisa never called back, nor did the Welsh dean, although I left two more recordings. I clipped the obituary and sent it to Alisa in a card, feeling this was the worst way ever to inform someone of the death of her ex. Then I put my ungrieving head down and worked. A few days later, I took Camille a copy of the department letter recommending her tenure and promotion.

Our decision, ratified during a subdued meeting that week, was not unanimous: Beth-Ann abstained. Yet the news about Alisa's partner of thirteen years seemed to have reminded the rest of them about what mattered. Not only did Sandra, Ralph, and Dan vote in favor of granting Camille tenure, as I felt sure they would have anyway, but as I added final touches to the cover letter, each commented on other ways Camille was wonderful. "Put in more praise for the digital humanities projects!" Dan emailed. "She really has extraordinary archival instincts,"

Sandra stopped by to mention. "Remember when she showed me how to send email attachments?" Ralph marveled.

It was a pleasure to hand the warmly worded endorsement to Camille. There had been a reserve between us, a tension I'd hoped would dissolve if I ignored it. She hugged me and gestured to a side chair.

"How does it feel?"

"Mixed," she said. Afternoon light striped Camille's shoulders, but her face was cool. "You know when you work toward something desperately for years, then you get it and realize, oh, damn, I'm still in exactly the same situation?"

I did know, but my shoulders must have sagged, because Camille, ever kind, leaned forward and changed the subject. "Now, tell me about Silvio's meeting with the Ice Maiden."

I huffed. "They offered him a one-year full-time replacement position starting September."

"Not a tenure line?"

"They said they couldn't open a tenure-track line while its current holder was battling leukemia."

"I guess that's not unreasonable. But what did they say about the future?"

"Well, the head of Psych acted awkward, because everything hinges on whether and when this poor woman steps down or dies. They will always need a person in developmental Psych, and they said Silvio would be a strong candidate when and if the job opens, but Barbara made a point of saying it would be a national search."

"Stupid," Camille said, and then shifted around irritably. "It's not like they should push a cancer victim out the door, but if they don't get smarter, they're going to lose a lot of people. It's like they still expect everyone to have a wife who'll put it all down and join the garden club."

"Well, he'll tell Broome State what the offer here is, and we'll see what happens."

Camille ducked as a beam of sunshine struck her face. This was my cue to let her get back to prepping class. I cast a wary look down the hall, but Alisa's door remained locked. I wasn't sure whether Fee had sent me on that fairyland head-trip or rescued me from it, but she was apparently still in New Orleans.

I found Silvio on our rear deck, leaning over books at the patio table in the absurd January warmth. He always worked so diligently, while I meandered and digressed. I sat down with him and tilted my face to catch the rays. "You're back," he said.

"There was no reason to stay all afternoon so I came home early. Last minutes of freedom."

"No, I mean you're really back." Sounding hesitant, he said, "You weren't fully in there for a while."

I watched him with one hand cocked like a visor, then settled in further and closed my eyes, feeling down through my blood to something in the soil below. As I did, I perceived an anxious vibration in the man beside me. My extra sense, whatever it was, remained acute as ever, waiting for me to tune in.

"I've been thinking, I guess. And I'm bone-tired. It's been such a bizarre year."

"Thinking what comes next?" Staring at the red glow of my eyelids, I heard him click his laptop shut and shuffle paper.

"Playing out the chess moves. But it's hard to see very far ahead. We just have to wait for other players to take their turns and decide from there."

Silvio was silent, though his stomach gurgled, or was that the creek at the bottom of the lawn? The sun felt delicious, and the air had that broken-earth smell, as if spring had arrived two months early and crocus blades were pushing up.

"If the North Carolina job becomes real. If they offer to hire me tenure-track," he said. "Would you ever leave here?"

I peered at him, dazzled. "A year ago, the question would have shocked me. But that's basically where I've been, thinking that over, whether I might be ready for a change."

His voice was soft. "Do you have an answer?"

"I'd have to know something about the nature of the change first. With a couple of years of chairing under my belt, I would be a decent candidate for some administrative positions. I won't get recruited on research credentials, and my writing feels stale."

"Maybe get hired as chair by a department that can't agree on an inside candidate?" He seemed to chew that over. "Or would you apply for some variety of deanship?"

I shrugged. "I'd have to be flexible if I want to be specific about the location. There are some lousy things about chairing, but I seem not to be screwing it up."

"I saw Sandra in the food store this morning, and she told me you were a brilliant department head." Silvio reached out and tapped my knee.

"She's just grateful she doesn't have to do it." I stood. "I would regret taking a job that didn't include *some* teaching. There's also money: college ahead, times two. I might not be able to relocate, unless Broome State pays better than we think."

Silvio stood, too, and checked his watch. The kids would be home any moment now.

"But you have decided something," he said. "I can tell."

"You don't believe I can tolerate radical indecision in a blissful state of zen?" He laughed but waited me out, watching my face, so I gave him the answer I had, vague and ridiculous and momentous as it was.

"I can change. I'm ready to take a different kind of control of my life. I just don't know what that difference will look like."

Pluto jumped down from his perch on the table just inside the patio doors, where he had been sitting to monitor our cruel flaunting of outdoor access. His mewing hadn't been audible, but now I could hear him thump onto the hardwood and run off. A door slammed, and Teddy and Rose's voices rose in argument. We were all home, family unit intact, resisting tides that wanted to pull us apart.

Sixteen

I inhabited my body differently since the new year's dream, my skin tingling with new awareness. I kept thinking, even as I sat at my desk like an ordinary person: I'm a hive of secrets. They buzzed with warnings—especially about what might happen if I tapped the current that I now sensed nearly all the time.

Silvio, still on break, stopped by my office at lunchtime and handed over an envelope. It was addressed to me in Alisa's hand. Opening the card inside, I skimmed the handwritten note for a mention of Sunshine, which I didn't find. I looked again at the envelope. "The postmark is before Christmas."

Silvio sighed. "Of course. What does she say?"

A couple of the sentences were in an unfamiliar language—Welsh, maybe? Even her English was cryptic: *Time passes differently here. The seasons seem strange.*

When I handed it to Silvio, he shook his head. "Maybe Fee could translate? The Welsh, I mean, if that's what it is?"

"I'll ask her. After class."

I hadn't told Silvio about the lost time on Fee's front lawn or the wishes that came almost true, in a twisted way. Whenever I imagined framing the words, I heard *crazy*. That's the judgment I'd pass in an instant if Silvio or anyone else told me, *Fee may be a wicked fairy who stole Alisa's place in the human universe—but I'm still trying to figure out the details.*

I might have used a stronger word than *crazy* if, before this year, a friend had said, *I might be able to perform magic.* Now objects containing iron called to me, and I felt the movement of blood through other people's bodies. Silvio would call that overwork with a garnish of hormonal dementia. I wasn't keeping anything from Silvio, not really, because what I felt was too slippery for words.

The secret of the teaching award would escape soon. I felt self-conscious during the first session of my seminar on Whitman and Dickinson. Next week everyone would know, and these students would look back at my opening moves and think, *She's an okay teacher, I guess, but not, like, a sorcerer or something, so what's the big deal?* Maybe I had summoned the award with magic—cheating, basically. Maybe everybody who won everything was a magic-worker and I was just late to the struggle. Maybe even suspecting magic had been at work in my prize win was a nasty echo of my mother's opinion that I wasn't praiseworthy.

My course was scheduled in the same third-floor classroom. Some students had followed me from American Gothic. Julene and Persis had decided on an English major, but not Anna, although she was back in school, wearing a leg brace. Ruddy with a ski-tan, Royall sat near the front. He might graduate on time after all, although it meant a full dance-card of English offerings.

After class, I found Fee's door cracked. She was spritzing her plants when I rapped on the jamb.

"I was sorry to hear about Sunshine," she said, sounding unlike a supernatural being whose self-serving enchantments caused collateral damage.

"Thanks. I guess." Fee raised her eyebrows. "My interactions with Sunshine over the last year were not friendly," I explained. "I'm not sure I should even show my face at the memorial. But listen, I want advice on reaching Alisa."

The smooth face opposite mine revealed no disturbance. "If she is not responding to messages, perhaps she does not wish to be reached."

"And that would be totally fair. But Sunshine's death is big. She deserves to know, and not by email."

Without answering, Fee nodded at the card in my hand. "Is that from Alisa?"

I passed it over. "Is that Welsh? Do you speak Welsh?"

Fee glanced at Alisa's cursive and sat down in one of the two side chairs, looking as tired as I had ever seen her. "I do speak and read Cymraeg, and I recognize the words here, but it's an older version of the language." The arm holding the card was extended, rather than pulled in to reading distance.

I perched on the edge of the other chair, feeling warm and prickly, but trying to keep an intellectual distance from the whirlpool of weirdness. "What does it say?"

"Nothing good." She lifted her eyes. "Sometimes mysteries should remain mysterious."

I felt my face change. "I don't like secrets."

"We are made of secrets," Fee said, still holding the message away from her body. "Like onions are made of onion. Keep peeling away the layers, and you will only discover more secrets."

My shoulders sank. While I did not want to supplicate the queen of the fairies, a pleading note crept into my voice as I said, "Please. I'm worried."

She eyed me for a few beats longer, then sighed. "My translation may not be exact; forms change over time and distance." Distance? I wondered fleetingly. Wouldn't linguistic structures work the same way on either side of the Atlantic? "But the sentences read something like: *Burn this with applewood branches and mark your forehead with the ash. Scatter the rest in running water and you will dream of me.*"

"I'm not sure about apple," Fee added, cocking her head. "Some other kind of fruit tree, perhaps."

I almost laughed with discomfort. "Whoa. Is that from a poem or something?"

"Not a poem I am familiar with. I believe these are instructions."

"Like, perform this ritual, and we can finally Skype?"

Fee was becoming irritable. "You have been unable to speak with Alisa, correct?"

"Well, we talked once, but the connection was bad, and email has been spotty, too," I conceded. "And your university is kind of remote, in the mountains, right?—I just thought that was why."

"Remote, yes." Fee paused. "Communication becomes unpredictable." She looked at the woodcut on the front of the card and remarked, "Hazel trees. But you worry, you said."

"I am concerned. Alisa does tend to disappear when she's really involved in something, writing usually, but this is turning into a really long radio silence. I've been telling myself Alisa wanted a clean break from her old life. She had a rough few months before the exchange came through." I remembered Sunshine on Halloween, how she clutched her quilted knapsack to her chest. "Did you know about Sunshine before your party, that they had been a couple, I mean?"

Fee handed the card back, and I turned it over, feeling unbelief turn over inside me, too, before she spoke again.

"I knew some other woman had left a mark on the house. There were two presences, Alisa and somebody else building portals and traps. Bad juju," she said, and smiled. "I loved New Orleans." Fee pointed at a heart-shaped charm pinned on the wall near her desk, sealed in plastic, full of beads and glitter and cut-out images. "Gris-gris," she explained.

"What is it supposed to do?"

Fee's serious gaze seemed focused elsewhere. "You could follow Alisa's instructions. They are not difficult. Nothing would be lost by the attempt. And you have visited before."

"Visited—Wales?" Now I was sitting forward again, preparing to dash away from this lunacy, as if I wouldn't carry it inside me as I fled.

"Once you have crossed the border, returning is easier."

I stared at her for a few beats. Then, without answering, I bolted.

Twilight had seeped into the backyard, but I felt drawn there, so I walked to the edge of the creek. It burbled, slipping over pebbles.

It was one thing to influence academic politics or dream of a changed life. Working spells—that's what Alisa's instructions seemed to boil down to—would elevate this fantasy to a vertiginous height.

I breathed, feeling my feet root into the damp ground. I noticed the wind beginning to rise, fiddling with my jacket-cuffs and loose hair, exhilarated by its own energy.

I did not feel crazy.

Wandering around the fringe of the property for a few minutes, I touched leaves and examined bracken, considering the state of things. Under the lichened crab-apple, I picked up some dead branches then laid them on a shelf in the shed to dry. They would burn more easily that way.

Everyone from English, except Beth-Ann, was sitting in the conference room when the Ice Maiden entered and shut the door. For a moment I absorbed her elegant costume. Lavender for preservation, and pearls for secrecy.

Barbara stared back at me, casting her eyes up and down with a quizzical expression. I wore my new color, the Christmas blouse with the silk scarf. "Red suits you," she murmured.

"Thank you," I said. "Please, sit by me. How would you like to start?"

The meeting went well: my colleagues bubbled with excitement over the proposed curricular changes, while Barbara listened and asked smart questions. Beth-Ann had just announced that she was leaving at the end of the academic year for another job; her departure meant no revamped composition sequence, no Strategic Communications track. Yet I admired Barbara's graciousness. She no longer seemed vengeful, but rather as if she were balancing the department's interests in relation to those of the College quite sanely. She scarcely glanced at Dan, and I could no longer detect a charge. An unruly electricity had been defused or, I supposed, redirected.

That night I cooked my favorite curry, a Bengali dish of eggplant and cashews, and told Silvio about the day. When it was simmering, I handed him a bottle of cava to uncork and poured a tot of pomegranate liqueur into two champagne glasses. The level in the liqueur bottle was lower than I remembered. I topped our glasses with fizz.

"Cheers," I said, and we clinked.

Teddy wandered in, sniffed the pot, tossed a handful of clementine peels into the trash, and asked, "So what are we toasting?"

Silvio raised the rosy liquid in Teddy's direction. "Your mother's latest triumph over the Sith."

"Cool." Teddy cracked a soda and lifted it. "The force has always been strong with her."

My repressed startle mutated into a shiver, but I took another sip, dryness and sugar buzzing together on my tongue.

Silvio left the day before his new term started. Nestled in a wool sweater, I walked through leaf-rot in the side yard to the shed to check the drying branches. As dinner cooked, I dragged out an old hibachi and scraped out the crusty ash. We owned a gas grill now and hadn't used this for years. The work warmed me.

After supper, I put cider on the stove to mull with cinnamon sticks and went outdoors again. I fetched the dry crab-apple limbs, arranged them in the hibachi, and buttressed them with crumpled newspaper—the killer of Tamir Rice found not guilty, photographs of flooded cities. The pages lit right away, shimmering blue-hot, but the wood took a while to catch, and it smoked.

After a bit, Rose stuck her head out. "Is it okay if I have cider now? And do you want some?"

"Yes, please." When she disappeared, I fed Alisa's card into the grate. A green tongue flickered up and sizzled down again.

Rose returned with two steaming mugs and dragged a patio chair up next to mine. "This is unusual behavior."

I wrapped both hands around the ceramic cup. I was wearing my jacket but was chilly, even tending an improvised witch's cauldron. "I just wanted fire. The real kind, not gas logs. I'll be going in soon."

"Yeah, I'm not going to make it for long," Rose said, peering around the faintly lit yard with a shiver. She had yanked a blanket off the sofa and wrapped it around her shoulders. "I get tired of listening to scales," she added, jerking her head toward Teddy's bedroom window.

"Trumpet practice is better than him sneaking around with sophisticated older women."

Rose snorted. "He did become a lady-magnet when we started high school." Her expression was disapproving. "There always seems to be some girl staring at him now and giggling to her friends. It's totally gross, and it's going to his head."

"Bound to happen. You're both so fabulous. You'd tell me, right, if one of you had a new girlfriend or boyfriend in the works?"

Disgusted noise. "No."

We swigged cider as it cooled, until we reached the gritty dregs and the house fell silent.

Seventeen

I sat in the unlit kitchen, charged and listening. I was a radio receiver tuned to static, finding patterns in noise. It was probably near midnight when I selected a saucepan and serving spoon and slipped out back again.

Slowly, to minimize clanking sounds, I removed the grilltop. It wasn't hot anymore, though the air still smelled smoky. I ladled soft piles of ash into the saucepan and dragged the spoon around the edges of the hibachi basin to make sure I had gotten most of it. Metal rang faintly against metal like a clapper scraping the rim of a bell.

I touched the ash in my pot tentatively, fearing a burn or I don't know what, but the night air had chilled it, too. I dabbled my finger in it and rubbed some on my forehead. Then I walked over to the creek and tried to scatter what remained. Soot fell out in an awkward clump.

Wings rushed by; a hoot blasted overhead. I jumped almost out of my skin, then a giggle erupted. I was performing embarrassing, unfamiliar feats in a backyard at midnight, which tends to put the senses on alert.

Yet this was an ordinary January evening on the edge of town. An owl hunted in its usual way, swooping through a vestigial stand of oak. A stream found its regular path through the watershed, carrying a new burden maybe, but patiently dissolving it. Water tries to swallow every poison spilled into its currents.

Wondering if I would be able to sleep, I went inside.

I clambered down into a curved bay backed by echoing cliffs. It wasn't the fairy ring landscape, yet I knew I had entered the same country. The light was somehow similar, and the vividness: the seaweed draping the rocks was impossibly green, and the ocean foamed silver.

Rose kneeled on the sand, whey-faced, weeping, next to, of all things, the iron telephone. I ran over, asking what was wrong. Color seemed to bend away from her.

"The magic, it's going, it's nearly gone," she cried. "It's bleeding out of me."

I woke in a sweat, slid out of bed, and walked to Rose's room, turning the antique knob as quietly as I could. She was sleeping with a crow-foot frown creasing her forehead. I closed her door and went to peek at Teddy, too. Great hairy feet stuck out of the covers, but his fuzzy face seemed younger in relaxation.

My heartbeat calmed, though my pajamas were soaked and I had that sick feeling of adrenaline wearing off, almost an ache in the veins. I wasn't sure I could sleep again, but I changed into a clean nightdress and drank some water. In the mirror, by moonlight, I could still detect a smear of ash on my brow. I settled on Silvio's side of the bed. When it approached five, I was about to give up. Instead, rain began to patter onto the tin roof, and I drowsed.

"Did you get my letter?"

Alisa, dressed in showy colors and seated on an enormous stump, looked faded but absolutely herself. She shook her head.

"About Sunshine?" I persisted, but Alisa waited.

I had to say it, somehow. "Alisa, Sunshine died."

Alisa recoiled without speaking; tears welled in her eyes. I hastened to soften the news. "In her sleep. An aneurysm, there was no warning. I know it's terrible, but no one could have known. She just didn't wake up one morning, right after New Year's." I was repeating myself, hoping to make that shocked expression change. "I'm so, so sorry. I tried and tried to reach you. I'm sorry, Alisa."

We kept company in silence for a while, until Alisa gasped and brushed tears off her face with the edge of her hand. "I should have known this would happen." Her voice sounded husky. "What Sunshine did was dangerous for her as well as for me."

"What she did?" I sat cross-legged on springy moss, opposite Alisa, in a pose that reminded me of a student before a teacher. I didn't quite feel able to leap up and hug her. She was familiar but strange, as if knowing her for so long had prevented me from seeing her. She seemed just as brilliant now, but more preoccupied, and a few degrees cooler.

After another deep breath, Alisa asked, "Remember those little landscapes in my living room and kitchen, the paintings Sunshine tried to steal?"

"How do you know about that?"

There was chagrin in her tone but, again, a chilly kind. "I think maybe you mentioned it in one of your messages? A couple of the early ones came through. Of course, when you live with someone for over a decade, she becomes predictable. Even her lies." Alisa scratched her head and pulled a bell-shaped flower by its stem from among the strands of hair and flicked it away. "And I can tell some of what's happening in your world by the way it's mirrored in mine."

Mirrors again. "Two landscapes, only six or eight inches wide. Watercolors. Kind of English-looking."

"Yes. I picked them up when I led that study-abroad trip. There was only one painting, or I thought there was only one, for ages. The bright one with the plain, grassy hills. We put it in the front room. Sunshine always liked it. She said the curvy downs looked sexy." Alisa picked at her hem, which was loosening—a thread had broken—before continuing.

"A year ago December, one of the dogs knocked it down and damaged the frame, only a cheap one, so I thought I'd get it properly set as a Christmas present. When I took it to the frame shop, the guy found a second painting behind the first."

I tilted my head, trying to visualize the dark watercolor that once hung near the kitchen window. "Was the other painting of trees, a night-time scene?"

"Not night-time." Alisa looked at me with asperity, and I understood.

"Oh. It's here."

"Yes. Here." Her laugh cracked like dropped pottery, and I could almost see air-quotes beading in the ether when she added, "Wales."

Somewhere a waterfall dropped curtains of sound. The moss under my hands, luminous, felt willful. "But what was she doing with them?"

"Well, she started wishing me away when the affair started, which was not long before the frame broke. Those watercolors—" Alisa hesitated, her fingers pleating, pleating. The light around her fluctuated. "They make a path from your world into this one. Sunshine left the paintings when she moved out, because she was nudging me through. Not that I was unwilling to get out of town, but this is not where I intended to go. I have been trying to see a way to return. I thought I had a decent chance of figuring it out, because I had a feel for how Sunshine's magic must work."

"Sunshine's magic? Is every woman I know practicing witchcraft?"

"Just the smart ones. Anyway, I was prying at it, like wrestling with a big knot, then the line just snapped." She sighed and added with a shake in her voice, "I should have guessed what that meant."

My body tensed. "The magic died when she did, so you can't get out? Does that mean Fee caused Sunshine's aneurysm to keep you there?"

Now Alisa jumped. "Fee? The one who got out?"

My legs tingled from holding one position, so I extended them, rotating my ankles, wincing as blood circulated again. "Her code name is the Changeling Professor."

"I actually miss your code names."

Actually? "Well, Fee got here all right, and she's taking over the joint. There's something frightening about her. Plus since she arrived, accidents keep happening, although Sunshine—Sunshine was the only one who died. And all these changes at work, and there's something going on with Rose and Teddy. It would take a month to explain it all."

Alisa reached a hand down to me, and I reached up. Although the dell was humid and filtered sunlight kept the moss warm, her fingers were icy.

As if to refute that connection, her next words crushed me. "I wanted to get far away from Sunshine and my stupid job and my stupid life. From you."

There was nothing to say and no air to say it with, so I listened while Alisa rattled on. "Yes, I know that's mean, but it's the truth. And for a while it was exciting. The good kind of dangerous. I had a torrid affair with a totally gorgeous person, really otherworldly." Well, whatever. I was breathing again, I noticed, as the pitch of her voice rose. "But I do not like this place. The world you inhabit is fifty kinds of messed up, but at least things can change there."

Look at my hurt feelings, standing slightly apart from me already, I marveled, as another part of me registered Alisa's frustration with something like sympathy. Even before news of Sunshine's death, Alisa had seemed diminished. Her face was so human with its pores and fine wrinkles, not perfect like everything else in this place, each painterly leaf. Her long auburn hair looked grayer, wispier. How could she bear such color?

Alisa was not as nice a person as I had imagined, but neither was I. "How can I help?"

Alisa fidgeted with her hem again. "Press Fee. She must know how the doors work, because she got one open for herself. And please keep remembering me. Of course," she said with a quirk of her mouth, "you probably won't even remember this conversation."

My first spring-term meeting with the honors thesis kids was scheduled for that morning. I felt heavy from a lousy night's sleep and upset from a sense of forgetting something, but somehow I closed the tinkling shop door behind me, purchased a tub of caffeine, and got them talking about their progress. Most of them left right afterwards, but the frizzy-haired young woman writing about female mystics with Sandra lingered, eyeing me, as if working up courage. I asked what was worrying her.

"This thing," she said, "about restructuring the major, adding a creative writing track. Will you be hiring a medievalist?"

Royall, also hanging around, said, "But you'll also need another tenure-track creative writer, right? One fiction specialist can't teach all those workshops."

"We do need both," I admitted.

"English should have a medievalist *and* a second creative writer." Royall used a deep, imperious voice that made me think of corporate CEOs, as if jeans and a North Face jacket were only the chrysalis from which a business-suited executive would burst forth. "It's a great department, and you shouldn't have to fight over scraps the STEM fields leave."

I couldn't keep amusement out of my voice. "You're preaching to the choir, son. I am the most devout member of the Church of English."

The frizzy-haired woman emitted a hiccupy giggle then clapped her skinny fingers over her mouth.

"I know," Royall said. What was that quality in his tone, his expression? Some captain-of-industry authority? He really had grown up this year.

Out on the street, I nearly bumped into Robin. He was holding the hand of his littlest child, a round-faced four-year-old with a mucous bubble at one nostril.

"Hi." I leaned down to regard the plump face under a cap of brunette curls. "Oh no, are you sick?"

"Head-cold," Robin said. He looked sad and shrunken, his jaunty confidence all dried up. "No school today, so he's coming to my office while I do student conferences."

"I hope you feel better soon," I said to the child.

Still holding tight to Robin's hand, the boy stared back with steady frankness adults would soon train him out of.

Except Fee had the same way of gazing at people, didn't she? Her attention always seemed full and unwavering until she turned away and forgot you completely.

Fee. Alisa. Suddenly I remembered the tree stump, the clearing. I shivered.

Eighteen

Hieroglyphic shards of the dream surfaced like puzzle pieces: Alisa's plea to be remembered; her cold hands. The mission she gave me, however, didn't come back for days, when Fee and Dan invited a bunch of us to a Burns supper. I pointed out leftovers to the kids, and Sandra picked me up at seven.

After the cock-a-leekie soup, Fee, Ralph, and the new comp-lit guy vied in reading aloud Robert Burns poems in the campiest brogue possible. Ralph, whose ordinary drawl was Tidewater plantation—he claimed dead Confederate generals as kin—was not bad. Their performances became more risqué, and their accents more atrocious, as the evening progressed, until Ralph began reciting love poems to Titania, much to Ralph's wife's impatience. Maybe I was tipsy but the clock kept skipping five minutes here, ten there. Finally, Sandra wrinkled her forehead at me, and I nodded, miming that I would be ready to leave soon.

In the dim hall, a beeswax candle burned in a silver dish. Noticing little rearrangements to Alisa's possessions, I tried to repress alarm at my friend's erasure. That's what she had said in the dream, wasn't it? That I would forget her?

Then, when I sat on the guest toilet and glanced up at the wall, the last element slid into place. Fee had rehung Alisa's two miniature watercolors in the bathroom—the paintings Sunshine coveted, that she had used to open a lane to another dimension. Faerie. UnWales. The top image was England, the bottom, elsewhere.

I was supposed to ask Fee about them. She might be able to help me bring Alisa home.

Zipping up, I stood to peer more closely at the paintings. I couldn't locate signatures or tell the period of composition; they could have been a century old or younger than the twins. There was no detail in the lower landscape that signaled otherworldliness, no alien tree, no figures or fauna. Yet the longer I looked, the more it disturbed me. My stomach lurched, as if in motion sickness.

Sweating now, I returned to the living room. Helen, who had endured enough, was standing by the door in her camel jacket, holding out Ralph's overcoat. Her husband seemed reluctant to abandon the entertainments, given omens of a less charming hour ahead.

"Wait," Fee cried when she spotted me. "Before you all go, if you can handle one more golden dram, raise your glass!"

"Fee and I have an announcement," Dan said with a proud grin, slipping an arm around her waist. "In New York City last weekend, I asked Fee to marry me, and she said yes."

For a moment we were silent, contemplating this change in fortune. Then Ralph kissed Fee's hand, and Camille hugged Fee and Dan at once, and everyone cried out congratulations.

"And there's more!" Dan said. "It's not quite public yet, but we just read the contract, and it looks like a go. Fee's first poetry collection has been accepted for publication." He paused. "By Norton."

The hubbub concealed my agitation. How had Fee tied herself to this place so fast, through contracts, even? Six months ago Dan had been sneaking around with Barbara, and before that, with a series of women. Had he altered so much, so quickly, that he was issuing marriage proposals? And didn't it take years to cultivate a literary presence through magazines and prizes before one of those big presses noticed you? I said, "What will it be called?"

She looked at me. "*Fey.*"

On the way out, I watched for toadstools.

On Thursday, the Ice Maiden phoned me. Good news for English, Barbara said, or at least I hope you will think so. You know Royall's father is one of our most generous donors.

Yes, I answered, remembering the son's authority at the coffee shop.

He has offered to endow a chair in Creative Writing, on condition it does not supplant the line in medieval literature previously held by Sandra.

Oh, I said.

He also asked that Sophia Ellis be considered for the position, with or without a national search. (For a moment the formal name didn't register.) She has exerted a positive influence on Royall, turning his academic career around, and they are very grateful for the transformation, Barbara said. They report Royall is almost a new person.

Yes, yes, amazing, I answered. I will talk to my colleagues immediately.

The emergency consult happened in bits and pieces. Beth-Ann didn't care to weigh in, she informed me. A quick tête-a-tête with Ralph, before he decamped to a Shakespeare conference, secured his approval. Dan had to recuse himself, given his conflict of interest, but he and I discussed his admiration for Fee as a poet and teacher.

He also conveyed, with great tact, that while I should talk to Fee herself, she did not wish to infringe upon Alisa's territory. Fee would be content to teach around Alisa's preferences, especially since Fee's load would be dominated by creative writing courses. Was this the price of Fee's help? Make room for her, and Alisa could return?

Sandra and Camille met with me in my office. I explained the offer.

"The endowed chair doesn't specify rank," I said, trying to stick to the real-world decision factors. "I propose we skip the national search and convert Fee's position to tenure-track, but with a shorter probationary period. We know she's a good fit, but it would worry me to hire her with tenure. This way we have an out."

"Not necessarily," Sandra warned, eyes bright. "Fee's resume is becoming so excellent that even if she turned into a monstrous colleague, we would find it very difficult to justify a tenure denial."

Camille, poker-faced, was nursing a cup of tea. "Fee would bring an awful lot to the department. The hitch for me is what Alisa would say."

Sandra sat up straighter at Alisa's name, as if Camille had uttered a word that broke a spell. I related what Dan had reported, including Fee's willingness to avoid Alisa's teaching areas and her interest in topics we hadn't been able to offer for years. "The overlap's minimal. But I hate making this decision without consulting the person who would be Fee's closest colleague, field-wise. I tried calling Alisa yesterday and again this morning, and sent her a message"— I jiggled the mouse for a quick glance at my screen—"but she hasn't responded."

And I failed to dream my way into fairyland a second time, I did not add. "I'll keep trying, but I don't know how long I can stall Barbara, because of course she wants to call the donor and promise him everything Royall's heart desires."

Sandra asked, "If Alisa were on board, would we endorse the proposal?"

Camille nodded once, firmly. "Take the money and run, is my vote."

Sandra said, "I agree," slapping her knees. Wow, was she energized at the prospect of getting out of here. "Cynthia, why not tell the dean we're interested in making an offer to Dr. Ellis, but we require more time to consult with our absent member."

Winter light suffused the office as we reflected for a moment. The books, the chairs, the bodies in the chairs were outlined with fantastically sharp edges. What world was this?

Sunday afternoon, I found fragmented texts from Alisa on my cell. *More power to Fee for making this happen, but. This could work if.*

The screen froze, I powered the phone off and on again, and the words were gone.

Tuesday, Groundhog Day, I found a garbled message on my office voice mail: "There are two boxes," Alisa explained hurriedly, "but you need to select *both* the rabbit *and*—." The recording cut off.

I checked email constantly and clicked twice a day on my spam filter to be sure I hadn't missed anything, but knew I wouldn't find answers.

Sleepless on Wednesday, I shrugged a raincoat over my pajamas, slipped my bare feet into Teddy's gargantuan boots, and clomped out to the shed with a flashlight. It was one in the morning, sleeting faintly. I ran my finger around the inside of the hibachi and rubbed the faint, damp ash onto my forehead. When I reentered the house, Pluto jumped and scratched me right above the boot cuff.

"What the hell, cat?" He glowered and stood his ground.

I had to wash out the bloody scrape as well as scrub soot off my hands before returning to bed. I closed my eyes and visualized Alisa at her office desk, scratching out a letter in longhand. Soon she would glance up and talk to me.

I eventually drifted off. I dreamed I was sitting on an examination table in a doctor's office, alone, wearing only a paper gown. In the room were two black cloth-covered boxes, each large enough for an English professor to crouch in. They were fastened at the top with fabric loops and shiny buttons. I watched them for ages.

The next day I sent a message to Barbara. We were still experiencing communication problems, but if I didn't hear of complications by Monday, we'd be pleased to offer the chair to Fee, with the conditions discussed earlier. I was astonished not only by the pace of events, but also by the dean's willingness to forgo a national search. A description of the open position had been posted on the Human Resources site, and I had received applications from three completely unqualified people. With no other advertisement, it was a formality.

In her application for the position, Fee included copies of poems, some hot off the presses, the others in galleys. The verses were full of chiming sounds. I said a couple of lines aloud without quite deciding to, then stopped, embarrassed.

I arranged to meet Fee the next morning at the coffee place. She waved to me from a table for two at the front window. While I placed my order at the counter, she chatted with a Geology professor. She was already accruing the kind of network it had taken me years to assemble. I remembered what Alisa said about women practicing magic: *Just the smart ones.*

When I returned to the table with my coffee, Fee was pouring a stream of green tea from a pot into a glass mug.

"Cynthia, how are you?"

I sat down without removing my jacket. Fee had chosen the best vantage point, but it was a chilly spot in winter. "Very pleased about Royall's father's gift," I said. "So carefully framed, too."

Balancing the steaming glass between her fingertips, Fee gave me an intelligent look. "I gather Royall was influenced by conversations with you."

I sat up, confused.

"In the senior honors thesis colloquium, about the future direction of the department. Royall listens, you know. He respects you."

"'Respect' isn't a word I'd associate with Royall."

Fee sipped and set the glass down, composed. "You mean his treatment of Camille. He and I spoke about that, too. Delicately, of course, on my part, but he sees that he behaved badly."

Ah. That was why Royall refrained from adding vitriol to Camille's tenure file.

"Fee. Can Alisa come back?"

"The position is an entirely new one. It doesn't affect Alisa."

I harshened my voice. "I'm not talking about tenure-lines and office space. You know what I mean. I obeyed the instructions." Then I added, realizing I believed myself, "I talked to her."

Fee sipped, and I sipped, and she poured a second, stronger cup. Her eyes darkened as the street outside was dimmed by clouds on the move. Finally, she spoke. "It was very difficult for me to leave—Wales. Like Alisa, I started somewhere else, tried to flee, and became trapped, cut off from my old life. I worked very hard, for a very long time, to position myself in readiness for escape. Then I had to wait even longer, always vigilant, for an opportunity."

I had a vision of a woman grasping a knife and dashing uphill, away from blurry pursuers, but I couldn't place the memory, if that's what it was. I wondered aloud about Fee's "opportunity." "Sunshine wishing Alisa away? Or did the paintings start everything?"

She shrugged. "Chicken and egg." Maybe she wasn't able to parse cause and effect, either.

I drank down to the sugary foam, and my empty cup clattered on the tabletop. I felt heartsick. "So your success requires Alisa's loss?"

Fee frowned, as if the dregs of her tea tasted bitter. "That's how the old formulas work. But rules can change. I hear Central Park was abloom for Christmas," she said, irrelevantly, or not. "I will contemplate open windows. You should, too. There may be ways. Trade-offs. A different price."

She looked out the window until Dan appeared on the street and her mien brightened. She waved at him and stood. "I must go."

Dan was already indoors, helping his beloved slip into her jacket-sleeves, smiling gorgeously, when Fee added, "And next week, I will deliver a gift."

Nineteen

I wanted a rest from gifts, especially Fee's. I longed to hibernate and let the power fill me before I faced her again. Nevertheless, one icy morning, when I opened the front door, I found a basket-weave tote, ornamented with ribbons and sprays of dried flowers, on the stoop. It contained two tissue-papered packages the size of the miniatures. I was reluctant to unwrap them.

Pluto, my familiar, sniffed the bag and pounded off to the back room. I set the tote on a kitchen chair, and he returned, leaped onto the table, and clawed the herb-stalks. I yelled, but he wouldn't budge. When I placed the whole shebang on top of a bookcase, he howled and climbed the shelves until he pulled down a hardcover Sir Walter Scott on his head.

I moaned. "Pluto, I'm at home to *escape* the insanity." Tail down, he sulked to the front windows to watch the renovations across the street.

Like Pluto, I tried to put the bag out of mind; I toiled over a stack of disappointing student essays on Emily Dickinson. Truth was, my concentration was poor, too. The hiring of Fee was out of my hands. Presumably the dean was negotiating a contract I would never see, one that would root Fee here for as long as she wanted to stay.

Just grade, I told myself. Hide and get some work done. I visualized icy feathers of snow wafting down, confining me to my burrow.

Silvio arrived Thursday night as sleety rain rattled down. He and I grew up in the northeast, where a couple of inches of snow didn't faze anyone, but this town didn't even own a plow. Anything more than a dusting foreclosed on all human movement for days.

I met Silvio at the front door, embracing him. "Thank goodness," I said. "I was worried about the roads." I had willed him home safely. I did love him, even if I couldn't tell him what was on my mind.

He set his bags down and shook melting ice out of his hair. "Nasty out there. Lots of accidents. I skidded a couple of times." Silvio hung his damp coat on a hook and bent to unlace his boots. "The radio said the sleet will turn to snow. They're predicting six to eight inches."

That made Teddy whoop. He came into the front hall with an enormous bowl of caramel-veined ice cream, probably half the gallon I had just purchased. "School is totally going to be canceled."

"Never a sure thing, so finish your homework anyway." Silvio hugged him and headed into the living room to tousle Rose's hair. "You seem distinctly less excited," Silvio said to Rose. She did look limp and wan.

"The high school already canceled a couple of times when back roads flooded. They'll start deducting days from spring break soon."

Silvio commended her on being sensible, and Teddy made a rude noise. Pluto was glaring at the top of the bookcase again, where I had stashed Fee's package.

Silvio and I sat up after the kids went to bed, figuring we should taste that fancy ice cream before Teddy devoured the rest. I turned off the lamps and opened the curtains, and we sat on opposite ends of the sofa, feet not quite touching, spooning it up by firelight, watching small flakes sift down and begin to stick.

"I wouldn't mind being snowbound this weekend," I said. "People just peck me to death with questions at the office, things they would otherwise figure out themselves."

"Mmm. What's up with Rose?"

I shrugged. "Obscure moodiness. Pretty standard. It was for me at that age." I was carving little paths with my teaspoon, mining for crunchy bits. "There's a lot for teenage girls to be angry about."

"Usually she saves the glowering for you and is sweet as pie when I come in."

I poked his shin with my toe. "Ain't that the truth." I closed my eyes to leaf through mental calendar pages. "Might be PMS. I haven't had my period since Christmas, but she's getting more regular now. It's like each cycle hits her harder."

I flashed back to that year of getting my first period—later than all my friends—then losing my father, then being assaulted. I kept burying these memories but they kept surfacing anyway. I changed the subject. "Oh, I never told you about the most excellent fight she and Teddy had a few weeks ago."

"Hit me."

"Teddy was whining about midterms, and Rose just started hollering. 'Don't you complain!' she yelled. 'You're not doing all this work while blood pours out of your vagina!'"

Silvio smacked his hands over his face, then guffawed.

"So Teddy goes, just as loud, 'You think I don't know that? There's blood all over the bathroom! It's like a war zone!'"

We dissolved in laughter.

At ten a.m., the snow was still coming down, and all the schools were closed, even the college. Finally, tiny flakes were succeeded by fat feathers, and then by a white sky. After lunch, Silvio and Teddy went out to shovel while I loaded plates into the dishwasher.

Rose was hanging back. "Ma, do I have to help? I don't feel well."

"What's the matter?" I asked.

"I don't know. Kind of tired and nauseous."

She looked pale, washed-out as the daylight, so I kissed her forehead, a gesture the kids only tolerated in the service of temperature-checking. "No fever."

"And cramps," she said. "There are only three snow-shovels anyway."

"Okay, go rest. But if you don't eat more and start feeling better, I'll be taking you to the doctor's office Monday."

"No one has time for that," Rose said with a spark of the crossness I was fond of. Once the kitchen was tidy, I glanced up at the package on top of the bookcase. Its presence was nauseating me, too, but I didn't want to unwrap it with Silvio home.

I went out and joined Silvio and Teddy, but I was distracted and useless. When Silvio shooed me inside again, I found a message from my mother on the landline.

I called Ariadne back, and her voice, as always during misfortune, sounded cheerful. Just checking on us, she said. She'd seen the snowfall numbers on the news. Not so balmy always in the south, was it.

We were fine, I reported, just digging out. Rose didn't feel well.

"Oh, fourteen-year-old girls, it's always something. So theatrical. You were impossible at fourteen, just impossible." As she nattered on, I groped my breasts for signs of premenstrual soreness, because Rose and I tended to synchronize, at least when I cycled.

Since, conversationally, we were down in Ariadne's bowels, I thought, well, nothing lost, and asked about her experience of menopause.

"What do you want to know about that for? Aren't you done with that yet?"

I was forty-eight, I reminded her, and the average age of menopause in the US was fifty-one.

"That late? My goodness. I was forty-six, forty-seven maybe. I suppose you were about Rose's age at the time."

Not long before my father's accident, then. "What symptoms did you have?" I ambled over to the front window, where Pluto was watching Teddy throw himself onto an undisturbed patch of snow and etch an angel with his arms and legs.

"Symptoms?" Ariadne sounded bemused. "No symptoms. I had my period every month for thirty years, except when I was pregnant, and then one day it didn't come anymore. I was too busy taking care of your father and the house and a moody teenage girl to worry about those things that bother women today, the hot flushes or what have you."

I pretended brownies were burning to get off the phone.

Saturday Teddy arranged to meet his friends at a good sledding hill not far from the house. Rose refused—she had too much homework. I wished, not for the first time, I could divide her diligence among the two of them, but I supposed it was too late for that particular act of will.

Before he left, Teddy sidled up to Silvio's desk. I was standing nearby, looking over Silvio's shoulder at the calendar to confer about March plans.

"Um, so I'm not keeping secrets," Teddy said.

Silvio's reading glasses slid down his nose, and he looked at Teddy over their rims, expectant.

"It's a group of us sledding. Also girls. Also one particular girl."

I leaned back against the desk and folded my arms. "Is this a date?"

Teddy fidgeted. He was wearing jeans and a flannel shirt, but the skinniest jeans, the newest shirt. "No! It's like, eight people. But I was supposed to meet this particular girl downtown after school on Friday, which I obviously didn't because of the snow, and she's coming along today. I just didn't want to act like I was hiding something."

"Do we know her?" I asked. "How old is she? What's her name?" Silvio touched my arm lightly, and I tried to relax. Shoulders down. Hands in the pockets of my long gray sweater, an old favorite.

"Chill, mom. She's a freshman too, and you probably have met her, although she didn't go to our middle school. Rose talks about her, they were sort of friends for a while."

"Were?"

Teddy's shoulders hunched. "Well, they're still friends, maybe, I don't know, but I don't think Rose is thrilled I'm hanging out with Lucie."

Pluto entered the study, and he didn't seem pleased, either. No matter how many secrets we unwrapped, how much snow we shoveled, it seemed like we would never stand on clean, bare ground again. I wasn't sure spring was even under there.

Twenty

The snow melted then refroze, turning the roads into ice-mirrors in which a person could watch herself procrastinate. Silvio returned to North Carolina, but the twins had Monday off. I went to work for a couple of hours, and when I returned, Teddy was upstairs, allegedly working. Rose had spread out her papers in the dining room, as I often did. A mug of peppermint tea steamed at her elbow.

"How are you feeling?" I asked as I flicked the electric kettle on.

"Better." Rose was terse, and I didn't want to antagonize her by fussing, but blood had returned to her cheeks. She was wrapped in an oversized sweater and leggings, sitting cross-legged and staring down her textbooks like a warrior. I fixed chai and left her to it, settling with my own books in the living room.

For a while I read Dickinson, Pluto strategically positioned three feet away on the floor. I had never met a religion I found plausible, but I did hope for an afterlife in which I could ask Miss Emily a few questions. I was sure some of those poems were spells. I wondered what she had wished for.

A bird glanced off the hall window with a clatter. More than once I looked up at Fee's bag still languishing atop the bookcase. Finally, sighing, I dragged the piano bench over to the bookcase and retrieved it. Pluto stood up.

"Behave," I warned him.

Loosening the ribbons and dried flowers looped around the bag handles, I tossed them to the floor, then pulled out one of two neatly wrapped squares and stripped off the tissue paper. It was the ordinary painting, the scene of grassy hills. I studied it, not knowing why such a plain composition should be so magnetic. I hadn't done any painting since adolescence, so I couldn't analyze it with an artist's understanding, but the strokes were fine and the colors lovely. Green shaded to gold, which is why it seemed like autumn, I supposed. I hadn't noticed the faint white path scaling one of the hills. It looked like chalk, implying the South Downs. I had only been to England once, in my twenties, and had stuck to London mostly, with a side trip to Oxford and another to Bath and Stonehenge. I remembered the sheep-grazed landscape, though, and riding in a bus past a giant white horse etched into a hillside. There were so many barrows and standing stones.

I placed the South Downs painting on the coffee table and reached for the second square. A thick leaf of writing paper fluttered out of the bag, with a note in Fee's hand. *Not safe around the twins,* she had written. *Be careful.*

I unwrapped the second package. The darker glade swam up at me, jewel-toned, eerie. I hated it but could not stop looking.

"What are those?" Rose had approached noiselessly and perched on the couch at my side.

"Paintings." Dumb answer. "From Alisa. I mean, from Fee, but they belong to Alisa. She loaned them to me for safekeeping."

"Safekeeping" sounded ridiculous—why would Alisa's house be unsafe?—but Rose was too absorbed in the watercolors to notice. Her shoulder pressed mine as she leaned in, and I realized she hadn't been so warmly present for weeks. I fought an urge to yank the otherworldly painting away.

"They're so different," Rose mused, tucking a tuft of hair behind one small ear. A blue teardrop glittered on the lobe.

She picked up the sunny image and held it above mine. "But look."

Rose pointed at the clearing in the uncanny woods—*don't touch,* I wanted to yell—tracing another ghostly path I hadn't noticed, a stripe of trodden grass. The curves of the two paths, green and white, lined up perfectly, divided only by wooden frames. "They match," she said.

Pluto uttered the *ack-ack-ack* warning he issued to birds he could not catch as he hunted them from behind windows he could not open. I tried not to snatch the frame from Rose as I reclaimed it and rushed the paintings upstairs.

Rose finished washing a frying pan, placed it upside down on the counter, and turned to me. "Mom, I want a second piercing in my ears. I want to get them done this weekend with Saara, at the jewelry shop downtown. I have money."

"Just what you need, more holes in your head," Teddy said, and tucked in his earbuds before trudging upstairs.

I wiped the pan with a dishtowel. "I guess that would be fine." Maybe this was a good time for my burning question. "So, what's this Lucie like, the girl Teddy mentioned?"

Rose deflated. "Gorgeous. Smart. Her father's a dentist. They came over from Honduras when Lucie was little, I think."

"Teddy said you and Lucie are friends?"

Rose stiffened. "We were lab partners last quarter, and I sit next to her in Algebra. Like I said, she's smart, so we go over work together sometimes. Speaking of," she said, scooping up the backpack to return to her private world.

Still at the Egg-Life. Dickinson's poems were chiming in my head. Well, at least Rose's shell had cracked, just a fraction.

I had taken to walking by myself, desperate for exercise and time to think, but the ice made that impossible. After Teddy and Rose, inadequately dressed, left for school, I turned on a yoga DVD and started faking my way through various stretches. I kept trying to clear my head, concentrate on breath and muscles, and sometimes that worked. My monkey mind was lively.

I had been reading about major design and senior capstone experiences, in light of the changes in English, and surprising myself by pushing further into the research. Then I got to talking with Dan, and before I knew it we were reconceiving the senior seminars. Maybe we would even co-author an article. Razing the major down to stubble and regrowing it more purposefully felt important. This was work I actually wanted to pursue.

Savasana, I told myself, lying down, imagining my belly as a deep mountain lake. Corpse pose. Breathe. Be empty.

But there was no putting aside desire. I wished more and more desperately to know Rose's trouble. I told Silvio there wasn't one, just her body's transformations, her justified rage at an America that could even consider Donald Trump for the presidency, but I was privately convinced otherwise. During her pallor of the last snowy weekend, a nightmare had recurred: Rose kneeling on a beach, colorless, grieving. What had she said? I glanced up at the iron phone on the hall table. It did not ring.

Rose was brewing her own spells. Her moodiness became, perhaps strategically, less outrageous, and she no longer spent every spare moment hidden in her bedroom. She ventured downtown with Saara for the piercing, returning with evil-eye studs above her favorite blue teardrops. But Rose did not join

Teddy's group of friends—and Lucie—at the movies Friday night, preferring to brood at home. She treated her brother and his trumpet practice with exaggerated patience. Teddy seemed careful of Rose, and watchful.

I volunteered to drive his friends back to their scattered homes after Friday's horror flick. Lucie lived the farthest out in the county, so I dropped her off last. She behaved shyly but seemed nice enough, and Rose was right—Lucie was pretty, with large brown eyes in a delicate face. There was plenty of intelligence in her expression, but she wasted none on me.

She told Teddy the time of her events at the next day's track meet, and he promised to be there. I watched her wave from the lit-up doorway and slip inside, then continued along the circular drive to return home.

"Is she a good runner?" I asked.

"The fastest of the freshman girls. Faster than lots of the older kids, too."

"She's built for it." I glanced sideways at Teddy and imagined I caught a blush. "Why didn't Rose join you guys?"

"I have no idea."

"I can't help but think something is worrying her."

"Mom, I've told you a million times, just because we're twins doesn't mean I know what she's thinking."

"Does it maybe bother her that you're dating?"

"That would be weird. And I'm not dating." Teddy reclined his seat and closed his eyes. Only the road spoke, crackling and rumbling.

On Sunday, the weather mild again, Silvio and Teddy went for a run. Both had tension to burn off. Silvio was striving to dazzle colleagues at every turn while being present to his family four hours away, meaning he was trying to defy the laws of physics. We did have a few things in common.

I was surprised to find Rose perched on my bed. She had removed the two watercolors from under it and laid them on the quilt so the paths aligned.

Rose glanced up as I entered. "I can't stop thinking about them."

Trying not to panic, I moved slowly, distributing clothes into various drawers, hanging a blouse in my closet.

"They belong to Alisa. Why do you have them, again?"

"She bought them in England, years ago. Actually, she bought one and only found the second painting recently, underneath, when the frame broke."

"The first was the open hillside, and the hidden picture was the woods." Rose sounded positive, leaning over the images, and I noticed her thinness.

"That's right." Disposing of the final pairs of balled socks, I moved closer. Sun from the window lit her up, and she touched one new piercing gingerly.

"Does that hurt?"

"No," Rose lied.

"There's antibiotic ointment in the medicine cabinet."

"The jewelry store gave me something. I just think these are magical," she said, drawing my eyes down to the watercolors again. "There's some relationship between the two, but I can't quite figure it out."

"Well, the paths, like you showed me." One of Rose's feet, in a colorful sock, was dangling over the edge of the bed, and I put my hand on it lightly. What I really wanted was to grab her toe and hang on for dear life.

Rose withdrew her foot. "Not just that. And look at that stump," she said, pointing at the darker image.

Pushing aside the vertigo the painting always gave me, I peered in. "I hadn't thought about it before."

"It's enormous. Imagine the size of the tree! It must have been ancient. Why would anyone cut it down?"

I considered the plant stalks around the stump's edge, their closed buds represented by just the tiniest dabs of pale green paint. "The stump makes the picture sad."

"Something's been lost." Rose tucked both feet beneath her now, pitched over the miniatures with fierce attention.

"We'll find it," I said, and for the first time in a while, Rose raised her eyes to me.

Twenty-One

Blood again. I barely made it through a discussion of Dickinson's volcanos. When I returned to my office, I found Fee in my side chair, studying the photo of my fair family.

She smiled, all innocent flowers and citrus scent. "I signed and submitted the contract to Barbara this morning. The university lawyers are straightening out my visa, although I will have to visit the embassy soon."

I didn't ask which embassy. "And the college president formally confirmed we may search for Sandra's replacement next year. Things are looking up for English." I parked myself in my desk chair with all kinds of relief.

Fee's luminescence increased. "You are a good leader."

The late afternoon sun had declined. I rolled back into a shadowy corner, feeling, as I often did around Fee, mousy.

No, not that again. I straightened my spine and willed myself to inhabit my body with conviction. "It's been quite the year. Alisa leaves, you arrive in her place, and within six months you secure a permanent line, a book deal, and an engagement ring. Plus Sandra retiring right after a conversation with you. I think you're the leader here."

Fee raised her eyebrows. "There were other forces at work in those events. Including your…wishing."

I shook my head violently. "No."

"And you wanted Beth-Ann gone, I think."

"I did not make that happen!" Two marriages had imploded, a psychology professor had leukemia, and I didn't want credit for any of it. "I helped Camille with her file. That's it."

Fee crossed one slim leg over the other and smoothed her skirt. "Some blood was shed this year. You were clumsy. But you steered a fractious department away from bad choices, towards better ones." She pointed the toe of one gorgeous boot in my direction. "You have worked more magic than you admit."

Feeling sick, I flipped the pressure. "Opened any windows lately?"

Now Fee pouted. "No. It is not time yet." She stood up. "Keep those paintings for a few weeks longer. A chance may come."

You big old fairy control-freak, I thought. Although she wasn't a fairy, was she? In the coffee shop she'd made it sound like she'd picked up a few tricks after being carried away, like Alisa. Or perhaps the word was *abducted*. So many tales blurred the line between a woman's wayward desires and her assault and kidnapping.

I said aloud, "Wait."

Fee paused in that ultra-still way, with antique courtesy.

"That day before Christmas, in Alisa's front yard." I still insisted on referring to the house as Alisa's. "Why did you save me?"

I watched her consider pretending she didn't know what I meant. Then she exhaled. "I let you wander away, but I gave you the wreath, a kind of charm I am good at weaving."

The wreath of pine, ivy, and mistletoe had guided me back. "But why?"

Fee's hair was down today, a black wing to shade her summery gaze. "I was still deciding if I liked you, Cynthia," she said. "Your blood magic repulses me. The way you oscillate between gauche bursts of power and complete denial is irritating. You would do less harm if you would own up to your capabilities."

I choked.

"But my own feelings aside, you are needed here. And I guessed, despite your ambivalence, you would help me stay, help me win my heart's desire. I guessed correctly."

Fee slipped out. My office was cool now, but I burned.

That evening, Dan texted. *Did you see Camille's post?*

I opened the social media site. Camille, visiting her beau for dinner, had stopped in a neighboring town to shop. A white male police officer followed her from one store to the next, then asked her to step out of a boutique and answer a few questions. Frightened, she stalled, and the policeman grabbed, handcuffed, and bundled her into the back of the patrol car. After hours at the station, they allowed her a call. Her lawyer-love arrived promptly. An explanation ensued about how Camille fit the description of a recent serial shoplifter. They released her without apology. Her post was long and fiery.

Should I call, text, or add a message of solidarity to the hundred or so comments her post had already attracted? I couldn't think what to say.

I clicked over to the news, wondering if local outlets had posted a story yet. There were headlines, instead, about the abrupt resignation of a school superintendent on whose computer child pornography had been discovered; a mother of two who had gone missing; and Ku Klux Klan fliers found on lawns. Everything was terrible and getting worse.

I had to get more information out of Fee. If there were webs of wishing and supernatural influence vibrating all around me, I needed to know much more about power and its limits.

I almost crashed into Camille in the mailroom the next morning. My breath caught in my throat when I saw the bruises on her wrists. She didn't have time to talk, she said. She wasn't ready for her ten o'clock class.

Two students, Julene and Persis, visited me jointly after eleven. They had come from Camille's Harlem Renaissance seminar and were upset. Rumors were already flying and a student had asked Camille directly what had occurred. She described the arrest before moving discussion back to Langston Hughes.

"I understand why she went back to the books," Julene said. "There are some idiots in that class, and who needs to hear their attitude? But that can't be the end of the conversation."

Persis's lashes were wet, but her eyes sparked. "Other colleges have Black Lives Matter rallies. Here it's just business as usual."

"There's a black students' organization," I said and searched for the club contact information. I wrote the URL on a slip of paper and handed it to Persis. "We could contact them and offer to set up a rally. I'll help, but if students announce the event, administrators and trustees will care more."

Julene looked over her friend's shoulder and nodded with recognition at the student name scrawled there. "I know her. Let's do it."

"I don't know what good a rally will do," Camille burst out, when I found her in her office. She was seated but looked ready to fly out of there at a moment's notice.

I hesitated. It had seemed like a powerful idea. "Maybe make visible that a lot of people want change. The students are thinking about you, but their idea is to focus on racial violence all over the country."

"That would be best," she said, leaning her elbows on the desk, her head in her hands. "What I need is no more spotlights. Just a mojito and a good night's sleep."

"Let me treat you to that drink." That was my zone of competence.

She never felt welcome here, she said as we walked through the darkening afternoon. Life improved once the downtown shop-owners knew her by sight, but tourists were always asking sharp-edged questions, implying she looked out of place. Greeters at the big box stores wouldn't pass her a shopping cart. Students like Royall were snide, and some university staff, too. Petty stuff, but it wore a person down.

Shame flooded me. "I didn't know it was that bad."

"You didn't want to know," she said.

We sat in a corner of the bar, and a blonde hostess handed us menus. Camille told me about a day during her first year, when a couple of scruffy white guys in a truck with a confederate flag decal had followed her back to her apartment, shouting slurs.

"What happened?"

"I locked myself in and called campus security, and they did some kind of ineffective investigation that led to nothing, and I started therapy."

That's terrible, I kept murmuring, and *I'm so, so sorry.* We ordered artichoke dip and mojitos and I texted the twins that I would be late. I said, "You're a wonderful colleague and I really, really don't want you to leave."

"I've wanted to get out ever since I got here. I nearly quit after those guys in the truck—I was scared to leave my own house next morning. My boyfriend was finally changing the math, and now this happens. It's like you all got acclimated to having one black professional woman around, just one, but as soon as I step past the city line, wham."

The dip arrived. I spoke again, hoping to keep her at the table despite how stupid I had been. "I'm sorry I didn't know. It's not right that you felt alone." I paused. "Alisa warned me. I've been hiding."

"You and the rest of America." Camille sighed. "At least we're going to Mexico City for spring break. A few weeks ago that felt extravagant. Now it seems like a stroke of genius."

We took turns dunking chunks of sourdough boule. "Getting away sounds perfect, but I'd like to help you feel safe here, too. *Be* safe here."

She said "hmm" and swallowed. "If you have the power to fix the whole racist country, by all means, work those magic spells. But I wasn't safe growing up in Georgia, and I'm not safe now. I just look at you and Silvio and the twins. Could I do that? If the tenure committee gives me the thumbs up and I get married, could I raise kids in this part of the country? Or if I move in with my man half an hour north of here, closer to civilization, is it possible? I find myself thinking a tenure denial just might set me free of this whole mess."

"Well, you *will* get tenure. The committee is reading files now. They always issue verdicts the week after spring break."

Camille sat bolt upright and lowered her skinny straw. "You don't think this whole thing—I mean, I'm not sure I want to stay here forever, but I would like the option!"

"If this had never happened, a tenure denial for you would look insane," I responded, confident I was speaking truth. "Your file is too strong. Given your highly questionable detainment by local police yesterday, wouldn't any vote against you look that much worse?"

She sagged. With a glance up at a television screen over the bar, muted but broadcasting something about the presidential primaries, she said, "The one thing I know is, never underestimate the crazies."

The mood around the department was low. When Camille and I met with Dan to hash out next year's senior seminar topics, he told me about endless "Where are you from?" questions, students asking him how to swear in Chinese, and a running partner's tiny-Asian-penis jokes. Camille nodded, but I had been unaware of any of it. As department head it was my job to know what happened. Sweat prickled my scalp.

"When Alisa and I were new assistant professors together," I blurted, "the chair of English was kind of handsy."

"Was that the Episcopalian from Birmingham?" Camille asked. "The one obsessed with Jonathan Swift?"

I nodded.

"You've told me stories about him. Why didn't you say about the hands?"

"I guess because it was so awful. I mean, Alisa and I developed strategies for staying out of range. And Sandra helped, without acknowledging how bad it was. But it was crushing how everyone else just pretended not to see it."

"Scary, when you're tenure-track," Dan said. "You wonder, if you make him mad, will he find a reason to fire you?"

"It was terrible. After he retired, I just wanted to put it behind me."

"Why?" Camille persisted, leaning forward, her palms on her knees.

I reached into a dark place inside myself for the real answer, and it surprised me. "Because I was so fucking mad. Because I had to keep working with these people who hadn't troubled themselves to help me, and if I acknowledged the anger, I was afraid I wouldn't be able to set foot on campus again."

Camille leaned back with a complicated expression. I wiped perspiration from my hairline and announced, "So, these seminar topics are going to be great!"

Dan burst out laughing, stood up, and opened the door. Camille was first out, heading to a class, and as she walked off, I heard Beth-Ann pronounce loudly at the copier that she was relieved to escape this backwards-ass state. No one responded, and I imagined Beth-Ann brooding there alone, bat-suit buffed to a high gloss, not sure if she needed a grappling hook to pull someone close or a thruster to zoom away.

I packed up and half-jogged my sweaty self to the parking deck so I could make a doctor's appointment. Finally, I was ready to get my joint pain and fatigue checked out.

"We need to order blood tests," the physician said an hour later, filling out an order slip. "And meanwhile, we're going to try some dietary changes and see what good they do."

So that was the weekend, shame and shopping for gluten-free bread at the co-op. When I explained my new diet to Teddy, he was horrified. Rose, experimenting with a paleo regime, smiled serenely.

I was fine for a couple of days. But when Sunday rolled around, I watched my fair-haired son toast his morning bagel with wheat-lust in my heart and resentment about everything he took for granted. When, in the late afternoon, Rose found a slice of sausage pizza wrapped in foil at the back of the fridge and polished it off with a post-Paleolithic shrug, I teared up like a fool.

At the Department Heads meeting run by the dean, I realized I had, indeed, been underestimating the crazies.

Barbara showed up with University Counsel in tow, a stoop-shouldered guy in a funereal suit whose bulbous nose was reddened by broken capillaries. Bourbon, Sandra claimed. She and Ralph had taught me dislike of the man, who tended to slow a meeting down to a crawl and suck all vitality out of its participants.

After reminding us about fall course lists due to the registrar, Barbara informed us the topic under discussion today would be the development of a social media policy.

Before the legal vampire could bare his fangs, the Mathematics chair shouted from the back, "Why? What in heaven's name is going on now?"

Barbara, calm in a gray skirt-suit and lemon-yellow blouse, touched the gold chain at her throat. "The controversy last week trended on Twitter."

"What controversy?" he shouted again.

"That English professor who got arrested," Physics smirked, with a sidelong glance at me.

"No charges were brought," Barbara began, and Sociology muttered, "Tempest in a teapot." The volume of her comment was nicely judged—apparently private but just audible to most people in the room. There was some uncomfortable shifting.

"Nothing happened to her, right?" Physics said. "Just taken in for questioning because she fit the profile, and then released. That's called police doing their jobs."

"What the hell, Stan?" I demanded as I looked around at the other chairs and registered: white, white, white. The interim head of our struggling Africana Studies program declared, after I spoke, "Seriously!" But he too was white.

Barbara was trying to wrest back control. "We're not in the business of judging the police here," she said loudly.

"The point is the university's brand," Nosferatu began, and she shot the lawyer an infuriated look.

"Its *brand*?" The Philosophy chair's voice was incredulous. "Is that the point? By 'social media policy' do you mean censoring the faculty, overthrowing the protections of tenure, and curtailing freedom of speech, so that we don't upset wealthy alumni?"

That's when the meeting really went south.

Over the phone that night, I described the furor to Silvio. About the Philosophy chair, I said, "I appreciated the guy's protest, but some people were shouting about freedom of speech and some about political correctness. I'm pretty sure I heard the head of Economics call Camille a 'malcontent.' The lawyer clutched his chest like he'd been staked, and Barbara may have actually perspired."

"Is the head of Philosophy the guy from Poland?"

"Yes, so we heard about dictatorships in Eastern Europe and the dangers of imposing a police state. I guess the bright side is we won't be asked to sign off on a social media policy anytime soon." I was squatting as I spoke, wiping down the front of the oven with glass-cleaner. I wrinkled my nose at the chemical smell, and my fingers tingled against the metal.

"Well, that's good. But you're worried about Camille, I guess? Isn't her case under consideration?"

"As in, right now. They're reading files this week, and the head of Philosophy is on the tenure committee. So is support-the-police Stan."

"Shit."

I moved on to the fridge, scrubbing a sticky fingerprint off the steel handle. "The thing I feel crappiest about is not finding language to explain anything to those morons, how much harder Camille's job has been than most of theirs."

He was quiet for a beat. "Yeah. It's hard to get through."

"Well, I'm going to have to get better at it. In the meantime, please tell me it's going to be fine."

"It is definitely going to be fine. Is that Windex I hear?"

"Well, off-brand. I hired a cat-sitter today, and as a result started looking around. This house is gross."

"Still planning to arrive Friday night?"

"With two sulky teenagers and a loaf of millet bread."

Twenty-Two

As I packed for North Carolina, I wondered about this current forking through me all the time, what Fee called my "repulsive blood magic." I had a feeling for machines, the red power in other bodies. But the electricity seemed to emanate, too, from dirt and rock. Would I have magic, if that's what this was, in another landscape?

Even that last morning, Teddy pleaded not to spend most of spring break in his father's apartment—he would be missing all the fun with his friends, especially, I gathered, Lucie. I started yelling about ingratitude. When they left for the bus, Rose was struggling to maintain an expression of high-minded neutrality.

I sank into a chair with the dregs of my coffee and the very thin local weekly paper, usually a ten-minute distraction at best. But the opinion page bristled with letters about Camille's detainment by the police, most of them offensive. I texted her a warning not to read it, and she responded, *I don't even subscribe.* I chewed my thumbnail, getting angrier and angrier, and finally drafted my own letter to the editor instead of grading quizzes. Pluto stalked from window to window as I typed, throat clicking.

Eventually I drove to campus, taught class, tried again to get my grading done, and ended up writing Alisa an email instead. Unlike Silvio, Alisa knew most paranoia was justified. I described Camille's ordeal, plus everything ridiculous said by a cast of characters my old comrade knew intimately. I wrote about how the bad old days were coming up a lot in my thoughts now. Then I confided my worries over Rose and Teddy.

My outpourings had no audience, unless some minion in IT was scanning my email. Alisa felt far, far out of shouting range.

Twenty years at the College, I wrote. *I've been penciling my children's heights in the same hall closet ever since they could stand. But I'm not sure I'll fight to stay, after all.*

I was supposed to pick up the twins fifteen minutes before the bell, to beat the traffic, but I dithered until the last second about whether to pack the paintings. If together they created a portal to UnWales, I didn't know how to operate the technology, so I was waiting until I received instructions or dreamed what to do. In the meantime, it felt unsafe to smuggle them around or to leave them unguarded, either. I ended up shoving them into the back of my closet before hopping into the car.

Rose leaned forward from the back seat for a while, in a gossipy mood. She and Teddy made fun of the World History teacher who had referred in class to a series of world leaders, starting with Alexander the Great, as "douchebags."

"It's World War Two after break," said Teddy. "You know Hitler is gonna be a total douche."

After an hour, chatter subsided. I watched the landscape change, hills surging and flattening, rivers glinting. Driving south in early March was like watching a time-lapse film. Bare branches began to bud, and a few of them bloomed. As spring advanced, Judas trees flowering purple, so did the evening. The sun dropped. Hot colors lit the horizon then faded. My gray mood deepened. Something had been lost. But we'd find it.

Silvio seemed delighted to welcome us to his bachelor lair, the third floor of an old house, rented with basic furnishings. We had helped him lug belongings up the narrow staircase in August but hadn't returned since, and the place was cozier than I remembered, nestled under eaves. His galley kitchen smelled delicious. Silvio had stocked the fridge with treats and set the small table for four.

We gabbed over dinner about weekend plans. Silvio had a notion to rent kayaks on Saturday. He wanted to show us his favorite restaurants and the new gelateria, maybe the second-run movie theater, furnished with couches and serving cappuccino and microbrews at the popcorn counter. On Sunday, we were invited to Silvio's department head's house for dinner, and Monday we would spend the afternoon on campus. That was a light teaching day for Silvio, but the kids could sit in on his class, if they wanted. Rose liked that idea, but Teddy's grumpiness returned.

"Extra school during spring break, uh, no thanks." He was even more outraged when he realized he would have to share the sofa bed with Rose or unroll a sleeping bag on the floor. As I lectured him about privilege and gratitude, my heart did its angry jumping thing.

Silvio and I finally retreated to the bedroom with wine and chocolates. He settled into a side chair, lifting his feet onto a corner of the mattress, and I propped pillows against the bedstead. There wasn't much room, but it was a relief to shut the door against our children and roll my eyes in synchrony with the man I'd chosen, long ago, for sympathizer-in-chief.

When Rose turned the shower on, providing a screen of white noise, Silvio said, "I have news."

I looked at his face and could tell right off. "Oh my god."

He laughed and ran a hand through silvering blond. "Yeah. This afternoon, the administration approved the tenure-track line in Psych, and they're offering it to me."

I placed my glass of red on the window sill. "Silvio!"

"I don't have the paperwork yet, so I don't know the numbers, but Ross says I'll have the offer next week."

I was hot-flashing, so I stripped off my cardigan and flung myself backwards onto the bed. I had wanted him to find a job that made him happy. Supposedly.

We decided we had better tell the kids before Sunday's dinner party, but not much before. We followed brunch at a funky café with a twenty-minute drive and a hike over wetland trails in a state park. A strange wood seemed like the right place.

Rose congratulated her father, emphasizing how much he deserved this, then fell silent. Teddy was winding up to panic, wanting to know if we were about to move.

"Maybe in a year," I admitted. "We just don't know yet. But for right now, there's no job here I could reasonably apply for, and I'm not ready to quit mine without an offer in hand."

Silvio shoved his hands deep into jacket pockets and fixed his eyes on the pine-needled path. "First, the terms. Then your mother and I talk to Barbara and see if it gives us leverage at home."

Rose's eyes met mine with a question. I gazed back, shrugging infinitesimally. No, Rose, I am not hopeful.

"If it doesn't," Silvio was continuing, "your mom starts looking for work down here, and I keep my eyes open, too."

Teddy teared up, and when he opened his mouth, I expected violent protest at the unfairness of it all. Invisible hackles rose on my back. Instead, he said, "I don't *want* to keep living apart for another year."

As my throat constricted with sympathy, Rose chimed in, scientific. "Yeah, Dad, conditions are not good. Teddy and I are a handful, you know we are. And mom's breakdowns are increasing in frequency and intensity."

I cracked up. We paused on a wooden bridge over low water, broken here and there by stands of tall reeds, reflecting heavy clouds. Disturbed, a heron rose with a few powerful wingbeats and disappeared into the trees, legs trailing.

We made it to the car as the first fat drops descended, and by the time we pulled onto the road, rain was bucketing down.

"If you've been finding the separation hard," I said, twisting to face the backseat, "that's important information. It can't be the only consideration—there's money and careers and everybody's happiness to worry about—but it matters a lot."

Silvio's voice was thick. "Living apart is terrible. You guys only have three more years at home before college, and I'm missing so much."

"Dad," Rose said in a pained tone. "You're not missing anything. Stupid school every stupid day of the week, and you're there almost half the time. We love you, and we want to be together, but you're doing the right thing. We just don't want it to last, like, forever."

I shouldn't have been astonished. Rose understood every angle, including what her tender-hearted father needed to hear. I was the person she refused to placate. I respected her for that, too.

Back at the apartment, where the pack of us had spoiled Silvio's regimen, we lounged around reading or working on laptops while taking turns in the shower. Silvio whispered to me in the bedroom, where I was deep in an N. K. Jemisin trilogy rather than composing the article I was planning, that he didn't think he should take the job after all. I couldn't read his expression.

I put the book down. "If you manage to squeeze a tenure-track job at home out of this scenario, you should take it, even though Broome State is the better department. If not, you accept the position here, and, just like we told the kids, we commute while I look around."

Oh so reasonable, but inside me, water welled out of the ground and low trees writhed. "If we're still stuck in different states this time next year, we reevaluate. One of us may have to give up so we can all live together, but it's not time for that yet."

The lines on Silvio's face deepened, and he hunched his stocky shoulders.

Silvio's department head was a warm, bearded guy our age, although his wife and children were younger. An eleven-year-old boy spirited Teddy away to the PlayStation, while a resolute seven-year-old grabbed Rose's hand and tugged her upstairs.

The couple, it turned out, had met on the job. When Laila was hired by Broome State's Education Department, Ross was already teaching in Psychology, and his first marriage was on the rocks. She shared details over zuppa inglese—I had informed Silvio in advance I would be breaking the gluten embargo, for professional reasons.

I liked Laila. Her sidelines included science fiction and knitting. We swapped book recommendations before she broached work. "We have this really cool Teaching and Learning Center for faculty development," she said. Despite her relaxed posture, she had been assessing me. "The person who directed it for a decade just announced he'll be retiring, so they'll advertise the position in the fall."

I forked up the last mouthful and asked how the center operated and what its programming was like. Laila told me about a recent faculty workshop as well as an interdisciplinary collaboration her husband and Silvio had become involved in—I had heard a bit about it before, but he and I didn't have much time for chat these days.

When she paused for a bite of dessert, I noticed the windows were dark.

"Anyway," she said, "the position won't be tenure-track, but they want a director with academic credibility. After Silvio told us about your teaching award, Ross and I Googled you." She laughed, unembarrassed. "We think you'd be a strong candidate, not that the final decision is up to us, but still. I hope you'll apply. Silvio has already made department life so much more vital for Ross. We have to transplant you both, somehow."

The retiring director of the Teaching and Learning Center was a quirky, squat old white guy with whiskers sprouting from his orifices, not the future self I was straining to see through mist, but I liked him. I strolled out of his office, Monday afternoon, with a stack of handouts, a brochure for a summer workshop in Atlanta, and a list of books to read pronto. I was not feeling electricity rising up through the soil in this place, but there were other sources of power. Maybe professional authority would be enough, and I could put aside the terrifying business of badly conceived wishes possibly coming true. Did I want to?

Early Wednesday morning, Silvio and I paced around his neighborhood, discussing the offer letter. The money was better than expected—heftier than his non-tenure-track paychecks, and more than double my starting salary in the late nineties. I should have felt light, heartened by expanding possibilities. This could only be good news.

He cooked breakfast, I packed lunches, and we gathered laundry and chargers and other sundries that had migrated to the medicine cabinet or rolled into corners. "You'll leave something behind, but I'll find it and bring it home the day after tomorrow," Silvio said as he hugged Teddy.

The roads were slower, clogged by accidents and construction, as if we were rowing against the stream. Rose still inhabited a castle overgrown by nettles, but she chatted from her turret. Maybe I was moated and palisaded, too—I felt solitary in my irrational unhappiness. Yet what I experienced was the inverse of fortification. As I neared home ground, with Silvio's buffer absent, there was nothing standing between me and this weird universe of making wishes and burning apple-wood in hibachis. Half an hour from home, I stepped out of the car to pump gas and felt a pulse of power leap through me from the earth.

Twenty-Three

I should take out those paintings, I kept telling myself. Take the frames apart, search them for clues like an indefatigable British detective. But I don't want to. I don't want the responsibility. I felt the uncanny painting throbbing at me—risky to repress, risky to acknowledge.

I'll know when it's time, I temporized, then didn't give myself a chance to think about it. We returned to a dusty house, our duffels stuffed with dirty laundry and backpacks with neglected homework. When Silvio arrived Friday, we were still catching up, cleaning, shopping. Pluto had found a bunch of pipe cleaners somewhere; I kept scooping up fuzzy wires without locating the motherlode. Teddy and Rose needed to finish projects for Earth Science—dioramas at their age?—and I was grading. At first I stayed busy but oriented to the objects in my closet. Then my compass needle started to wobble until I couldn't sense north anymore.

The following week, in addition to a flurry of classwork and conferences, I had to finalize the department's fall schedule for the registrar. Alisa had not responded to requests about her teaching preferences, so I hazarded a guess.

The low point was the hour Silvio and I met with Barbara. We gave her the details of the Broome State offer and asked again whether a tenure-track job could be opened here. She blushed and repeated, "The person now holding that slot is very sick, but she is only fifty-nine, and she has not retired. What can I do?"

Nauseated by my own words, I said, "Sandra tells me she just entered hospice." I explained that if a secure position could not be found here for Silvio, I would have to search for a job to the south. Barbara told us she would keep exploring possibilities, but her body language was not encouraging.

The high point was the news that Camille had been recommended for tenure and promotion, although, rumor had it, after a divisive discussion. Now it was up to the president and trustees at their May meeting.

At home, Pluto seemed chastened for about thirty-six hours by his abandonment to the house-sitter, then in a single day scratched each of us in turn, Silvio twice. Silvio and Teddy were running together more often now, and for longer distances, but when they left the house in their gear, Pluto stood at the window and released throaty howls.

"He might be part hound," Rose said, stroking the creature.

"And all Satan." I bent to pick up another pipe cleaner.

Rose seemed controlled and steady. She was sharp-tongued and visibly down, but a good girl, earning straight A's while her twin's grades oscillated, and staying in weekends while he went out with his friends.

It wasn't until after Silvio's spring break ended and he hit the road again that I halted in our front hall, quiet but for a ticking clock. With fingers resting on the iron telephone, I thought, *What am I doing?*

I was pretending competence but I was afraid.

Worst case scenario: the daylight world was full of holes. People could fall through portals and disappear. Some people, like Fee, could even push an unlucky soul through a crack between universes for their own obscure reasons, or save her again, if they wished.

I might have power of a related kind. If so, I faced a new kind of work with no handbook or research cohort—and in the meantime, fumbling around, I was creating suffering. Leukemia, maybe. Broken hearts. One-way faculty exchanges for grieving friends, power-mad Writing Program Directors, and unfulfilled spouses.

The other scenario was my verifiable life, in which blasts of adolescent misery were relieved by the peregrinations of a spouse building a nest in another state. A choice loomed between my job and love. Real threats existed to the physical safety of friends and children, and to the safety of other people's friends and children. Glaciers melted, and refugees drowned. I inhabited a world in which a grandstanding racist misogynist, a man who wanted to punish women for abortions and build a concrete wall at our southern border, was running for president. This world I knew was not preferable to the one that frightened me.

Further, Alisa was lost, and I might be the only person who sort-of-wanted to rescue her. It was time to focus. Maybe I could help, addressing one puzzle at a time. Or two.

Pluto watched while I ransacked my closet for the paintings. Behind too-small dresses in unfashionable lengths and a shoebox full of audiotapes, I found Fee's basket-weave tote, empty.

I stepped back, turned in a circle, surveyed the room. Pluto, purring, reached his front paws up my thigh, and I leaned down to scratch his thrumming head.

My neck prickled. It seemed unlikely, but I followed an impulse to Rose's room.

She hadn't dealt with her clean laundry, so I lifted a pile off the nightstand and started placing socks, bras, and shirts in drawers. No miniature paintings were nestled among the leggings. I did discover a bin of craft supplies upended on the floor between her desk and a bookcase—the pipe cleaner spawning ground. I bent to pick up the mess and spotted a worn cloth bag pushed behind the desk. I slid it out.

She had decorated this tote at some middle-school slumber party, drawing her name in glitter glue above a sparkly flower and attaching feathers and sequins. Inside the sack were the two watercolors, her diary, and three orange vials of pills.

Vicodin, a year-old prescription from a doctor whose name I didn't recognize. The patient, however, was Ross, Silvio's boss in North Carolina. I shook the vial then removed the safety cap to check. More than half full, as if he had taken some pills after an injury then stopped.

Percocet, in Saara's mother's name, same story.

Xanax, prescribed to me a year and half ago, expired now.

Shaking, I opened the diary and read a few pages. I stopped to call Silvio. He had just crossed the state line, but he pulled over to answer my call. I'm turning around now, he said. I'll be home by lunchtime, and we'll talk to Rose together.

After phoning in sick, asking Harriet to cancel my class and office hours, I lay down on Rose's bed. In my fugue state, I saw black specks flocking on the ceiling, the way she used to as a child. She had cried that they were ants, bugs, something terrible, could she please sleep with us? Sometimes we found her in Teddy's room in the morning, either curled in his bed or lying on his rug in a swirl of quilts.

I sat up and counted the Xanax. I remembered taking one, maybe two, feeling unpleasantly dizzy and angry, as well, that another doctor had read my pain as depression or anxiety. I had put the vial away and forgotten it. Seven were now missing. Unless Rose had stolen multiple bottles of narcotics and antidepressants, working through each then disposing of the containers, she wasn't using pills heavily. Either she had just begun experimenting, or she was stockpiling.

Terrified, I opened the journal and read from the beginning. The first entries, from August, concerned high school's mutating cliques, lunch table dramas, who was crushing on whom, and friends' boasts about sex and drugs. At Saara's Halloween party, a flask of Southern Comfort was passed around. Teddy swigged from it, but not freaked-out Rose or straight-laced Saara. A couple of entries referred to Gina, the senior double-bass player, as a *skank*. Rose thought Teddy smoked pot with Gina and her friends.

Entries from around Christmas described me as *seriously wack* and *on the rag*. Rose called me a hypocrite for coming in so late from Fee's that night, no explanation, while demanding details of Teddy's whereabouts and questioning him about drugs. She assumed I had gotten high with "that Welsh poet" because my pupils had been dilated. She missed Silvio, who kept me *under control*.

After New Year's, the entries changed tone. Lucie's name came up a lot, with descriptions of how beautiful she was. There was even a poem for her friend, drafted in loopy cursive, deploying clever metaphors to play on the name. Darkness fell when Lucie left the room.

The passion changed nature with one shocked page in red ink: Lucie was scheming to get close to Rose's hot twin. Rose confronted her, and Lucie said *horrible things*. Lucie and Teddy started to hang out together, and Rose felt bereft.

A short entry followed about running into Fee in the bookstore downtown. "O Rose, thou art sick," Fee said. Rose searched the phrase and discovered the poem by William Blake. She transcribed it in her diary, now half-full of longing and heartache, and double-underlined the last two words: *life destroy*. The underscores, in a different ink, grooved the page.

Pluto posed on Rose's carpet, front paws extended, blinking. I said in his direction, "I will obliterate that woman if any harm comes to my daughter." He purred.

I closed my aching eyes, thinking. Rose had a crush on Lucie, who had the hots for Teddy. No hope for an erotic awakening between my daughter and the not-so-demure Atalanta. I remembered my own infatuations with girls in high school, and androgynous rock stars. I'd never been certain of my desires until I'd met Silvio.

Yet I should stop projecting, seeing Rose as a version of myself with the slight uncanniness of a mirror image—blonde to my brown, Japanese to my French, Khan Academy to my volume of Hawthorne. Comparisons pissed her off. She would write her own story.

Sitting on that blue comforter, shivering because I had perspired through my clothes, I was losing time again, shimmering between uncertainties. A clock ticked. The cat sighed. A distant washing machine beeped and stilled. I was prying into Rose's *dark secret love,* and it felt wrong.

I opened my lids to equinoctial light and saw the prescription vials. They cured my ambivalence. I read on.

A place must exist somewhere, Rose wrote, *that I could just be normal. Not weird. Not secret.*

Many of the remaining entries concerned the second painting, the forest glade. First she described how beautiful it was, strange and frightening but beautiful, and how she wished she could sit on that tree-stump and breathe that air.

Gradually the glade became the place she could escape to and *be normal.* Angrily, Rose described how I had hidden the watercolors, keeping her from sanctuary, trapping her in the awfulness of the real world. She found them anyway, searching while I worked late.

There seemed to be a path, she wrote, from the everyday to that other place, and she had discovered it. Each night she removed the paintings from their new hiding place and puzzled it out. The paths brightened; buds opened. Xanax helped her find the way. Percocet just made her sick and sleepy.

She had an idea how to cross over in the flesh, to step through the watercolor as if it were a window, but had to wait until Silvio returned to North Carolina. I was oblivious, but he was unenchanted.

I showered a second time, dressed in clean clothes, fetched a tall glass of water, and returned upstairs.

Pluto heard Silvio before I did and pounded down the stairs to greet him. When I heard Silvio come in, I called, "Up here." Silvio took the stairs two at a time, the cat racing behind him.

I showed Silvio where I had found the bag then pointed to its contents, spread on the quilt. As I summarized the journal, I handed him the glass. He drank. While he read over the last few pages, I refilled the cup at the bathroom tap.

He was holding a miniature in each hand when I stepped back into the room, looking from one to the other with confusion. "Tell me again why you have these?"

I reminded him of Sunshine's attempted Halloween heist. "Fee thought I should keep them out of the way."

He shook his head. "Are they valuable?"

"That's what I was wondering." How would it help to describe them as magical objects, to a man who would regard this idea as a dangerous delusion? For now, the only goal was to help Rose.

Silvio, caught in the tangle of his own guilt and fear, wasn't even looking at me. "Did you find out? Whether they're worth a lot of money?"

"No, I put them away and forgot them until this morning."

He sat on the bed. I moved a chair closer. The sun was strong, picking out dirt on the window glass, snout-shaped prints from Pluto. It was somewhere around noon, on the day winter and spring hung in balance.

Silvio rubbed his face. "Her—superstition. Clearly it's wrapped up with sexual feelings. But do you know what she means about the path, or the paintings changing?"

I explained how Alisa found one painting behind another, stumbling when I remembered she had told me the story *in a dream*. I moved to sit beside Silvio and felt relief at the warmth of his body, the breadth of his shoulder. Bodies, at least, were honest. I showed him what Rose had shown me, how one path led to the other.

"The first couple of times I saw the paintings I didn't even notice the paths. The light wasn't so good, I guess." Okay, here goes. "One unsettling thing," I said, pointing at the downs, "is I could swear this circle wasn't here, last time I looked." My finger traced a line of pale white dots in the grass, a fairy ring.

Then I took the more disturbing watercolor from Silvio and pointed at the flower stalks growing next to the weeping stump. "And I am positive these buds were closed. I remember admiring the brushwork."

Instead of pale green leaves closing on a promise, the stalks now bloomed in unearthly colors. In the bracken behind the stump, a single wild rose gleamed.

Silvio pulled back slightly to examine my face, then gestured at the craft bin open on the floor. Yes, there would be old watercolor paints, a childish set. "I didn't know she had the skill," he said, "but either you're mistaken, or she altered the image."

I gazed back him. I didn't believe Rose had retouched the painting but didn't want to admit it. Silvio sensed my skepticism but didn't want a scary argument. Our shoulders dropped at the same moment, and we embraced. Silvio wiped his eyes.

"What now?"

"Something to eat," he said. "I could use a cup of coffee. Then we pick her up from school."

"But what will we say? We can't tell the front desk we have a family emergency but leave Teddy there."

He handed the second painting to me and put the pills and journal in Rose's bag. His voice was grim. "Doctor's appointment. We really do have a meeting scheduled at two with a therapist. I made calls from the car."

Twenty-Four

Silvio, Rose, and I had teary conversations in the car and with the therapist. Silvio and I said over and over that we loved Rose and were proud of her. Whomever she loved, whatever she wanted, it was fine with us. Then she stayed to talk to the counselor alone. Silvio remained in the waiting room while I returned home to meet Teddy.

I did not explain Rose's crush on Lucie to her twin—that was her secret. I did tell him about the stolen prescriptions and her feeling out-of-place. His face hollowed out as he listened.

Rose had shot me an incredulous glance when, in the therapist's office, we began to discuss the watercolors. Silvio asked if she had painted in the flowers. No, she said, no, she wouldn't do that, even if she could have.

I tried to be true to the strangeness but not embellish or explain it. Yes, I also thought the paintings looked different. Yes, I agreed this defied logic.

The woman running the session, whose gray hair brushed the shoulders of a vivid dress, asked Rose how she thought flowers in a painting could have blossomed.

Rose answered that flowers blooming and toadstools growing in a watercolor didn't make sense, but few things did, not really. Everything changes, sometimes in ways you couldn't anticipate.

Puberty, for instance, she said. Breasts and hair and blood. How weird is that?

After the session, Silvio treated Rose to ice cream in the next town over, where Camille had been harassed by police. Its residents smiled at my blond husband and daughter, whose strangeness was not visible.

Our dinners were late and mismatched. Rose and I shared leftover meatballs over spaghetti squash. I grilled a cheese sandwich for Teddy, the way he liked it, and opened a box of tomato soup. Silvio ate soup, a ham sandwich, and the remainder of a hummus tub with tortilla chips, then tore into a box of cookies.

At some point he asked if I thought Alisa would mind our removing the paintings from the frames. Tingling all over, I said no. We pried them apart with a flathead screwdriver. With the mattes removed, the watercolors seemed tiny, edges frayed. No markings appeared on the back of either, but when we turned them over and compared them side by side, we realized that the glade had been painted on different paper—more textured, yellower, fractionally larger. Handling it triggered my vertigo.

Teddy said, "Maybe the hills were painted after the woods, even in response to the older painting. Maybe that's why the paths seem to match."

As Teddy flipped them again and brought them into alignment, I reached out to grab Rose's hand, and she squeezed back. But the paths touched, chalk and grass, sunlit and shaded, and nothing happened. No one was sucked through a portal; existence did not shimmer and change channels. We sighed.

I moved the watercolors back to my bedroom. When I woke after three hours of sleep, Silvio was snoring. He had canceled his Tuesday obligations. The therapist recommended a consultation with a psychiatrist about medication, and since Silvio knew the local specialists, he would take Rose while I met my class.

I turned the pages of the past few months in my mind, examining the plot twists. Becoming agitated, I tiptoed downstairs and stroked a blacker patch of darkness rumbling at my calf. I whispered to Pluto, "What kind of story am I in?"

The darkness did not answer. I fished my cellphone out of my purse. I had forgotten to check it all evening, and the charge was low. 3:27 a.m. I scrolled through contacts and called Fee.

She answered after three rings and sounded throatier than usual. "Cynthia?"

"I need to talk. It's urgent."

She did not ask why. I arranged to visit her house around eight, on my way to work.

Everything ached, my head, my hips, but I did not take pills. Tucking myself in beside Silvio, I descended back into sleep.

Fee was dressed in a skirt and heels when I arrived, books and purse stacked on a chair by Alisa's front door, sipping from a china mug. I placed the unframed watercolors on Alisa's kitchen table, refused her offer of tea, and fetched myself a glass of water straight from the tap.

"You wanted Alisa back, so I gave you a door." Fee said. "There's always a price for opening it."

"Not Rose! I would never pay the price of Rose!"

Perfect Fee sat there, poised as always. Mona fucking Lisa.

"*Alisa* would never pay the price of Rose. She may really, really want to come home, and we weren't the perfectly devoted friends I imagined us to be, but she's not a monster. The price of the ticket could never be the sacrifice of an innocent human being."

The luminous smile lost wattage. "Then she is a better person than I." She took another sip, set the cup down, and gestured at the paintings. "Shall we burn them?"

I was startled. "Does that destroy the path?"

"This path. There are many entry points, but most people find them hard to see."

"Then yes. There has to be another way to bring Alisa home, beyond a one-to-one trade. And if there isn't, so be it."

Fee disappeared to the living room. When I followed her, watercolors in hand, she was extracting a tall match from a paisley box on the mantel. I offered her the painting of the uncanny glen.

"No, first the South Downs," she said, and, crouching down to the fireplace, lit the paper's edge. It burned quickly; she didn't drop it onto the empty grate until the flames were almost touching her fingers. It crisped there, an effigy of itself resting on iron bars.

"Now," Fee said, still balancing improbably and holding out one slender arm in its pale blue knit. I handed her the painting that had obsessed Rose.

The second watercolor wouldn't light until Fee struck a third match against the sandpapery bottom of the box and ran it back and forth along the top edge of the paper, heating the fibers persuasively. It burned in colors with a hot sizzle, dropping through the grate to the hearth bricks as fire devoured each painted petal. The smoky scent made me long for something I couldn't name. Fee brushed the ashes into a pan she had ready. I shadowed her as she turned toward the back door.

We stepped outside and walked over the soft ground to a sunny back bed, neatly mulched, where narcissi bloomed. Elegant tulips stood in bud. Fee dug a hole with the brass fire iron and tipped the ashes into the soil. Then she buried them and smoothed the mulch over.

When she stood again, one heel sank into the ground. Her hair looked ever so slightly disheveled.

"Is Rose safe?"

Her slender shoulders shrugged. "No one is safe. But one door is closed."

My class had read some of Whitman's *Calamus* poems as they had been arranged in the 1860 edition of *Leaves of Grass,* and today's assignment was "Live Oak, with Moss," twelve lyrics not published in their original design until long after the poet's death. In sequence, they framed a much franker tale of Whitman's love for "an athlete" than any single poem suggested. *But toward him there is something fierce and terrible in me, / I dare not tell it in words—not even in these songs.*

Royall recited a few lines, then a theater student with a beautiful baritone and black eye-liner took a turn. It was good to hear the verse in living voices. While the students discussed the poem, I reserved a corner of my brain for Whitman's *dream of a city,* a place where he could love openly. *Is there even one other like me—distracted—his friend, lover, lost to him?*

When class dispersed, Camille popped out of her office. "It was 'manly love' day in Professor Rennard's class."

I smiled back. "How are you?"

"Jealous of your *eleves*. One student talking over another, all excited."

"Well, millennials just can't get enough nineteenth-century poetry. How are you doing?"

"Oh, you know. Enraged." We cackled.

I didn't stay in the building long after my class ended. Phoning Silvio, I learned the day had gone well. None of the clinicians found Rose suicidal—the idea seemed to incense her. The psychiatrist prescribed an antidepressant and continued counseling. Rose wanted to go back to school the next day. I packed work to keep me on track at home, just in case.

On the way to the parking garage, I stopped under a tree. Not a live oak—they don't grow this far north—and taller trees were just beginning to bud. From whatever precocious specimen this was, *I plucked a twig with a certain number of leaves upon it, and twined around it a little moss, and brought it away.* I would place this in Rose's room, as Whitman had arranged the token in his own space. Or maybe that was a poetic gesture, a pretend emblem for real feeling. The boundaries blurred.

Silvio and Teddy were working at the dining room table, munching chips. Both of them kept glancing at the patio doors. Rose loitered out back in a thin jacket, but Pluto, standing guard, seemed calm. This reassured me to an inappropriate degree.

I stepped out and walked downhill toward her post at the edge of the creek.

Rose glanced over her shoulder at me, cheeks pink in the chilly air, hair wild and growing in dark at the roots. "They're gone."

How did she know? But no more evading my daughter, who understood everything I didn't intend to tell her. "Fee and I burned them this morning." I stood next to her, hands in pockets, studying how the water braided and unbraided itself, always on the move although it appeared to be the same water. Today you could see right through lucent glass to rocks and leaf-litter on the creek bed.

"I felt that. I swear I felt them go." I turned toward her closed face as she said, "Why didn't you tell Dad what the paintings could do?"

Kicking at clay, I said, "I never lied."

Rose huffed.

"Look, I don't know what's real, and neither do you. Except, like you said, everything changes."

Now she stared back at me. "It's real. You've been there. You know this is a terrible world, and there's a worse one just underneath it."

"Yes, it's terrible." A chill, dry breeze lifted and plucked at me, teasing Rose's loose hair into denser tangles. *Without any companion it grew there, glistening out joyous leaves of dark green.* "But there's love, too. I'm not good at happiness. I'm always dreading and regretting instead of being present. But there is love, Rose, and people can work to make the world better."

"I know you and Dad and Teddy love me. It's just hard to believe anyone else ever will."

"People will love you! High school is a bad place, but the world is big. One reason I made my life at a university is that great people cluster there, artists and intellectuals who care about the same things I do. Young people who haven't made up their minds yet. You will go to college, and you will feel less strange there."

Rose emitted the loudest, most exasperated sigh ever, stomped her feet, and socked me in the shoulder, hard. I yelped, fending her off, then grabbed her in a hug. She relaxed into the embrace.

"It felt good when they burned," her muffled voice said into the seams of my coat. "I felt a little bit more free."

Twenty-Five

Part of me wanted to bury the ashes of this awful year and keep trudging through the hours, focusing on Rose and all the other real and present people to whom I had responsibilities. Yes, Alisa was an old friend, but wasn't I finally liberated from obedience to her instructions? Magic could stay off to one side, glittering, untouched. Yet I never ceased being conscious of it, even as Silvio called Ross and received a week's extension on the offer; as we talked about the hateful bathroom bill just passed by the North Carolina legislature; as I applied for the August pedagogy workshop the funny little man had recommended to me; and as Rose returned to school. I desired certain outcomes, but wanted to be sure my wishes were wise before I exerted any power that might or might not be available.

I abridged my work hours but agreed to a lunch date the following week with Camille and Sandra. By some alchemy, they were friends now.

On the way home, I shopped for chocolate bunnies, marshmallow chicks, and paper grass for Easter baskets. We had talked Rose into one more backyard egg hunt. Seasonal time, all cycles and repetitions, worked a counter-magic to the ruthless progress of my children's growing up and my body's dissolution.

What a pleasure, to stay up late stuffing coins and dollar-store prizes into multicolored plastic eggs, cheap ones we had bought a dozen years ago. My fingers stung with energy. We rose early Sunday to hide them in dewy grass while an indignant cat mewed at the window. Only after breakfast, when the kids were slipping into sneakers and jackets to begin the search, did I remember that, yet again, I had forgotten to count the plastic eggs before we concealed them.

"Commuter relationships are so hard," Camille commiserated, layering a slice of pickled ginger onto a spiral of sushi. She had sustained a graduate school romance for a full year after moving here.

"But the sex is good," Sandra said, and Camille choked on her California roll. The piece of tuna I had just secured with chopsticks splashed into wasabi-laced soy sauce. "Absence makes the loins grow fonder."

"This is true," I admitted, and Camille laughed harder. "I'd forgotten, you dated Nina long-distance for, well, it must have been years. Where was she, Rutgers?"

Listening to Sandra describe the affair, I heard those open Massachusetts r's I rarely registered in her speech anymore—she once told me she could trace some ancestors right back to the Mayflower. "Immigrants, old-style," she had said. I also remembered how Sandra's relationship with Nina had petered out around the time we'd hired Camille. "Then she was diagnosed with Alzheimer's," Sandra finished.

Having never known this, or forgotten it, I uttered a noise of surprise.

"Nina's in a nursing home," Sandra said as she poured more jasmine tea, its pale stream catching the light. "Assisted living, I'm told I should say. I visited and phoned for a while then left Nina to her children's care. She was such a big personality, it was like watching the moon wane. With each visit there was a little less of her, until finally only a sliver remained."

After lunch, Camille and I parted ways with Sandra and strolled back to campus together. Business owners had adorned the sidewalk with pots of flowers. The petals were shivering.

"That's kind of heartbreaking," Camille said, wrapping the soft greens and oranges of her scarf more closely around her neck. "To be with someone, even long distance, for ten years, and then just wash your hands of the person. I'm not sure I hold with that. We owe things to each other."

To our children most of all, I thought, but to ourselves, too. "That's another difficult thing about living in a small town for decades, how you get to know everybody's business, the feuds and affairs. People take sides." I adjusted my purse, which dragged on my shoulder. "I just tell myself that no outsider knows what really goes on in a marriage. It may look like one person has all the power and is abandoning the other, but it's usually more complicated."

Camille made a skeptical sound.

I said as we crossed an intersection, "Maybe Nina and Sandra had a deal: good times only. Or maybe Nina did something to break Sandra's goodwill before she got sick, but then the diagnosis actually made Sandra hang in there longer."

Camille stepped onto the curb a beat ahead of me. "And of course, it couldn't be marriage, not back then, which puts another kind of strain on people."

I blushed and loosened the jacket I had buttoned five minutes before. "Right."

We walked in silence for a moment. Then Camille touched my arm. "I'm so sorry to hear about Rose's troubles, but I'm glad you told us. And I can't believe Silvio will have a tenure-track job in another state! What a year."

"Worlds clashing, and no manual about how to live in them."

Camille gave me a funny look. I realized that speaking my thoughts more often had tipped me from oblivious professor to something weirder. Oh, well. Some people would like what I was becoming, and some wouldn't—I couldn't control that.

We reached the edge of campus, crossing onto pretty paths maintained by the university.

"Worlds blowing to smithereens, maybe," Camille said. "But coming together, too." She was wearing a new ring on her left hand. "I hope Alisa gets back in time for all the parties."

In my office, I closed my eyes and visualized the glade, a prison of unchanging summer. I couldn't see Alisa but felt the former boss of my life around, somehow. She hadn't actually wanted to be my mother-two-point-oh. I asked: *Do you want to get back in time for all the parties?*

A staticky fizz told me we were connected. *I want to get back,* she answered. *But I could give a damn about the parties.*

I guess I knew that. *So for real, why do you want to return?*

Because this is a terrible place. Because I have work to do. I always wanted to be someone, the conference keynote speaker, the guest editor, the dissertation adviser everyone maneuvers to work with. Instead I played house with Sunshine for all those years. I'm so mad at myself. Cyn, I really need you to focus.

Nostalgia for life here—not to mention friendship—were conspicuously absent from that list. Okay. I would help her, but I wouldn't put everything else aside immediately. Other people deserved my attention, too.

The new family schedule meant picking up the kids from school on Thursdays and delivering Rose to a 3:30 appointment with the therapist. This was just outside of town, but in the opposite direction from our house, so Teddy and I elected to wait out the appointment at a nearby diner. The diner's coffee was burnt, but Teddy liked the blueberry pie. We got out our homework and set up shop. "I like your ribbon," I said, nodding at the rainbow flag pinned to his backpack.

"Finally joined the sexuality awareness group that's not allowed to put up posters in the high school or announce its meetings over the loudspeaker." Then, through a purple-black mouthful, he said, "Past time, too. Rose joined right off in September, and I should have done it then."

I twisted my pen cap. "Did you know?"

"At some level, maybe. I was fixated on my own drama and didn't want to deal. Which makes me an asshole."

I shook my head. "I'm the asshole. You were just being fourteen."

He regarded me with his deep-water gaze and shrugged. "Anyway, she and I are talking about it. Also, I hereby proclaim I broke up with Lucie for good. She guessed about Rose and had a bad attitude." He inserted a large chunk of crust into his mouth.

I leaned back against the vinyl-covered booth. "Does that mean everybody knows?"

He held up a finger for a few seconds while he chewed then answered, his voice made gruff by pie. "Prob'ly. And there are some dickish kids for sure, and teachers. I told you about that guy with the tee-shirt in October, right? 'It's Adam and Eve, not Adam and Steve.' Talk about douchebags."

"Seriously, Teddy. If it's getting bad, tell me."

"Don't worry, Mom, I have the situation under vigilant surveillance so you don't have to," he said, unaware he had wiped a long streak of blueberry across his cheek.

I worked on clarifying my intentions. When in company with others, I tried to stay focused. I failed, but I kept trying. If I had two hours to prepare my class, or twenty minutes to spend in conference with a struggling student, what was the best possible use of the time? What did my sad colleague Robin, perched speechlessly in my side chair and playing with my stapler, really want me to say, or ask? If I felt frayed and balky, what could I do to restore my sense of direction?

I was not good at living in the moment, as Pluto kept reminding me. He threw himself down at my feet for a good scratch when I was rushing to get dressed, make dinner, or grab the phone. When I wouldn't make time to worship him, he administered a nip to the ankle. Even when I did pet him, he sometimes bit me anyway.

Summoning Alisa home occupied part of each day. I sat somewhere quiet and visualized her dialing an office landline, making a long chatty call to her sister, describing her plans to return. It didn't seem real. The next day, assuming corpse pose but unable to imagine myself as a deep mountain lake, I conjured Alisa at a decrepit internet café, setting the return date on her open plane ticket, sending me flight information. A little flare lit in my belly then sputtered out. I sensed connections clicking while showering on April Fool's day, so I put Alisa in her cottage, extracting a suitcase from under a lumpy old bed and rolling up winter sweaters to stash them in readiness. The threads of her adventure were beginning to pull tight.

Often I felt foolish. Alisa was trapped in a world below the world. I would need a more powerful trick to free her.

Silvio organized homemade pizzas—laying out grated cheeses, chopped artichokes and olives, tomato sauce and pesto, plus pepperoni slices for a certain carnivore. He and I were avoiding all kinds of conversations, but concern for our daughter made that easier. On that subject, our views were married.

On gluten-free flatbread, I laid out thin slices of roasted red pepper like spokes, dividing the circle into four quarters.

Herbs for spring, tomato for summer, olives for fall, pepperoni for winter.

"You okay there, Ma?" asked Teddy the vigilant, whose less aesthetically pleasing pizza shared my cookie sheet.

"Just having fun." I set the tray in the oven then mixed a vinaigrette.

Silvio assembled a green salad in a wooden bowl, pausing occasionally to talk with his hands. He described Ross's research into attention, particularly literary transportation, meaning the trance state some people enter when they read. They were designing a study together, to occur this summer, involving adolescents, technology, and attention. Silvio trailed off at this point. Before the crisis, we had decided he would keep the North Carolina apartment through the summer, a home base for collaboration. Now Silvio, not falling for Rose's calm-down-I'm-fine act, wanted to work from Virginia.

"Actually," Rose told us, "I did something today."

We looked at our wild-haired girl in leggings and oversized flannel shirt.

"Yesterday my therapist asked what made me feel strong and confident, and I told her. Math."

Teddy, perched on the counter, shook his head.

"She said I should find more ways to spend time in that mental place, so I thought of Ms. Wolff and this summer program she recommended."

Your geometry teacher? Silvio asked, and Rose nodded. It was, she explained, an engineering camp for high school kids in coastal Virginia.

"Anyway, I went to Ms. Wolff's classroom first thing this morning and asked her about it, and I'm applying. I have a few forms for you guys to help me with this weekend." She turned her feet sideways, balancing on their outer edges as she twisted her face nervously. "It would be in June, for three weeks."

Panic rose in my throat at the idea of sending my girl off for that long. Also, filmy dollar signs danced in the air. I brushed these ghosts away and tried to beam out good energy. "Good for you, Rose."

"That sounds great," Silvio echoed. He hid his chagrin by opening the oven to rescue our pizzas before they burned. For one reason or another, the family would spend the summer flying off in different directions. Our divergent trajectories were increasing in velocity.

Twenty-Six

One lilac-scented Saturday, I unloaded the bags I'd filled at the farmer's market. I was glad for the sunshine on my skin and dirty new potatoes in my hands. Rose and Teddy, still wearing the clothes they had slept in, set up their chessboard on the dining room table, next to the book on fairy chess I had given them for Christmas.

"How does it work?" I asked, finding refrigerator space for fresh eggs and dropping a roll of local goat cheese into the bottom drawer.

"Apparently," said Teddy, "if you alter one rule of the standard game, it's fairy chess. Like if you change how a particular piece is allowed to move. Or if we say," he continued, blocking part of the board with his left arm, "the whole A row just disappears. *Should* we eliminate a row?"

Rose, kneeling on the opposing chair, rose up on her shins. "No, I want to go bigger. Imagine the board extends a row to the left and right." She moved a white rook out past the board's edge. Teddy mirrored her in the other direction.

I sat down to watch. Even though I taught them the game's basics when they were little, having learned them from my own father, it had been years since I could hold my own playing them. I could sometimes spot a problem or opportunity. I felt pleased when Rose or Teddy moved a piece as if in response to my thought. Often, however, they put each other in and out of check so fast I could barely follow the threats and evasions. Once Teddy scooped up a sacrificed pawn and set it on an empty square. I was confused until I remembered they had mislaid a black pawn from the old set a while ago and simply played without it, mentally holding what should have been its place on the board until someone's bad move allowed them to swap in another.

"This changes the whole game," Rose said, chewing her lip, then she clicked a piece into a new position and Teddy said, "Oh." A flurry of moves ensued and Rose took his outlying rook, placing him into check.

"I forgot the extra rows were even there."

"You haven't lost. There's still something you could do."

"Yeah," he said, sliding a bishop across several squares. "Let's play through."

I had an idea, from which I was temporarily distracted by a thump of carrots onto the floor. I had left a bunch on the kitchen island, forgetting how much Pluto loved dangling leaves.

I rummaged through attic boxes for art supplies. I had never been good at watercolors, learning to paint with acrylics instead and eventually moving to oils. I wasn't a terrible painter, although after girlhood, I'd never put in serious hours. I found the watercolor pencils, never used, that I was looking for and a pad of good paper, empty except for a few sweet sketches of the children. I also took some charcoal pencils, which I sharpened, and a big eraser.

I carried my art supplies, kitchen scissors, and a ruler out to the back deck, then looked at the yard from various angles. After moving the hibachi under the apple tree, I sat down, measured a rectangle about the size of the miniatures, and started working.

It was easier to clear my head and fall into a groove while drawing than it had ever been during yoga. Drawing wove a kind of spell, in which vitality poured through me, finally, along clear channels. Working small was difficult, however. Apple branches could curve a little differently in my drawing than in actual life, but my sketched hibachi looked implausible, so I flipped the page and started again. I lost myself for a while, not feeling the breeze pick up, hardly noticing dark clouds blow in.

When shapes were in place, the patio doors opened and Silvio called, "What are you doing?"

"Meditating," I answered, hoping to discourage further conversation.

Silvio yelped. Pluto had slid around his leg and leapfrogged across the back yard, making one jump across the deck and two jumps to the left, toward the shed.

Silvio zigged after him and I zagged. We triangulated, but Pluto stopped near the shed door, shot a paw out, and rolled a green plastic Easter egg from a tuft of grass. He pushed it a few steps across the backyard then stopped, sat on his haunches, and looked expectant.

"Crazy cat," said Silvio, picking up my familiar and scratching him under the chin. "We haven't played this game all winter, and now he escapes again. Must be spring fever."

I picked up the egg and cracked it, knowing what I would find. From its hollow, I extracted a party favor, a cheap metal key chain attached to a plastic rose. It delivered a tiny electric shock. Shoving it in my sweater pocket, registering the threat of rain, I picked up my materials and followed Silvio inside.

I ate alone at the dining room table, watching branches blow, feeling expectant. My heart palpitated. The rain spattered down in sudden gusts, as if someone were throwing marbles at the patio glass.

Something was coming. Halfway through my rice and beans, I reached for my phone, checked the weather, put it down, and swallowed a couple more forkfuls. Then I picked up the phone again and thumbed through to email.

There it was: a message from Alisa with the title *our place in the causal matrix of space and time.*

The content was just a link, so I followed it to an article about skillful and unskillful desires in Buddhism. I read patiently, absorbing the piece on its own terms, not skimming for coded messages or ritual recipes. Unskillful desires, I learned, lead to harm or suffering, or simply to transitory pleasures not worth the effort of striving.

I pushed the bowl aside, pulled my pad over, and looked at the most successful drawings. They weren't skillful in the artistic sense, but they were recognizable. I pulled out the watercolor pencils, and added winter tones, smearing them with drops of water. Shades of green for grass and the straggly laurels; pinkish gray for tree-bark. Bits of the creek flashed brown. It was a path.

The path in my drawing, when I examined it on Sunday, could have led to the unearthly glade, as I remembered it. I had an idea that even though the original paintings or portals or whatever they were had burned, I could still create a way out of UnWales for Alisa if I pictured the route powerfully enough. Intuition suggested that a second—or fourth—piece of art, mapping a path away from the glade into Spring, would complete the circuit. Besides intuition, what did I have to go on? I was basically inventing my own religion.

Spring was difficult to visualize, because here in the real world, rain still fell in sheets. Monday morning afforded another hour for sketching, but construction noises from across the street grated against my concentration. Men were unloading a port-a-john from a truck into the neighbor's yard, next to the dumpster; apparently the builders would still be at it for a while.

I packed pad and pencils into my satchel, in case of inspiration, though the day ahead, beginning of our last week of classes, looked busy. Harriet, right now, would be selecting refreshments for the honors thesis presentations.

I slipped into the presentation room a few minutes before four-thirty. Royall was fiddling with the projector, looking spiffy in a striped tie and navy blazer. He seemed calm and ready, so I helped myself to some berries and said hello to his divorced parents on my way to the front of the room. His exquisitely turned-out mother stood at one end of a row of chairs, chatting with Fee, his father at the other end. Barbara, fingering her statement necklace, was chatting with him, her knees angled flirtatiously close to his.

The room was filling up nicely. My job was to welcome everyone, introduce presenters, and vamp as students transitioned from one slideshow to another. Royall's parents beamed at him proudly as he stepped next to the projector cart.

Royall had always been a good public speaker, so his charm didn't surprise me. His thesis focused on Yeats in relation to Irish folklore. He hadn't made any astonishing discoveries or ingenious arguments, but his work under Fee's tutelage was decent. He parsed difficult old verses astutely. He leavened his presentation with photographs of Yeats' tower, Coole Park, and various gorgeous landscape shots that he had taken on a father-son jaunt to the west of Ireland, of *woods and waters wild.*

I watched Fee clap for Royall, and Dan lean forward from the seat behind to whisper in her ear. She remained too perfect, her black hair swept up with old-fashioned combs above her pale neck. Draped over her shoulders was a loosely woven apple-green sweater, plain but, in the elegant way it hung, suggesting expense. I didn't entirely like her, but Fee was no longer an alien exotic. She had made the town and college stretch to receive her, and now she fit the ecosystem. We were, in fact, better for having welcomed her.

My end-of-year optimism crashed when Barbara called. A member of the Board of Trustees—which would convene for its final meeting of the academic year shortly—had telephoned our jocund, glad-handing, not-very-bright president to express "concerns" about Camille's candidacy. The agitated party was the same fisher for conflict who had lately been raising questions about the college's high tenure rate. These CEO trustees were all about downsizing and thought we should be firing more people in sacrifice to their capitalist gods.

The non-unanimity of votes on Camille's case had raised flags where this board member was concerned. Further, he had wound up two other men, also trustees, who had followed the social media controversies after Camille's detainment by the police, and who were disturbed by her less-than-wholly celebratory comments about the college. Prejudice? What, here?

The situation was not good. Barbara, Camille, and I needed to meet with the president, and not just to help him devise a game plan. The College president, Barbara informed me, would himself need persuasion. She may not have been Camille's biggest fan, but she was clearly pissed-off by this attempt to short-circuit her power.

"The president thought Camille's response to the police interrogation was, well—"

"Spit it out, Barbara. What exactly did he say?"

Her laugh was also a growl. "He called her behavior 'unbecoming.'"

My specialty.

Twenty-Seven

Our conversation with the president was scheduled for eight-thirty the following morning. At seven-forty a.m., the twins rushed out, barely in time to catch the bus. At seven-fifty, I realized my car keys were missing from their hook. I checked my purse, backpack, and the pockets of various jackets. No dice. I searched around the car, eyes peeled for a glint on the driveway or along the front path.

By eight, I was frantic. The second pair of keys to my car was on Silvio's fob in North Carolina. I had stayed up late studying the faculty handbook, conferring by text with Camille, Sandra, Dan, Silvio, and even a couple of friends at other universities, readying spells. I was exhausted.

Breathe, Cyn. When had I held the keys last? Could I visualize them?

They should be in the right-hand pocket of my new red raincoat. Again I patted it down, turned the pockets inside out, and scanned the closet floor, which held only a pipe cleaner. I swore.

I recalled having had a third key cut, once upon a time. Where had I stashed it? It wasn't among the rest of the spares, dangling by the door. A visual memory rose up of strays gleaming at the back of what we called "the sharp drawer." I picked through the serrated grapefruit spoons, kebab skewers, corkscrews, and paring knives, and found it at the back with several other keys. I hurried out to the car in triumph.

The red-nosed university lawyer sat at the president's right hand, and the young Title IX coordinator sat to his left. She was almost completely powerless, but it was good news that across some administrator's brain had floated the word "discrimination." The president himself, despite his freshly pressed shirtsleeves, looked uncomfortable.

Across the table, Barbara sat next to Camille, who looked sleek in an indigo blouse and charcoal pantsuit; they were movie-star versions of themselves, straight from central casting. I sat on Camille's other side, thinking I looked marginally professional, though only if I kept my blazer on to conceal unattractive pit stains.

Given the floor, I reminded everyone of Camille's stellar accomplishments as a teacher and scholar, the extra, unheralded service she performed as a mentor, and the unusual circumstances behind Beth-Ann's abstention. The president just yessed me to silence.

I considered testifying to the hostilities Camille navigated in our community and on campus, but decided another approach held more promise. My skin prickled as I spoke. "Of course, even raising the social media issue, as I understand certain trustees have done, is a violation of the faculty handbook."

The president looked startled, and the lawyer lifted his veiny head. I feigned calmness. "See page thirty-seven. Information not in the final tenure file is not permitted to influence deliberations." The lawyer pulled his laptop closer and began paging through a document.

"Yet," I continued, "an influential member of the tenure committee issued derogatory remarks about Camille's police troubles publicly, in a meeting of department heads, shortly before the committee vote. That person was prejudiced against her because of information extraneous to the file. Here are copies of the notes I recorded immediately after that meeting," I added, extracting a manila folder from my bag and placing it on the table. Camille's eyes sparked.

"Cynthia is correct about those derogatory public statements," Barbara said. "They troubled others, as well, as documented in emails sent to me shortly afterward." Barbara's binder, prettier than mine, was already laid out in front of her like a grimoire. "I cannot, of course, reveal what various members of the tenure and promotion committee said behind closed doors, nor how they voted, but a clear record exists of procedural irregularities."

Perspiration beaded the lawyer's lip, and the president slumped in his chair.

Camille and I left the presidential suite together. We didn't speak until clear of the building and out on the lawn, where a pearly fog was burning off.

"You've been keeping secrets," she said.

"A chronic problem. I'm working on it."

Camille's brow creased despite the hope in her next words. "If anything can force the trustees to back off, it's the specter of a lawsuit."

That was, of course, the assumption underlying my tactic. "And the president will always take whatever position results in the least conflict with the board. I don't want to jinx this, though."

"Well, the worst that can happen is I don't get tenure. Maybe that would be a blessing in disguise."

"Don't even say that!" I yelled. "And transcribe your notes right after class and send them to me so we have a timestamp. I'll do it, too."

"Yeah, yeah." Camille smiled.

On the phone that night, I told Silvio how the meeting had gone. "The Board has already received summaries of the cases up for promotion, and they vote on Saturday to affirm or deny."

"I know you're petrified, but there's absolutely no way they'll overturn the faculty ruling. I mean, has that ever even happened at the College?"

I was pacing in the twilit yard, inhaling its fragrance, regretting that the lilac's bloom was already passing. "Once in recent memory, according to Sandra. Nineteen-nineties, just before I was hired. A woman got approved by the tenure and promotions committee then fired by the Trustees. She was fighting to start the Women's Studies Program, and it all seemed totally political." Appreciating the intensity of Silvio's silence, I added, "I don't like the precedent."

"But that was twenty years ago. And Camille has a book and articles and a fantastic teaching record and all this service on searches and task forces. The community held a frigging *rally* to show solidarity with her."

I stopped, as I often did, at the edge of the creek, peering down. "You don't have to tell me. But I'm learning I've never lived in the same world as anybody else. Best you can hope for is a little friendly overlap."

Rose was lying on the sofa reading manga when I went back into the house. I grabbed her big toe, but she ignored me.

Unable to sit still, I returned to the sharp drawer and sifted out the rest of the mysterious keys. My own ring—containing two sets of car keys, as well as keys to the house and my office—was still unaccounted for, even after Teddy and Rose ransacked their bags and pockets. The spare I had located this morning was now hanging at the door by a twist tie, so what were these?

A big silver thing marked *Toyota* should, I realized, have departed with the minivan trade-in. I chucked it. Two smaller keys looked as if they might fit our house doors. I tried them, and they did, so I marked them as more spares.

What about the small silver key, though, at the back of the drawer? It wasn't sturdy enough for a serious lock. I pulled the novelty key chain out of my sweater pocket, the one with the plastic rose retrieved from the Easter egg, and it sparked with static at my touch again. Loosening the metal ring with a thumbnail, I slid the small key onto it and dropped it on the counter.

Just then I heard a jingle and scrape from the hall. Pluto was batting my missing keychain at speed across hardwood. I hollered, and he fled, but not before one last swipe sent it under the upright piano. To retrieve it, I had to lie on the dusty floor, sweeping a yardstick under the piano cabinet, while Teddy watched and laughed.

If further discussion occurred among board members concerning the threat Camille posed to the genteel traditions of our oh-so-ivory tower and Western Civilization in general, we never heard about it. The case was good. Concentrating on that with all my puny force of will could do no harm, although magic was surely beside the point.

Barbara called Camille on Saturday with good news, and Camille called the rest of us. The party was on.

Ralph and Helen hosted cocktails at their large brick Federal-style house in town. Silvio said he'd stop by if the chess tournament ended early enough—he was chaperoning both twins—but I went on my own for one strong gin and tonic authored by Ralph, followed by a sobering-up period downing three glasses of sparkling water and a large quantity of peanuts and potato chips.

Robin arrived not long after I did, with warm congratulations for Camille and her fiancé. "The first Robin of spring," Ralph whispered to me, and it was true I had hardly seen our surviving compositionist, aside from one anguished conversation about his plans for the following year. Robin sought me out during my first recuperative glass of Perrier, raising a light beer in my direction.

"I'm glad this year is finally ending, and on a high note," he said.

"How are you, Robin?"

"Better." He met my eyes for once. "I'm going to spend the summer near DC with my wife and kids. She's willing to give me another shot."

I wished him luck and happiness with perfect authenticity, and I wondered if he would become yet another commuting spouse as of September. Fee would live with Dan right in town, but Camille and her fiancé planned to move north, and Robin's wife's DC suburb stood at an even further distance. Commuting was possible, I supposed, but traffic would be miserable.

Robin's outlook was better than Beth-Ann's. Her soon-to-be-ex, the IT guy, remained firm about keeping his job at the college, as well as the house and custody of the kids. Beth-Ann was leaving the state solo. I fidgeted whenever I remembered my ardent wish to halt Beth-Ann's curricular carnage. Skillful desires do no harm.

During my second glass of water, I talked to Harriet, who stopped by to hug Camille and sip sweet tea. "What a different department we are than this time last year," she marveled.

"I feel like a different person," I said.

She placed a hand on my arm. "Well, you are crossing the bar now."

"What?" I must still be tipsy.

But Harriet's voice was low and thrilling. "The *change*," she said, as if I must understand her. "You are almost one of us." Then, calling thanks to Ralph and Helen, Harriet rustled out.

To drink my third and clearly necessary non-alcoholic beverage, I thumped down onto a chair between Sandra's roost on an ottoman and the sofa where Camille nestled against her lawyer.

Sandra was saying, "I was demented on your behalf, Camille. That's why you were calm. I siphoned off all the psychic poison and drank it myself."

"I helped, too," I said. "I focused all the mystic energies of central Virginia into a force field that held the Board in stasis until they tenured you."

"Mystic energies, huh?" Camille raised her eyebrows.

"Why not call it praying?" her fiancé asked, and Camille laughed.

"That sounds suspiciously like the power of positive thinking," Helen warned from behind Camille, her fingers balanced lightly on the sofa. "You'd better watch out. I asked Silvio about positive psychology some years back and received quite a lecture."

I wrinkled my nose. "No, he's not fond of advice to 'visualize the ring on your own hand.'" Positive psychology had moved on since then, as had Silvio's peeves. Yet I kept recalling those tirades. They helped me practice discretion.

I drew another miniature, quickly this time. I had observed how blossoming dogwoods, from a distance and without my glasses, seemed composed of horizontal streaks. Slender branches reached skyward, but the flowers lay flat, like empty platters.

I sketched three pink dogwoods along the verge of our road, with blue pavement stretching past and vanishing around a bend. I didn't pencil in a frame first this time, but the finished scene was about the right size. I put it aside.

Later, when I entered the English building in a red blouse, the classrooms were full of hushed students writing examinations. Cheerful professors tried to keep their voices down.

Camille and I whispered in the mailroom. "You know I was on the market this year, right?"

"No," I said. "What happened?"

"Finalist at two places and an offer from a state school in the Midwest. That's when the engagement happened. He proposed to keep me here, and I turned down the job offer."

Local entanglements. "I'm glad you're staying."

"Not forever." She looked into my eyes, and I looked back as steadily as I could. "Not if anything remotely decent opens closer to the city."

I couldn't wish against that anymore.

Camille's phone vibrated in her pocket. Glancing down at the screen, she said, "Another school shooting."

"Oh, no." Out of the ether, I felt some event rushing toward me, larger and larger until it I could almost feel its hot breath. The inverse of a wish.

"Cyn." Camille was scrolling and searching now. "I don't know if it's real or a hoax or what. But this says Broome State."

Twenty-Eight

I strode to my peaceful, sunny office, straining to hold off fear. An hour earlier, I had received a text from Silvio, as usual on Monday mornings: *Just pulled in.* As a rule, on arriving, my husband walked to his office, worked for a few hours, taught class, and drove to his apartment. We wouldn't talk until after dinner, unless some problem arose.

Camille followed me down the hall and stood in my doorway, staring at her phone. "I'm reading about a gunman and hostages in the Waddell building, but it's not confirmed."

Waddell. Psychology.

My body sat down in a desk chair with mismatched armheights I had never bothered to adjust. I closed my eyes and performed the small magic of visualizing the man I loved walking from the parking deck toward Waddell, then up to the fourth floor, using the musty back stairs. He passed two bathrooms whose female and male symbols were plastered over with fancy purple glyphs—to protest House Bill 2 and memorialize Prince. Elsewhere on campus guerrilla signage had been stripped down, but not in Psych. Still, the taped-up pages were beginning to peel at the edges. I could see it.

After Silvio unlocked his office, his stomach rumbled. I saw him pat pockets for his wallet and phone, grab his briefcase so he could eat and work in the student center café for a while, and jog back down the cement-block stairwell. He planned to order panini and coffee. Silvio, I declared to myself, was safe.

Then, as if it were an explosive device to be defused, I plucked my cell off the desk. One text had arrived before I picked it up. *I'm safe in the student center.* Another popped in as I looked: *Surrounded by people including security. Watching it on television.*

I read this to Camille, who must have been waiting in confusion. She exclaimed in one wild exhale, "Thank god." And then she left, to give me privacy.

I tried to call Silvio, but the line wouldn't connect, so I texted that I loved him. I then texted both twins, in case someone was following reports at the high school. They weren't supposed to have their phones in class, but neither was especially obedient, I'd noticed. *Dad is safe, don't worry.*

Oh, Sister Fox, what next? My fingers hovered over the computer keyboard as I asked, *Help me.* A few appropriate words sprang to mind. I typed them into the search engine and found news reports dated a few minutes ago.

There was video of an anchor with a map of campus projected beside him. "Broome State University is in lockdown. This is not confirmed, but witnesses say shots were fired shortly after eleven a.m. eastern time in Waddell Hall at Broome State University in eastern North Carolina. Many people are said to have fled the building. Police are cordoning off the area."

Silvio was safe, but what about everyone else?

Another text flickered. *Ross is still in Waddell. And some of my students.*

No more exchanges or sacrifices. No more lost pawns.

"People are tweeting from inside the building," the newsman continued, "describing the gunman as a fellow student who walked in this morning with a duffel bag." He gave a name and I searched in another window as the anchor cited more unconfirmed reports, this time of hostages in a classroom on the second floor of Waddell Hall. I found a selfie of a fair-haired young man, maybe the gunman witnesses had identified.

The anchor touched his ear. "More shots."

All right.

I reached out with my left hand, sending a push to the metal in the doorknob, and my door rocked shut. I lowered the volume on my computer, shut my eyes again, and imagined a classroom, blinds closed, door latched. Student desks were arranged in a circle. For some reason, the vintage telephone Alisa had given me, the one that liked to wander, was sitting on the teacher's work table in the corner.

Sit down, said the fair-haired boy, and everyone did, some swiftly, some tripping over themselves. I saw an older male professor. A middle-aged woman, apparently a student, was the calmest. Most of the others were female and young. Two women of eighteen or nineteen held hands until he told them, Stop that.

But the fair-haired boy was standing in the middle of a circle, a wheel. That would help.

Although my eyes remained closed, I heard my office door creak open and then close again, the lock clicking. As I tried to hold the image of a classroom in my mind, I smelled that lemony-earthy scent and heard Fee's demand. "What are you doing?"

A chair was pulled up next to me, hissing against the low-pile carpet. When Fee's cool right hand grasped my left, my skin recognized her.

In my imagining, the blond boy held an automatic rifle. This was a straight-edged blur, dark, because I barely knew what guns looked like, even after forty-eight years of movies and television, twenty years of living in the south. I knew so little, having held myself apart, cast my glance aside.

He wore a bullet-proof vest. A shadowy bag sat at his boots. The fair-haired boy, like school shooters before him, had probably packed a rifle, handguns, ammunition.

I heard Fee murmuring rhythmically but didn't attend.

I was considering how to make an object vanish from the known universe. I had relocated a heavy antique that one morning without consciously deciding to, and, days later, a car, on purpose. I could move the gun and the bag. Maybe I could erase all guns everywhere, wish them elsewhere in one blast of will. Yet I didn't understand how to desire this skillfully. Even if I had the power, no one could foresee all consequences, some of which might be terribly harmful. Besides, if all the guns melted away from this world, what dimension might they land in?

Instead, I pulled back the force of my wishing and regarded the scene. I whispered *safe, safe, safe* around the circle, reassuring the students, soothing the professor, building a sort of loop, a chain of energy. I was sure this spell would damage no one, not even the fair-haired boy.

Suddenly a phrase popped into my awareness from among the hushed words Fee was reciting. *Come away.* I heard more rhythmic syllables then, lucidly, from the strange body beside me: *for the world's more full of weeping than you can understand.*

I opened my eyes and stared at Fee, the otherworld made visible. Her focus was faraway. "No, everybody's safe now," I told her.

Fee shook wings of glossy black hair. Her lips kept forming the softest possible words. *Away with us he's going, the solemn-eyed.*

"Fee! Stop it!" I tried to pull my fingers out of her grasp but she was strong. You would think the hot animal of my hand would slide from her grip, but we remained linked.

I recognized the verses now, from near the end of Yeats' poem "The Stolen Child": *Round and round the oatmeal chest.*

I squeezed my lids shut again and saw students weeping, the professor blank-faced, beaded with sweat. The fair-haired boy turned and gave me an uncertain glance, squinting. He was so young.

Fee stood near him, like me an apparition in the dim room, one more inexplicable phenomenon amid the muffled uproar of feet and engines and shouting.

One of Fee's hands still gripped mine. The other was lifting the metal base of the telephone.

I wanted to wish Fee herself away, gone from the world, but she had work to do, and she needed me to help her do it. I felt power pooling, wanting to race up my spine, down my arm, into her. Nothing could happen unless I committed. I would have to take responsibility and make the best choice I could, a choice that could be irrevocable, that could be wrong.

I sucked in a deep breath, clenched my fingers more tightly, and zapped out all the energy my body could channel.

Fee finished her recitation, smiled at the fair-haired boy, and slammed the hunk of iron down on his head.

Silvio said, "Don't drive down. It's over, but police are still talking to people one by one, and folks are hysterical. I want to help. At least I want to wait with the people from the student center. I want to make sure they're all okay."

I yielded to his skillful desire but picked up the twins early. We drove home, watched the news, petted Pluto, brewed tea, answered messages. Rose faltered in the front hall once, registering some change she couldn't put her finger on. The vintage phone was gone.

It was too soon to check if my vision of events resembled the experience of the hostages in that room. Eight, some articles declared, while others said ten or more. Some people were carried away on stretchers, but the only fatality was the shooter, who reportedly killed himself. The picture I had glimpsed online was indeed the gunman, although in other photographs, especially the yearbook image most often broadcast later, his hair looked brown. Except in that selfie I had glimpsed first, he did not resemble the cute boy I adored in high school, the one who had raped my unconscious body in his brother's bedroom.

After the six o'clock news, which I hadn't watched in years, I called Silvio again. "I can't stand it. I want to drive down now."

"I'd rather come home," he said. "I'm packing as we speak."

Silvio was fine, as we confirmed with our senses, crowding around his warm solidity that night. He was upset, worried about students and colleagues—especially those who had hidden in the building, waiting for the worst—but present, breathing, smelling of recently laundered clothes and spilt drops of gasoline and truck-stop french fries.

We sat on the bed that night and I said, "Silvio. This bizarre stuff has been happening all year, and I've been afraid to tell you." He stiffened, and I rushed on, "I mean, it's not, it's more—well—supernatural, and I feel stupid even saying it aloud. I'm afraid you won't believe me." He waited, silent, so I struggled on. "I've been making wishes. A lot of them seem to come true."

"I'll keep an open mind," he promised. "Tell me."

I told him about wishing Alisa away right before the faculty exchange was offered.

"And me," he said, his voice gruff. "You wished me away."

"No, I did not!"

"I'm not an idiot," Silvio said. "You pushed me to apply for the job in North Carolina, you pushed me to take it, and now you're pushing me to keep it."

"Because you were miserable!" I grabbed his hands. "Silvio, I wanted you *happy.* I swear to God, I've been terrified you won't come home. I wanted the marriage we used to have, when the kids were little and we were happy, but we can't have that anymore, and I was trying to let you change." Now tears and snot were erupting from my face.

"What do you want now?"

"I want to be married to you." He waited, so I said, as calmly as I could, "I also want to become whatever I'm becoming. The space between us, which I thought was about giving you room, turned out to be something I needed, too."

I wasn't sure he believed me, but he listened. I thought about how much better I could see him now, with this strangeness between us. It was the familiarity, the safe routines, that distorted everything.

Silvio handed me tissues, and I wiped my face. Then he pulled me against his chest until my breathing calmed. "I swear," I kept saying.

"You made wishes, and some of them came true. One of those wishes was to send Alisa away. What were the others?"

Speaking into his damp shirt, I said, "That time Pluto escaped and ran into the road and the car nearly hit Teddy. I wished the car would veer to the side."

He did not answer, although the tension in his body might have decreased by some fraction. I thought about conjuring trouble for Fee at Halloween and how she redefined my desires to coincide with her own. That was too confusing to articulate. Then I talked about stopping Beth-Ann. "Fee had something to do with it, all of it," I insisted.

"Some of that was chance. Other times, you wanted things and made them happen," Silvio said. "Fee's very charismatic, but as far as I can see, the actual changes were initiated by you."

Then he straightened, pushing me away. "And the paintings?"

I sat up and clasped my knees. The paintings were part of a spell—Sunshine used them to banish Alisa, and maybe Fee enchanted them to bring Alisa back, and then they trapped Rose. But I had never breathed a word of that to anyone in the living world besides Fee, although I'd hinted something to Rose after they burnt to ashes. I looked at Silvio. While I was never perfectly sure what he was thinking or feeling, I thought: well, he already knows I'm superstitious, and he can live with that. If he decides I dragged our unstable daughter into my delusions, I could lose everything.

"I thought they were spooky. That's it."

His expression was a forest.

"If paintings could be portals, and I could work magic, everyone I loved would be safe and happy and gainfully employed within a three-mile radius of this house, except for my mother, who'd have a one-way ticket to fairyland."

He snorted and relaxed a little more. Then he reminded me of the psychological literature—that one is more likely to remember a dream if some event the next day echoes it, while forgetting the non-prophetic nightmares. Yes, I agreed, we are hard-wired to appreciate coincidence.

A current of understanding flowed between us. I wouldn't tell him what he could not bear, but I would walk right up to that line and give him what news I could.

I continued sending a little crackle of light to the professor with leukemia, whose illness I had refused, for so long, to take responsibility for. I imagined another beam flowing to the shooter in his underworld, the one he had consigned himself to, I wanted to believe, before I intervened.

Silvio and I touched each other more as we moved around the house, doing chores. When word came that the Waddell building would remain closed but classes would resume Thursday, he decided to return to Broome State for a couple of days. Sitting in the backyard, failing to read student essays, I visualized his safe navigation of empty rural highways.

When I received word he had reached campus, I got out my two sketches of the winter creek and the spring road. There had been no time to try my own magic before Fee's intervention. I felt sure my conjurations were worthless now, but I might as well send them to Alisa the only way I could.

I lit each on fire, holding them over the hibachi as they burned, dropping them when I had to, poking the paper with a stick until every inch charred and shriveled. The grill wasn't even hot when I finished, except from sunlight it had absorbed. I dumped its sooty contents into the fast-traveling creek.

Fee stood in Alisa's garden when I arrived. She wore a sun hat and work gloves and carried pruning shears. She looked more like a drawing from a nineteen-sixties ladies' magazine than an actual gardener at risk of mud exposure.

"Why, hello." She was holding her hat on, thwarting a breeze.

I ducked past flowering hedges, soiling my sandals, into the most private part of the yard, where Fee had set up wrought-iron chairs and a matching table. I was lugging my nasty blood magic into her sanctuary. "We murdered that boy."

"We stole him," she corrected, placing the shears on the table so the points faced me. "Gave him a push down a path he was already traveling."

I was practically panting. "There were other spells to try first. We might have been able to save everyone without killing him."

She shrugged. "You are always stalling. He was the right sacrifice at the right moment. No *innocent human being,* you said, and he was not innocent." I forced myself to breathe evenly, and I remembered Alisa's warning at the airport so long ago: *pay attention.* See what's in front of you and be ready for change. Perhaps I had been the problem that was creeping up on me.

I watched Fee watch me come around. Without hurrying, she removed her gloves, finger by finger. "You know I'm right. My wishes came true, and so did yours. I don't know if 'safe' is the right word, but good people who might have vanished from this world remain here to strive and suffer and grieve. And one young man stricken by desire, who yearned for all the wrong things and conceived a terrible road toward them, is released from pain." Here her tone became impatient, a little rancorous. "You dragged us into that thicket. There was no better way free."

Placing her gloves by the shears, standing by me in blossomy shade, Fee removed her hat. Her black hair was now tarnished by a single streak of silver.

"You're inhuman," I said.

Fee laughed. "I learned from inhuman people some tricks they didn't mean to teach me."

I looked at her shining face, her invisible stains. Some more-than-human forces had marked Fee, but that was true of a lot of us. It might be a relief to have this psychopath in my life, a woman who admitted to having crossed a few borders in her day.

Fee was staring right back at my clumsy, volatile self. "Are you a fox-woman, a *kitsune?*"

I felt my shoulders loosen. "That would be cultural appropriation." She guffawed unbecomingly, and I added, "I don't know what I am. I always had a feeling about foxes, but maybe I just wanted to be smarter than everyone else, while also hiding in my burrow." I paused. "If my magic has something to do with blood, where does yours come from? And what about Alisa and Barbara and Sunshine and Rose? Is it a woman thing?"

She clasped her hands and cocked a hip. "When you steal almost every spell you know, you have an incomplete sense of the logic. If there is logic. I suspect power is just out there and people can learn different ways to channel it. But children and old women are most likely to have their eyes open."

"I'm not old."

Fee rolled her eyes. "Hag."

I sniffed.

She played with a branch, deadheading a blossom, but her tone was much crankier than her body language. "That was a compliment. The magic will get stronger as you age. Unless you refuse to believe in it, in which case it will twist and rot."

Damn. "Is it tied to place? When I went to North Carolina, the power didn't feel the same."

"It should work everywhere, but with quirks. You have to get to know a place, and each location offers different gifts, with different requirements."

"You're new to Virginia, and you seem strong."

"I am not *new* anywhere, in any sense of the word." Her mad green gaze shifted again, focusing somewhere beyond me.

The silence between us opened, withered, died back to feed itself. It was a complicated thing.

"Here, before you go," Fee said, picking her way back to a sunnier part of the yard. I realized, as she bent over, that this bed was where March narcissi once bloomed, where we buried the ashes of Alisa's paintings. Tulips, barely spiking up then, had shriveled in the weeks since. A thorny shrub was beginning to flower.

Fee twisted a rose from a branch and handed it to me. In the apparent ease of her body, I sensed the slightest restlessness. I was reading her like a person reads a friend. I took the flower and met Fee's eyes. "Why did you come here? What is it you hope for?"

Now she smiled with a wideness anyone would take for genuine. "I don't know what I want. But I want it very much."

Twenty-Nine

At home, I kicked off one dirty sandal by the door, protecting the rose with a cupped hand. As I wobbled on a single bare foot, I looked at the empty place on the hall table, the spot my iron telephone had disappeared from for good.

As I kicked off the other sandal, my glance caught on the small cabinet mounted on the wall, its bottom lined with metal hooks, its hooks full of keys. The mysterious silver key on the novelty ring had found its way there, and a pipe cleaner, lying bent across the row of hooks.

I lifted them both and held the keychain's plastic rose next to the tender flower Fee had plucked. I twisted the pipe cleaner around the green stem and frail chain, binding them together, clamping them tight. It felt like the right thing.

My cell chirped. It was Silvio. He and other Broome State professors had been discussing the future of the department and their students, how best to take care of everyone after the tragedy. It was good, he told me, to feel like part of something—the work of repairing a small, damaged universe. His voice on the phone had an open sound.

"I just got back from Fee's," I said. "I'm not wishing her away anymore."

A few beats. "Do you believe you could do that? Make her go?"

She kept escaping from one universe, building a life there, getting restless, fleeing again. What I wanted was small magic that didn't break people or worlds. I sought to enmesh the people I loved more firmly, creating a hundred points of contact so that if someone needed to change, the rest of us could adapt without all bonds smashing.

What I said was, "I know it defies the laws of physics. But I think people have more power than they understand or know how to use. So even if I feel uncertain, I should try to help good things happen. Prevent harm."

"Like praying, even if you have doubts."

I sagged with relief at this concession. "Yeah."

Through the ether, Silvio conveyed noises of hesitation. "When you talk about Fee." Another pause. "You know you're attracted to her, right? That you've had just a tiny obsession with her otherworldly beauty all year?"

I reddened to the roots of my hair. "Um, no, I hadn't quite put that one together. I guess I see your point." I laughed, and suddenly he did, too, a little too hard.

"Anyway," I finished. "It's just desire. I choose what I do." And I would keep choosing, as I kept changing.

Before we hung up, Silvio asked me to check the mail. The Broome State dean had sent the final, counter-signed contract to this address the morning before the shootings.

I dropped the keychain I had been fiddling with onto the hall table. Still barefoot, I tripped down the steps to the mailbox. "Yes, it's here," I said before opening the mailbox lid, but I turned out to be right. I unsealed the flap and reported all was in order, or, at least, in the partial order we had to settle for. Beneath it in the stack, as I knew it would be, was my formal acceptance to the summer pedagogical workshop. Beneath that was the newspaper, with another headline about a missing person. Maybe someone else's yearning had gone terribly wrong.

I constantly prayed, you could call it, for remission for Sandra's friend with cancer, as wholeheartedly as I could. If she died anyway, Silvio would apply for her job, and my family might benefit from her suffering. In either case, I would send in my curriculum vitae for the Directorship of the Teaching and Learning Center at Broome State, and for any other plausible opening in the vicinity. Rose would keep seeing her therapist and taking pills that had actually been prescribed for her, except for three weeks in engineering camp, during which she would amaze everyone with her brilliance and find a tribe of teenagers among whom she felt at home. Maybe there would even be a girlfriend. Teddy would keep calculating the minimum amount of work required to earn grades his parents would tolerate, all while growing taller and handsomer, and not-dating every willing young woman in the high school, one by one. Unless he wanted to change, too.

I stood in the breezy sunshine until we hung up. The air smelled lovely. Maybe I could try again to work in the yard until time came to pick up the twins. What kind of person wanted to stay inside during May in Virginia?

When I pulled open the door-handle, Pluto flew out, rose keychain in his teeth.

I cussed. He streaked past me diagonally across the yard, toward the road. Dropping the mail, I gave shoeless chase, muttering "ow, ow, ow," then holding my breath as I watched his furry black body traverse the road without injury. I hesitated at the verge myself, looking both ways. Nothing but blue sky.

The cat seemed to be aiming at the new garage just erected across the street, with the small apartment framed in above. Construction was nearly complete. Just one man was painting trim today, and the neighbors' cars were absent.

I followed Pluto, who swerved around the building, toward the dumpster. I yelled, but Pluto never slowed until he reached the black port-a-john.

He waited for me by the door, which was unfastened and stamped with a unisex figure, a Rorschach test of a biped.

When I approached, puffing and irate, the cat slipped inside the narrow space.

I pushed the door open wider to admit light, wrinkling my nose at the smell. The cat stood near the toilet with the silver key and bound-up roses dangling from his jaw. I thought of Frodo and Samwise at the lip of Mount Doom.

"This cannot be a portal," I informed Pluto as I picked him up and jimmied the keychain out of his mouth. It sparked in my fingers, conveying an iron message. Alisa wanted to come home, and soon, after a few more weeks of study and preparation, I would possess enough magic to make that happen. Sighing, I tossed the key into the steel toilet.

By the end of May, I hit a productive rhythm in my research, heart palpitations notwithstanding. It was the article about senior seminars, intended to broaden my job qualifications. Silvio was home most of the time, and my joint pain was easing, so we took long spring walks through neighboring pastures. Rose and Teddy wrote exams at school and itched to be free. Fee and Dan flew out to a writers' retreat in California, after which they planned a small ceremony at Dan's parents' home. I agreed to look in on Alisa's empty house.

One morning I drove to Lord Fairfax Street. I managed to turn Alisa's spare key in the sticky lock, grabbing up fliers wedged inside the screen. Fee had left the place very clean, with a bowl of potpourri on the hall table to sweeten the air. I walked through the rooms downstairs, then upstairs, making sure the taps were off, the windows sealed.

The house felt expectant.

It had been, what, nine months? That was a nice number. I gazed into the upstairs bathroom mirror and saw Sunshine flicker in it, just for an instant.

Instead of heading to the college library, as I'd originally planned, I drove to the airport. The weather was dreamy, and I felt light-headed in the warm car, so I rolled down a window. When I parked in the short-term lot and shut the door, I didn't bother to lock it. My car was mildly decrepit and invisible to most people, like me, even in my red sundress.

The regional airport tended to be sleepy mid-day, midweek, even during summer travel season. Attendants in polyester uniforms gossiped at the counters. I rode the escalator up to Arrivals. The officer at the front security desk looked bored. He was leafing through a magazine, occasionally leaning back to joke around with people staffing the scanners.

I glanced up at the electronic board. A small commuter jet from Charlotte was scheduled to land soon. I sat down in the Arrivals Lounge. Hands idle in my lap, I inhaled and exhaled.

A few people went to the security desk and showed their IDs and boarding passes. Others checked the mounted screen as I had and either sat down or viewed the landing through plate-glass windows.

Soon travelers started to exit the gate area, singly or in pairs. Business types dashed past. A grandmotherly woman was joyfully greeted by a preschool-aged child and his father. A sixty-ish guy in a pastel polo hugged another man, grinning but saying little. They headed down the escalator or the stairs.

I watched the whole plane empty out, seat after seat. All these complicated lives were in flux, some spells well-cast, others gone awry, counter-urges burning.

Finally, one of the flight attendants wheeled his bag through, talking over his shoulder to a person I couldn't yet glimpse. "Will someone be meeting you?" I imagined he asked.

"Yes," said a slight woman in her early fifties, gaunt and tired. She limped slightly and wore a bandage on one arm, its gauze pad stained brown. Her hair was grayer than I remembered and cropped short. It hadn't seen a comb in a while.

Alisa spotted me, did a double-take, then composed herself. "There she is."

I walked forward. Alisa was managing awkwardly with a rubber-tipped cane, but I smiled at her, and she smiled back. I slid a bag from her arm onto my own. The flight attendant waved at us and moved away.

As I helped Alisa cross the lounge, she steadied and pulled herself erect. "Took you long enough. That was purgatorial," she announced. I started to ask if she meant the flight, the thatched cottage, the faculty exchange, or the whole country of Wales or UnWales. Then I thought: best to begin differently.

"Well, you wanted to get away."

Her mouth fell open. I laughed. After a few seconds of strangled outrage, Alisa cracked up, too, and then we were standing there like addled old bags, wiping tears from the corners of our eyes.

"Friends are always imaginary," I said.

Alisa picked up the thread without hesitation. "But we can still help each other out. Which I appreciate, by the way." She held open a purse so I could see my letters and cards there. "The mail was finally delivered. I had a good read on the trip back."

In sync, we stepped onto the escalator. The scenery slid past us, with a flash of glass and steel girders. It was early still. "I see lunch in our near future," I said. "Maybe that fancy Italian place."

"Real coffee! Oh my god," Alisa groaned.

On solid ground, before the revolving door, I looked at her again. "Maybe we could trade notes."

Alisa was staring at pretty blue foothills beyond the windows, but she nodded. "Yes, I'd like that. I hear you're pretty good at breaking people out of paradise."

"'Something there is that doesn't love a wall.'"

She harrumphed. "That's enough of *that.*"

"I'll use spells if I want to." I smirked when her face snapped in my direction. "If it feels right."

Alisa stared at me, not sure how to react, then something in her posture changed, and she shook her head. Her assent was a funny noise, laughter on its way elsewhere.

We walked out together, taking our time. No one would ever guess about the stolen hours.

Author Biography

Born in New York and raised in New Jersey, Lesley Wheeler is the author of five poetry books, including *The State She's In*, *Radioland*, and *The Receptionist and Other Tales*; the latter was shortlisted for the James Tiptree, Jr. Literary Award. Her poems and essays appear in *Ecotone*, *Lady Churchill's Rosebud Wristlet*, *Poetry*, *Strange Horizons*, *Massachusetts Review*, and many other magazines. The Henry S. Fox Professor of English at Washington and Lee University, she blogs at lesleywheeler.org and lives in Lexington, Virginia. This is her first novel.

Made in the USA
Las Vegas, NV
16 July 2024

92383633R00142